The
Lodge

ALSO BY KAYLA OLSON

The Reunion

This Splintered Silence

The Sandcastle Empire

The Lodge

A NOVEL

KAYLA OLSON

ATRIA PAPERBACK

NEW YORK AMSTERDAM/ANTWERP LONDON
TORONTO SYDNEY NEW DELHI

ATRIA PAPERBACK

An Imprint of Simon & Schuster, LLC
1230 Avenue of the Americas
New York, NY 10020

First Atria Paperback edition January 2025

ATRIA PAPERBACK and colophon are trademarks of Simon & Schuster, LLC

For information about special discounts for bulk purchases, please contact Simon & Schuster Special Sales at 1-866-506-1949 or business@simonandschuster.com.

The Simon & Schuster Speakers Bureau can bring authors to your live event. For more information or to book an event, contact the Simon & Schuster Speakers Bureau at 1-866-248-3049 or visit our website at www.simonspeakers.com.

Interior design by Kyoko Watanabe

Manufactured in the United States of America

1 3 5 7 9 10 8 6 4 2

Library of Congress Cataloging-in-Publication Data
Names: Olson, Kayla, author.
Title: The lodge / by Kayla Olson.
Description: First Atria paperback edition. | New York : Atria Books, 2025.
Identifiers: LCCN 2024019303 (print) | LCCN 2024019304 (ebook) | ISBN 9781668033197 (paperback) | ISBN 9781668033203 (ebook)
Subjects: LCGFT: Romance fiction. | Novels.
Classification: LCC PS3615.L75252 L63 2025 (print) | LCC PS3615.L75252 (ebook) | DDC 813/.6--dc23/eng/20240429
LC record available at https://lccn.loc.gov/2024019303
LC ebook record available at https://lccn.loc.gov/2024019304

ISBN 978-1-6680-3319-7
ISBN 978-1-6680-3320-3 (ebook)

For my parents, Mark and Dawn, who always believed I could (and would) go on to do something great—if *American Idol* hadn't said no to me in the first round of auditions, I might have ended up on a totally different path! Thanks for loving me through all the twists and turns of this creative life.

And for anyone who:

- Loves a hot celebrity tell-all
- Had *Tiger Beat* posters covering every inch of their bedroom wall
- Spent hours trying to nail every beat to Britney's "Oops! . . . I Did It Again" choreography (this book has nothing to do with Britney, but you are my people if you can relate)
- Had a favorite member of NKOTB, Backstreet Boys, *NSYNC, Hanson, 98°, One Direction, and/or BTS
- Is still in their boy band era and, frankly, never intends to leave

This one's for you.

EIGHT YEARS AGO

True North Lead Singer Jett Beckett Vanishes without a Trace

By Alix Morgan // Starslinger Daily, *Staff Writer, Arts & Entertainment*

Late this afternoon, the music industry—and world at large—was rocked by a press release of seismic proportions: international boy band sensation Jett Beckett has vanished.

It's been eighteen hours and counting since Beckett was last seen.

Here's everything we know so far:

· The lead singer of boy band True North—and arguably its brightest star—was last seen around midnight in Boston Harbor Hotel's John Adams Presidential Suite, where he was staying with his four bandmates during this leg of their sold-out stadium tour.

· Beckett was reported missing after failing to show up for both a meeting with the band's record label and the sound check for tonight's (since canceled) concert. His personal belongings—wallet and identification cards included—were found undisturbed in the suite.

- Two hours prior to the time of Beckett's disappearance, which is estimated to be around midnight, he had a backstage clash with bandmate Sebastian Green; their heated exchange was partially captured in <u>this viral video</u>. While emotionally charged, the video lacks the necessary context to show us what, exactly, sparked their disagreement and such a fiery fight.

- Despite that contentious clash, <u>sources close to Beckett report</u> there is no obvious evidence of foul play. The investigation is currently ongoing, but with no body and no evidence, it is presumed that Jett Beckett will be categorized as a missing person and therefore no criminal charges will be pressed at this time.

So where do we go from here?

Management has announced that True North's Diamond in the Sky Tour has been postponed for the next week, projecting optimism that Beckett will reappear to wrap up this month's leg.

Bandmates River Wu, Charly Johannsen, Ayo Okeke, and Sebastian Green could not be reached for comment. The band's manager, Jason Saenz-Barlowe, provided a statement via his social media channels:

"There isn't a person in this world who doesn't know Jett Beckett's face," he remarked during a video posted this evening, striking a confident, comforting tone. "It's unlikely he'll be missing for long."

For the sake of the fandom, not to mention Beckett himself, let's hope he's right.

Congrats, everyone—the news is out! Go celebrate tonight!

Everything feels buzzy as I take in the new email at the top of my inbox.

There's hardly anything to it, just that short note—sent from my editor, Maribel, to the whole team—along with a screenshot. I zoom in, see the Publishers Marketplace deal listing for Sebastian Green's book.

For *our* book.

I've been sitting on this secret for what feels like forever. It's a feat, honestly, considering how many times I've almost let it slip.

With the announcement now out, it's finally starting to sink in that I'm writing a memoir—a *celebrity* memoir that will likely take up permanent residence on the *New York Times* bestseller list for at least a year. Not only that, but I'm on a train, headed to a ski lodge in Vermont for an entire month, all expenses paid.

These are the things dreams are made of, and not just because I quit my day job last year to pursue freelance work. Ghostwriting the memoir of Sebastian Green, arguably the most famous member of my all-time favorite boy band?

Yes. Yes, *with enthusiasm*. I signed on in a heartbeat.

But I haven't breathed a word about it, not to anyone.

I've been dying to tell my best friend, Chloe. She's easily starstruck, though, and notorious for inadvertently spilling secrets. Not even my sister, Lauren, knows—and she's been crashing with me in New York for more than a month while doing an internship at the Metropolitan Museum of Art. In retrospect, maybe she would've let me get some work done if I'd told her.

I had almost nothing to show on my most recent Zoom call with the book's publisher. That wasn't entirely Lauren's fault, but her presence in my apartment has been distracting, to say the least. My editor—the infamous Maribel Tovar at McClendon & Murphy—though gracious, took the opportunity to emphasize our not-so-flexible deadline. Every single aspect of this book is being rushed so it can hit shelves before the holiday season, and as it is currently early March, the deadline felt tight enough even before Lauren made my work hours nonexistent.

Enter Sebastian Green.

Sebastian is a lot of things, but *thoughtful* is not the first word that springs to mind. Trendy to a fault? Yes. Aloof, flighty, a touch self-obsessed? Yes, yes, more yes. Handsome and he knows it? Absolutely.

But he's also a well-connected multimillionaire who wants his book to release in time to cash in on the holidays, for which I will be forever thankful, because as soon as I told everyone about my distracting living situation, he offered to hook me up with an all-expenses-paid writing retreat at an incredible-looking ski resort.

Why would he offer this? No idea. Maybe it's to make sure I want to show his best side as I tell his story? Maybe it also eases his guilty conscience about how he blew off two meetings before we ever got to this point—we'd been planning to meet up for a series of interviews but he took a last-minute trip to Los Angeles, and then another one to Spain, and promised we'd connect soon.

We haven't. Not yet, anyway.

Hence, I am on a train. To Vermont. Where Sebastian will—at some point, hopefully—meet up with me to discuss the more nuanced details of his life story.

In the meantime, he sent over roughly eighty hours' worth of voice memos. Thankfully, the ski resort should provide a quiet place for me to sort through them in peace while also affording the privacy someone like Sebastian needs to meet face-to-face.

As long as he shows up this time.

It's snowing when we pull into the train station.

Sebastian told me to keep an eye out for the driver who'll take me to the lodge, but it's harder than it should be thanks to the weather.

"Alix Morgan?"

I hear my name before I see him, the man holding up a sign meant for me. He takes my luggage as I climb into his sleek silver SUV, an Audi with leather seats and the biggest sunroof I've ever seen.

The ride is beautiful and peaceful, aside from a few disgruntled yowls from Puffin, my cat—Lauren wasn't confident she'd remember to feed him, so he's along for the ride. As we make our way north, the snowflakes gradually become smaller and more delicate, spiraling gracefully outside the windows.

We turn, and the world opens up: it suddenly feels like we're driving straight toward the canvas of a massive, masterful painting.

Snowcapped mountains pierce the lowest clouds; at their base is a sprawling lodge, grandiose and picture-perfect. It looks warm and cozy even at a distance, lit inside and out with the glow of yellow lanterns.

I feel like a starlet as we pull up to the lodge.

This close, it feels absolutely colossal—the covered drive at the entrance stretches at least three floors high, with stone and steel and wooden beams to scale. Entire humans could fit inside the iron frames of the glass-paneled lanterns, if said lanterns weren't ablaze with actual fire.

We come to a stop just outside the main entrance. One of the valets appears with a cart, and my driver steps out to take care of my luggage. Puffin yowls again, bristling at the cold air as we get out of the car.

I rummage in my wallet, pull out a twenty; it was not a short drive, and my bags are not what one would call lightly packed.

When I offer it, the driver waves it away.

"Save it for the next guy." He grins, tucking the last of my bags onto the luggage cart.

What sort of driver refuses an extra tip?

The sort who has already been paid generously, I realize as soon as I've had the thought.

Thanks, Sebastian.

"This way," the valet says, luggage cart in tow.

I follow him through the gigantic double doors and into the atrium.

The inside is every bit as oversized as the outside. Just past the entrance is a massive fireplace, possibly taller than I am, lively flames flickering in its grate. The atrium ceiling extends four stories, held up by the thickest wooden columns I've ever seen—it's like something straight out of a redwood forest. And then there's the book-shelf wall: it's as tall as the atrium itself (yes, *four floors high*) and filled with books that are mostly out of reach, purely there to serve the cozy aesthetic. Lush leather couches—with ottomans to match, and what appear to be hand-woven throw blankets—make me want to curl up with one of the books I packed and a mug of hot cocoa.

But alas, the valet leads me right past the seating area to the concierge desk.

"Ms. Morgan?" a woman greets me, her dark hair neat in a low bun.

I must look surprised, because she nods toward the luggage cart, at Puffin's carrier. "It isn't every day we get to make preparations for a cat."

Oh. Right.

"Your suite is all ready for you—I'm not sure how much Mr. Green told you, but your penthouse is in our Exclusive Access Complex, just down the path from the main lodge, where we are now. I'll page the tram for you unless you prefer to walk—it takes about eight minutes on foot."

"The tram sounds great, thanks."

The tram turns out to be a glorified golf cart with a few extra rows and some clear plastic flaps to keep the cold and the snow at bay. We wind down the path, only a little bit freezing.

It's hard to get a great view through the protective flaps, but what I can see looks magical: twinkle lights everywhere, sparkling against the snowy afternoon sky; a quaint mini village full of shops and cafés, the entire scene extremely warm and cozy and inviting. I even spot an ice-skating rink, positioned perfectly against the backdrop of the resort's main attraction: Black Maple Mountain.

We pull up to my building, which looks like a more modern addition to the resort. Apparently, some people live in this building year-round, while others treat it like a vacation home. I'm guessing Sebastian might be the latter; his attitude screamed *owner* when he offered up this place so cavalierly, but I'm not sure he's ever actually lived here.

"Your key card will give you private access to the penthouse floor—those elevators are around back, just down the sidewalk," the driver informs me. "Would you like assistance finding your way?"

I shake my head. "Got it, thanks."

"If you ever have any trouble, use the intercom and someone will be over to assist you."

He waits until Puffin and I have rounded the corner toward the elevator vestibule before driving off. One flick of my key card against the sensor and I'm in the building—one more, and I'm in the elevator itself. There's only one button: *P* for Penthouse.

I hear the faint vibration of my phone in my bag. It's a text from Chloe, asking where I am.

It's possible I haven't mentioned this whole month-in-Vermont situation to her yet. I know she'll forgive me for keeping secrets—but still, there's a part of me that worries she'll be hurt that I didn't tell her sooner.

I'm supposed to keep as quiet as possible about the fact that I'm ghostwriting for Sebastian. According to my editor, it's best for the book if we don't call attention to the fact that he didn't write every single word himself. Maribel did give me permission to tell Chloe everything once the deal announcement went live, though, so I guess I'm in the clear now as long as I trust her to be discreet.

The elevator opens onto a landing that's even more private than I anticipated—and even more beautiful, with stylish wood paneling, black furniture, a gilded mirror on the wall, and a sprig of greenery in a slim vase. There are apparently only two residences on this entire floor; a pair of battered boots sits neatly outside the door on my left, so I guess the other door must be mine.

I head that way but can't help glancing back at the boots. They're so large they almost certainly belong to a man—a man who recently got back from a long trek through the snow, judging by the sizable puddle underneath. I hadn't even considered the possibility of having a neighbor, especially not a maybe-tall man who could be fairly athletic. *Interesting*.

I call Chloe before I get too carried away. It rings only once before she picks up.

"Hey! Are we still on for happy hour? I started to worry when you didn't text me back."

Last night, in between last-minute laundry and placing an overnight order for more cat food, I had the sinking feeling I was forgetting something, but I couldn't put my finger on what.

Now I know.

"So, um, about that," I say, tapping my key card to the sensor outside my room. The lock opens on command, and I head inside. "Holy. Crap."

"Alix—what? Are you okay?"

I blink at the room before me.

Room is not a sufficient word for what's before me.

Alpine haven for millionaires with expensive taste is a more apt description. *Heaven with a view*: even better.

Sprawling is an understatement. And more than just gigantic, this place is utterly gorgeous. I suppose I should have expected as much, given that it's a penthouse—and yet.

"Alix?"

"Sorry, Chlo," I finally say. "No happy hour today. But I have a good explanation, I promise. Give me five minutes? I'll call you right back."

"That's quite the cliffhanger, but okay. I'm setting a timer—do *not* leave me in suspense for too long!"

Dewdrops · For You Page

#superfresh #freshdrops #breakingnews #sebastiangreen

u/SebGreen

2:32PM · March 1

heyoooooo

news is out, i'm writing a book.

wanna read it????! (jk i know you do)

preorder here but sorry, it wont land on your doorstep until later this year bc i still have to write the thing. gonna be SO WORTH IT THO

love,
seb

COMMENTS

⬆ **u/TruestNortherner**
TOP

I have been waiting for this announcement for
LITERAL YEARS and just preordered a copy for
everyone I know—Teenage Me is SCREAMING
CRYING FALLING OVER. How are we all doing,
everyone?

↳ **u/jettbeckettconspiracytheorist**
Ok as we all know, I am forever a Jett Beckett
stan. BUT. I will binge this in a single sitting the
day it's released bc it might be the closest we
ever get to finding out what happened the night
Jett disappeared

↳ **u/TruestNortherner**
STAHHHP it did not even OCCUR TO ME that
we might get details on what happened that
night, now I seriously cannot wait (PS: SEB
IF YOU SEE THIS WE VOLUNTEER TO READ
ADVANCE COPIES IF YOU GET THEM)

↳ **u/BoiiiBandBoiii**
CAN CONFIRM, would read Seb's grocery list,
idgaf what he writes I am here for it

↳ **u/jettbeckettconspiracytheorist**
If anyone wants to talk Jett Beckett theories,
you know where to find me

↳ **u/TruestNortherner**
Too depressing at this point,
u/jettbeckettconspiracytheorist,
I think he's gone forever :(

↳ **u/BoiiiBandBoiii**
UGHHH this thread started out so happy and
now I want to cry into a pint of chunky monkey

↳ **u/jettbeckettconspiracytheorist**
idk, I still haven't given up hope . . . but admit it
doesn't look good :((((

↳ **u/TruestNortherner**
It's been eight years

↳ **u/BoiiiBandBoiii**
EIGHT. YEARS. (make that two pints of chunky
monkey)

↳ **u/SebGreen**
it's rocky road on my grocery list, bruh, chunky
monkey is the worst (thx for ordering the book!)
–seb

2

"I'm sorry—you're doing *what*?!"

I yank the phone away from my ear a split second too late. The damage is done: Chloe's unbridled enthusiasm has pierced a hole straight through my skull.

"Alix. *Alix*. Say it again."

After so many years of heartbreaking almosts and outright rejections, my news still sounds unreal even to me.

"I get to ghostwrite Sebastian Green's memoir," I repeat slowly.

I've spent weeks holding this burning secret inside, wondering if it would all turn to ash if I exhaled in just the wrong way—now is the moment it finally feels *real*.

"Stop it," she says in disbelief. "I cannot. Sebastian Green? What?!"

I'm not easily starstruck, which is probably a substantial part of the reason I landed the job, but Chloe's specific brand of enthusiasm is contagious. I catch a glimpse of myself in the bathroom mirror of my home away from home, grinning like the naive writer I once was.

"It's surreal," I say.

"It's *incredible*," Chloe agrees. "Are you sure you can't make it to happy hour? Drinks on me tonight—we could go somewhere special to celebrate, there's this new rooftop bar in Williamsburg—"

"I'm not in Brooklyn right now," I interrupt before she gets too into the idea.

"Wait—you're not going out celebrating with *Sebastian Green himself* tonight, are you? Alix. If you're going out with Sebastian Green, I will literally die of envy!"

I sit down on the buttery leather couch near one of the many floor-to-ceiling windows in this palatial suite and take in the view of the resort's most prominent mountain. It's absolutely stunning.

"I'm not even in *New York* right now," I say. "Like, not just the city—the state. I'm in Vermont."

"Alix?" I hear Chloe say on the other end of the line. "You cut out for a bit, did you say *Vermont*?"

"They're putting me up in an amazing penthouse so I can write without distractions," I say.

It's not *technically* a lie. I'm just keeping it vague as to who, exactly, made all the arrangements and is footing the bill.

"I need pics, like, now. How long will you be there—and when can I come visit?"

I put her on speaker, snap a quick photo of the breathtaking landscape, and hit send. The snow-covered mountain outside my window is exactly the sort of postcard-perfect vista I imagined it would be.

"I'll be here for a month," I say. "That's the view from my living room."

"*Stop it*, Alix, holy— I will most definitely be crashing your vacay, and *soon*. Wow."

"It's not a vacation," I say, though I admit that fact has been a little slow to sink in. The fancy soaps and modern bathtub, the sleek wineglasses and well-stocked bar, views from every window, multiple shaded balconies, and even a game room with a pool table: literally everything about this place screams *vacation*. It's going to take some work to . . . well, remind myself to *work*.

"Why don't you plan on coming to see me halfway through?" I suggest. I could get lost in here, it's so enormous. "I'll do a ton of work these next two weeks so I can take a good break. We'll have cocoa and sit by the fire—"

"Say no more, I'll be there. Also! Keep your eye out for any hot ski instructors who might be interested in cozying up to a petite brunette with big golden retriever energy, please."

I laugh. "Sounds like a plan."

"If you happen to see any hot ski instructors for yourself, don't be afraid to step out of your comfort zone a little, okay? Just ask yourself, 'What would Chloe do?'"

"Not this again," I say, glad she can't see how hard I'm rolling my eyes.

"It's been *two years* since Blake," she says delicately, treading lightly over my sore spot. "This is the perfect opportunity to test the waters again."

If Chloe has golden retriever energy, I'm the cat who hides under the bed whenever anyone new gets close.

Blake was a lion.

The only good thing about dating him was that I met Chloe; she was dating one of Blake's Wall Street bros at the time. Of the six guys in that group—and their revolving door of significant others—my friendship with Chloe is the only relationship that survived.

"I probably won't have a lot of time for skiing, Chlo. Or guys." It is the flimsiest of excuses.

"You work too hard as it is," she counters. "Promise me you'll make time for *fun*, too? You can work your way up to scouting out the guys, I'll give you that. But you are in freaking ski heaven right now, and you will regret it if you don't make the most of that mountain while you're there."

"I'll regret it, or you'll make me regret it?"

"Do you really want to find out?"

I laugh. "Okay. No promises on anything else, but I'll agree to ski at least once on this trip."

"At least once *this week*," she says. "Do it tomorrow. Get up early, knock out some words, and then take a break in the afternoon—if you love it, you'll be glad I made you do it."

Chloe is one of the most productive people I've ever met, yet she somehow manages never to seem stressed out. It's possible I could learn a thing or two from her approach to the whole work-life balance situation.

"Only if I get enough done tomorrow," I concede.

The mountain really does look tempting. So does the little village over near the main lodge, and the ice-skating rink.

If I'm honest, it's been a lonely two years since Blake. Spending all my time in this gorgeous penthouse, all by myself—even if I'm technically on a tight deadline—might only amplify that loneliness. At least I have Puffin to keep me company. And Sebastian, though I'm not sure yet when he'll be coming.

"Text me a picture tomorrow of your skis in the snow," she says, and I can hear it in her voice: she knows she's won. "And if you happen to run into Sebastian Green on that mountain, you'd better believe I'm going to need a picture of him, too."

~

This penthouse is the coziest place I've ever set foot in my entire life.

I've settled in for my first writing session of the retreat, ready to finally make some significant progress on this project. There are a few workspaces to choose from, but for today I'm going with the sleek desk by my bedroom window. The view is calm but energizing: the hypnotic spiral of snowflakes against the majestic backdrop of Black Maple Mountain, with the resort village nestled in between.

It even *smells* cozy—I've got a steaming cup of jasmine tea on my desk, its fragrance mingling with the candle I lit (orange, cedarwood, and more jasmine).

The silence is almost overwhelming.

No garbage trucks banging around outside this building. No noisy neighbors threatening my sanity with their subwoofer that—on a semiregular basis—makes actual ripples in my water. No Lauren barging in uninvited to talk my ear off for an hour.

I fill it, instead, with Sebastian.

His voice memos are an absolute mess.

I'm not sure I've ever heard someone flit from one subject to the next quite like Sebastian does. Chloe is like this sometimes, but her detours are usually more like little fireworks, distracted bursts of energy she just has to get out before returning to whatever she was talking about before.

Sebastian's detours, though, are something else. It's as if the entire history of his life is detached from any sort of linear timeline in his mind and, instead, is more like an intricate spiderweb.

Fascinating—but not exactly straightforward.

I've wondered about so many things over the years: Was his infamous rivalry with Jett Beckett actually real or convincingly staged for media attention? If it was real, was it pure and simple envy, two gorgeous guys with inflated egos who were forced to share a spotlight, or was there more to it than that?

Will he spill any secrets about the night Jett Beckett disappeared?

Will he spill any secrets about why the band disintegrated a few months later?

Will he spill any secrets that aren't on anyone's radar at all?

As many articles as I've written in a professional context, I've never truly had the freedom to ask the questions *I* wanted answers to. Theorizing and speculating are common on the gossip blogger side of things—but at the various news outlets I've worked for, I've only ever found myself in a position to objectively report the truth.

Now is my chance to dig deeper.

The titles on Sebastian's voice memos are super vague and incomplete, judging from the few I've already listened to. I'm praying the rest won't involve anything more about school talent shows, or how he took his first piano lesson at age four, or how his mother drove him all over the place throughout his childhood to try to get him in front of the right people.

All of that is fascinating in its own right, but I already have enough about his early years to fill more than an entire chapter. That's probably already too much—people want the *juicy* stuff.

And so do I.

I hit play, and Sebastian's voice echoes off the walls and the polished concrete floor. As soon as he starts speaking, I know this particular voice memo will deliver.

File: sebgreen_empty promises.mp3
Date Recorded: February 7, 2025

SG:

The first time I met my manager, Jason, I had this *feeling*—it's hard to even describe. I had no idea who he was, no idea how much power he had. How much power he would *gain* once the band was a thing.

I remember seeing him for the first time out at the record label's office in LA. Even just the way he thrust a bottled water at me whether I wanted one or not made me feel like my life would never be the same—and that he would be the one to change it.

He acted like he owned the place. Anything he said, he made you feel like the world was at his fingertips. No worries, no doubts, just absolute certainty that he could speak an idea and it would become reality. Jason had the sort of instincts and energy that could make anyone a star, and he had his sights set on me.

It would have been nice to know they weren't set on *only* me.

We had meeting after meeting with all sorts of powerful people at the label, hours of back-and-forth about which demo would be the perfect one for me to record as a breakout track, more meetings and studio sessions with producers to turn a few of those tracks into reality. They loved my work, they said. I was going to be *huge*.

After all that, though—all those meetings and recording sessions—Jason took me out to this fancy lunch just so he could drop a bomb on me: the label was giving the song to someone else. They thought my solo career had potential, but they had other ideas, other plans—they wanted me to be the front man of a group they were putting together. A boy band.

It was only supposed to be for a little while, and *then* we'd circle back to my solo career.

What they didn't tell me was that all of this—all the meetings and schmoozing and flattery and promises—all of it, even the exact same fancy restaurant where Jason broke the news—

All of it happened to Jett, too.

They fed him the exact same lines, made the exact same promises.

Jason made him the exact same promises—

And we both believed him.

3

I can't write fast enough.

I make furious notes in my journal, scribbles only I will be able to decipher when it's time to transform them into an actual chapter. I'm fascinated by this backstory—not just because of the implication that Jason Saenz-Barlowe is a total snake (which I've suspected for a while), but because both Sebastian and Jett were manipulated into joining the band with empty promises of solo careers. Every making-of-the-band piece I've ever come across has painted a much rosier picture.

Sebastian did eventually go on to release a solo album, but I always assumed it was just his plan B after the band fell apart. It's also a wonder those demos never resurfaced. Did no one ever think to look?

Honestly, I always assumed Jett Beckett was the problem in their rivalry. His name was constantly in headlines back then; drama followed him everywhere. I had the displeasure of interviewing him once, right before he vanished. It's not an exaggeration to say I've never been treated worse by a celebrity in my entire career. He came off as entitled and demanding, sullen and sour and on edge.

I won't go so far as to say my entire paradigm has shifted now that I know Sebastian and Jett were both manipulated into joining the band—but it's illuminating. Jett Beckett had a reputation, for sure.

Maybe—*maybe*—he was pushed into that, too. All publicity is good publicity, as they say.

I make a list in my notebook, trying to capture all of my stray thoughts before they evaporate. I use a purple pen for all things Sebastian, a green pen for all things Jett, and red for Jason, their manager. It's a total mess. I highlight the most compelling parts, draw arrows connecting bits of information, make even smaller footnotes in a few places—it looks like a serial killer's bulletin board when I'm done.

It's good work, though. A story is starting to form in my head, a compelling narrative.

From an outsider's perspective, the story of True North looks like this: a group of five handsome, talented guys were hand-picked to form a boy band—an industry plant that, unsurprisingly, skyrocketed to fast fame. Their overnight stardom looked like a dream come true, transforming them from guys next door to universally beloved cultural icons. Anyone could see their material success: the platinum records, a veritable army of awards statues, single after single played relentlessly in every place a person might hear music. The contentious relationship between Sebastian and Jett only fueled their popularity—Sebastian was the golden boy, Jett the brooding bad boy, and both had enormous fan bases.

Already, though, Sebastian's revelations about how he and Jett were brought into the group feel like an undercurrent of red-hot lava, a persistent, pervasive force that cracked the band's foundations right from the start and possibly led to its eventual demise.

I need to talk with Sebastian, ask some questions. He and our editor both strongly urged me to text if I need to get in touch—apparently Sebastian's email is, and I quote, "a black hole"—but it feels like it's getting too late to text someone I've only spoken to twice. One glance at the clock tells me I've been in the writing zone for longer than I realized; it's nearly midnight, and I completely forgot to eat dinner.

I'll text him first thing in the morning.

Hey, Sebastian, I type on my phone as soon as the clock hits eight. I have a few questions . . . can we set up a call for later today or tomorrow? Or, if you're planning to come to the resort soon, we can wait until then.

It still feels weird that I have his number—that I can text him like we're friends.

Unlike texting a friend, however, I have no clue when to expect his reply.

I'm running on six hours of sleep right now; I crashed so hard last night that I completely forgot to shut the blinds. Even if the sun hadn't rudely awoken me, Lauren would have—she called during her seven a.m. run to vent about her boss at the museum. I spent most of the call ordering room service through the resort's website since I couldn't get a word in edgewise.

Someone brought up a fully stocked breakfast tray about half an hour ago, complete with the best vanilla latte I've ever tasted in my life. I'm picking at what's left of my food when my phone vibrates on the desk.

When I see Sebastian's reply—a simple who is this, sans question mark or capital letters—I nearly choke on a blueberry.

I'm not sure whether to be offended that he couldn't be bothered to enter the contact info of the person who's writing his memoir or mortified that I expected him to save my number at all.

Also, hi, exactly how many people does he have tentative plans with re: meeting at a resort?

Alix Morgan, I write back. Your ghostwriter?

I hesitate before hitting send, rethinking my punctuation. A question mark feels passive-aggressive, possibly insulting. I switch it to an exclamation point instead, but that feels like enthusiasm overload.

In the end, I delete everything but my name.

At the ski lodge in Vermont, I type out instead. Working on your book and just have a few questions when you get a minute

After a few minutes of staring at my phone, willing him to write back, I give up. His phone has to be within reach, and my questions shouldn't take long—but I'm the one whose entire month is dedicated to writing this book, not him, so maybe he's just busy with other things. Hopefully he'll get back to me soon.

I open my notebook, pick up where I left off.

It takes a moment to reorient myself. My notes—while thorough—are a mess, and the momentum and magic I felt last night are slow to return. I scan all the highlighted parts, read over my many questions. It's enough to get started, I decide. I can draft a skeleton chapter and flesh it out more once I've talked to Sebastian.

Four hours later—after I wade through another long voice memo that mostly focuses on Sebastian's musical influences and the idols who made him want a solo career in the first place, followed by two writing sprints and some edits on the pages I drafted last night—I'm in need of a break.

Sebastian still hasn't written back.

When I opened my closet upon arrival, I discovered several boxes, all adorned with the simple gold-embossed logo of one of the village shops, along with a pair of skis and a helmet. Affixed to one of the boxes was a handwritten card: *If these don't work, they have more in the village. Charge whatever you want to the room.* —Seb

I don't want to know how Sebastian Green guessed my exact size based purely on my social media feeds and our two Zoom meetings, but the ski clothes he gifted me all fit to perfection. Everything is in my favorite colors, too—lilac and white with gold accents—and the snow goggles are iridescent pink Oakleys. I feel like an Olympian, or possibly even an astronaut; I've never worn such fancy ski gear in my life, only decades-old hand-me-downs from my mother and her sister.

I tie my hair into a pair of short braids, pulling out a couple of sandy-blond strands at the front like snowboarders always do, and tug on a cozy knit hat. It's mustard yellow with a faux-fur pouf, the only thing that doesn't quite match the rest of my outfit.

It feels strange to wear ski clothes again after all this time. Our family went every year while I was growing up—until we didn't. Lauren was a late surprise, born just before my twelfth birthday.

After she came along, our vacations stopped: our parents didn't want to travel with a new baby, didn't want to travel with a toddler, three kids were outrageously more expensive than expected . . .

I blame my brother's appetite for that; he hit a gigantic growth spurt around that same time and devoured everything in sight. I devoured pop culture instead, books and movies and music, an escape that erased—at least temporarily—the bitterness I felt about how drastically our family dynamic had changed.

Silver lining, at least: I never would have pursued a career in entertainment journalism had pop culture not been such a refuge for me in my teens. I wouldn't be writing Sebastian's book at all, let alone writing Sebastian's book in a place like *this*.

I head out to the elevator landing, ski gear in hand. My eyes land instinctively on my mystery neighbor's door—the boots are gone, the puddle of water wiped away like it never existed.

I happen to be staring at the door when it opens.

Out walks a guy with shoulder-length wavy hair and a slightly overgrown five o'clock shadow, chiseled cheekbones, and the lean, muscular build of someone who's led a very athletic life. My gaze flickers down to his feet—sure enough, there are the boots—then back up to his remarkably handsome face. His eyes are an intense shade of deep brown; his eyebrows are dark and unusually thick. He looks vaguely familiar, a little like one of Chloe's favorite tennis players, the one from Greece.

After the briefest flash of surprise—to see a stranger on this private penthouse floor at all, no doubt, let alone one who's staring a hole through his door—the corner of his mouth turns up into a cocky half grin.

"What?" I say, hugging my skis and poles close to my chest as my cheeks grow hot. "It's a really lovely door."

A really lovely door. That's the best I could come up with to explain my staring? I'm going to die.

He turns, crossing his arms as if to study the frosted-glass placard that reads PENTHOUSE B. "Oh, yeah," he says with a serious nod. "People come from all over the world just to see it."

"Clearly," I reply. "I just got in yesterday."

"Have you seen any other interesting things in the short time you've been here? Coffee tables, footstools?" He pulls his door shut and comes to stand beside me in front of the elevator.

Only when he reaches past me do I realize I forgot to push the button.

My cheeks grow even hotter. Who stands in an elevator lobby just for *fun*, without pushing the button, only to get caught staring at someone else's door?

"Honestly," I say quickly, hoping he won't get the wrong idea, "I haven't left my own place since I got here, so I'm taking in the sights for the first time."

"Ah," he says. "Going up on the mountain?"

The elevator dings, and he gestures for me to go first. The skis and poles are unwieldy—one of the skis gets caught on my way in, and he has the decency to help me instead of giving me a hard time about it.

"Maybe not *all* the way up," I admit. "It's been a minute since I skied."

"They've got great instructors at the ski school," he says as he presses a button marked with a star. "Private lessons, too."

Sebastian did tell me to charge whatever I want to the room—maybe a private lesson wouldn't be the worst idea.

"Where do I sign up for those?"

"Right here," he says, flashing a grin that rivals that of any of the celebrities I've spent my entire adult life writing about.

"Right here," I repeat. "In the elevator?"

He laughs. "I teach at the ski school and give private lessons."

"So, by 'they've got great instructors at the ski school,' you were talking about *yourself* and not some other guy?"

"Hey, the other guys are great, too," he says with a grin. "But I've got an opening at two if you want it?"

It would be perfect, actually. Enough time to explore the village a little, get something warm from the café. "Is this how you sign up all your clients?"

"Only the ones who seem like they might get lost touring the furniture on their way over to the mountain."

I laugh. "Okay. Tell me where to meet you and I'll be there."

Once we're outside, we split off down different paths. I take the one marked for the main lodge and the village; he's headed to the mountain.

"Oh, wait!" I shout suddenly, a few seconds later.

He turns, thankfully still within earshot.

"What's your name?" I call out.

"Tyler!" he shouts back. "What's yours?"

"I'm Alix!"

"See you at two, Alix!" he replies, loud enough that the entire resort now knows we have plans.

And then it hits me: I have plans.

Plans with an undeniably attractive guy. One who didn't mind me acting like the most awkward human on the planet.

No, no, *no*. He's a ski instructor, and that's it: nothing serious, nothing deep.

But that smile.

And those eyes—and his kindness. The way he made me laugh.

Chloe pushed me to leave my comfort zone, and she's insufferable when she's right. She would never let me hear the end of it if my ski instructor turned into anything more.

Which is why he absolutely, definitely cannot.

Black Maple Lodge

Stowe, Vermont

Welcome, Guest—

Thank you for choosing Black Maple Lodge as your home away from home! Whether you're here for the skiing or simply to get away, we hope you'll have a delightful and memorable experience at our resort. We are proudly family owned and operated, and it is our privilege to serve you.

The Village Café

Start your morning off right with a beverage from our espresso bar and a fruit pastry, or check out our selection of complimentary maple candies and hot cocoa samplers in the afternoon.

Harmony Spa

For tired muscles after long days on the powder, we invite you to spend an hour or two with our award-winning staff at Harmony. Now offering Swedish, deep tissue, and hot stone massage, as well as manicures, pedicures, facials, and scrubs.

Redfern Ridge + Maple Hollow

For casual dining options, including buffet and à la carte selections, Redfern Ridge is open daily from six a.m. to eight p.m. For more formal dining, Maple Hollow (two Michelin stars) has both indoor and patio seating available starting at six p.m. until eleven p.m. *See room service menu for specific listings at both venues; room service available 24/7.*

Ice-Skating Rink

Set against the stunning backdrop of Black Maple Mountain, the lodge's ice rink is the heart of the village. Skate the night away under starlight and the warm glow of the village. Skate rentals on-site, cocoa and soft pretzels available at the snack bar.

Honey & Thyme Lounge

Experience Black Maple Lodge's signature beverages at Honey & Thyme, our premiere lounge where you can kick back and relax by the fireplace in wingbacks made from custom Italian leather or enjoy the fire pit and twinkle lights on our outdoor patio. *Ages 21+*

Life at the Lodge

To extend your time at Black Maple Lodge into a vacation that never ends, inquire inside the main building at Concierge. *Select townhomes and penthouse suites now leasing. Subject to availability.*

4

I've got just over an hour to kill before I head up the mountain to find Tyler.

I make my way down the winding path that leads into the village, stopping to snap the occasional photo—this place is overflowing with scenic charm—and text the best one to Chloe.

You'll be happy to know I've got a ski lesson booked for 2pm

YESSSSS, ALIX, I'M SO PROUD, she writes back immediately. Plz don't break your beautiful neck

That's what the lesson is for, wish me luck

I tuck my phone away and head inside the café I read about in the welcome brochure. According to its little blurb, there should be complimentary maple candies right now—and sure enough, I spot a table full of them over by the far wall.

"Welcome," a barista with short, dark hair greets me; she's probably around my age or just a little younger. "I'll be right with you—there's a rack on the patio for your skis, if you'd like."

I would very much like. They're bulky and awkward and I almost dropped them six times on the walk over from my building. I head outside again, wondering how on earth I missed a rack full of skis, only to find it hidden around the corner.

Back inside, the barista seems remarkably chill for being alone behind the coffee bar, unhurried as she pours steaming milk into a mug. Only a few other customers are here right now, and all of them seem to be on dates with their smartphones.

"Cappuccino for Mark," she says calmly—but with authority—sliding the most perfect drink I've ever seen across the pickup counter.

Her entire vibe is a mood, the sort of silence that expands to fill the space. It's a precise one-eighty from the energy I'm used to with Chloe.

"What can I get for you today?" she asks once she finally makes her way over to the register. Up close, I can read the neat white lettering on her name tag: MAKENNA.

I'm torn between the honey nut latte and my usual no-whip mocha, feeling unusually indecisive.

"Dealer's choice?" I finally say.

"You got it." She prints out a receipt and slides it across the counter. "Just write your room number and sign on the line, unless you'd rather pay with cash or card."

I charge it to the room—thanks again, Sebastian!—then go over to check out the maple candies while she gets started on my drink. Each tray is marked with a little handwritten sign proclaiming things like CLASSIC and CAYENNE PEPPER and PECAN. I take one from the cayenne pepper tray—I've got a weak spot for all things sweet and spicy—and settle in at a table near the window.

The mountain looks gigantic from down here in the village, where we're right at its base. It's a stunning view; this cozy little corner could be the perfect work spot if I ever need a change of scenery.

A few minutes later, Makenna brings over two mugs: a simple

white one full of intimidatingly dark coffee, and another that looks like a work of art. From the drizzle of honey on top of the perfect white foam and the artful sprinkle of pistachios, I'm guessing it's the honey nut latte I was eyeing. I take a sip and sigh: it's heaven in a cup, sweet and smooth.

"No offense to whatever that is"—I gesture to the black coffee—"but it's, uh, probably not for me."

"You're not alone," she replies. "You'd be surprised how many people come in here and only want cocoa. First time on the mountain?"

"First time on this one, yeah. I'm doing a private lesson this afternoon so I can remember how not to crash into a tree."

"Smart," she says, wiping down a nearby table that honestly already looks pretty clean. "Which instructor?"

"Tyler."

My cheeks feel hot even as I say his name. I guess it really has been an embarrassingly long time since I've had plans with a guy one-on-one, even something as innocuous as a ski lesson.

"Oh, Tyler's great!" she says, eyes lighting up. "He comes in pretty much every day. First time I met him, he told me to surprise him, so I made him the weirdest combo I could think of. He kept a totally straight face—he drank the entire thing, as if a quad-shot peppermint-hazelnut latte with matcha powder was *exactly* what he was craving."

"That sounds terrible!"

Suddenly the plain black coffee seems more appealing than before.

"Oh, it was bad." She grins. "But now it's like a game between us—he always tells me to surprise him, and I always try to get a reaction out of him with disgusting drinks. He wins every time."

I laugh. "He sounds like a lot of fun, honestly."

"Best part of my day by a mile," she says, with one last wipe of the table. "Keeps things interesting around here."

A bell on the café door jingles as another customer comes in; Makenna gives me a little wave before heading back over to the bar.

My own words echo in my head: *He sounds like a lot of fun.*

It's been years since a thought like that has invaded my mind.

Two years, specifically.

Ever since Blake, I've closed myself off to the possibility of dating. Why put myself in the position to be strung along by a guy who takes himself—and *everything*—way too seriously? All he and his Wall Street finance bros cared about was themselves: if they looked good, if they felt good.

Well. That and their money.

It took me way too long to see it.

At first, all I saw was Blake's (admittedly gorgeous) exterior: tall, dark, and handsome with bespoke suits to match; a Manhattan apartment that's been featured in more than one movie; flashy themed parties every Halloween, Christmas, and New Year's Eve. He took me on the fanciest dates, where the fanciest people would see us being fancy together—so many yachts and galas and impossible dinner reservations.

Chloe was dating one of Blake's friends at the time. The Wall Street bros never dated anyone longer than a few weeks—Chloe and I were rarities. We became fast friends, seeking each other out when the nights inevitably devolved into conversations we couldn't care less about, all Scotch and stocks and sports cars. I often felt distant from Blake after he'd had a few drinks—we went through too many cycles of him saying things that cut deep, then swearing he didn't mean them the next morning. Daylight always made his shadows disappear, always made me wonder if my unsavory feelings were real or just left over from a bad dream.

The beginning of the end was when I caught Chloe's boyfriend cheating on her one New Year's Eve. She was home in Ohio taking care of her mom who had a bad case of the flu, which somehow made her boyfriend's indiscretions seem all the more heinous.

When I told Blake about it, he shrugged it off.

The glittering, twinkling aura I'd come to associate with their whole group sharpened into blinding focus in that instant. His unbothered reaction said everything—he wouldn't think twice about doing the same thing to me.

I asked him point-blank if he'd ever cheated on me.

He had. And he didn't even try to look sorry.

How had I not seen it?

Nothing about our year together was great, in hindsight, but one of the worst parts was that it did considerable damage to my confidence that I could accurately judge a man's character. Everything seemed so obvious in the rearview, but Blake's charisma had blurred my ability to see it as it was happening—and that *terrified* me. How would I ever trust myself to not make the same mistake all over again?

Chloe has reassured me a thousand times that anyone could have fallen for Blake's act. That their whole group was full of selfish, manipulative gaslighters, and how our boyfriends treated us was no reflection on who we are—that none of it was our fault, that we were young and naive like so many other New Yorkers who go through a finance bro phase. Chloe always insists there are a million other guys out there who would be equally horrified by their behavior.

I *want* to believe her.

I want to believe I could find someone good. That I could trust myself when I think I've found one and have it turn out to be true.

In the meantime, I've sworn off men who take themselves and

their money too seriously, men who don't care how rotten their souls are so long as they're perceived as attractive and desirable.

Chloe's taken the opposite approach: she's gone on over a hundred first dates in the last two years, but never lets them get anywhere close to serious. She worries I've closed myself off *too* much. And the fact that my upcoming ski lesson feels like a potential date based purely on the merit that it will involve one-on-one time with a man—well—

I admit it probably means Chloe is right.

Today is for the Chloe approach: nothing too serious, nothing to overthink about—just me and the mountain and the hot guy who's going to remind me how not to crash into a tree.

Dewdrops · For You Page

#traveldrops #freshdrops #tahiti #islandviews #sebastiangreen

u/SebGreen
1:57PM · March 2

thing i wish i'd learned a long time ago: they treat you right in tahiti

wish all 70mil of you were here (jk don't you dare show up, it'll scare the fish)

love,
seb

The ski school is housed in a modern log cabin that sits at the edge of the village, an A-frame lit from within by warm, glowing light. I arrive with two minutes to spare and check my reflection in one of its massive front windows—not bad. I rest my skis against the building and take a quick second to tuck some flyaways back into my braids.

"It'll only get worse on the mountain," someone says behind me. I whip around so fast both of my skis clatter to the ground.

"Holy—*Tyler*. You shouldn't sneak up on a girl like that!"

He laughs. "I thought you saw me in the reflection."

"Clearly I did not."

"Clearly," he agrees. "Ready for your lesson?"

"Don't I look ready?"

He eyes my skis, still lying haphazardly on the ground like soldiers wounded in battle.

"Oh, yeah. Totally."

He leans down to rescue my skis at the exact same time I do, nearly giving me a concussion before I'm even out on the slopes.

Only now do I realize my helmet is still in the closet.

Tyler notices, too. "Daredevil or just forgetful?"

"Neither, normally. Any chance you have extras?"

"There *is* a chance," he says. "But unless you wear the same size as a six-year-old, you're gonna have to just take mine."

My cheeks heat up despite the chilly breeze. "Oh, I can just run back over to my place—or go to the village—"

"We'd only get twenty minutes in, at most," he replies. "I've got another lesson at three."

"What will *you* wear?"

"An abundance of confidence in my ability not to need a helmet?" he says, and I laugh.

I can't quite tell if he's serious.

A moment later, though, he's holding his one and only mint-green helmet out to me. Now that his shoulder-length waves are no longer confined beneath it, his hair is unruly, but it smells *very* good—an unexpected and rather pleasant hint of floral shampoo.

I nod at the helmet. "You're sure?"

He grins. "We won't be leaving the Zen Zone today—I could ski it in my sleep. Also, that helmet is good luck."

"Because wearing it will automatically turn me into a pro?"

"Because it's just like the one my mom gave me when I was a kid," he replies. "It was a limited-edition color, super rare, made only that year—the year I started skiing. Finally found it on eBay in an adult size a few months ago."

He leans in close, and I get another heady whiff of . . . freesia, maybe?

"Don't tell the six-year-olds I'm going without," he whispers conspiratorially as he hands it over. "They'll never want to wear theirs again."

"Don't make me regret this." I accept the helmet. "Your face is too pretty, and it would be a shame to break it."

I did *not* just say that out loud.

I did not.

I did.

He laughs as if he hears it all the time, as if it is a completely normal thing to say—never mind that what I said doesn't even make sense, since the only part of his face a helmet would protect is his forehead.

"Too late," he says, going along with it, pointing to his ever-so-slightly crooked nose.

"How did *that* happen?" I ask. Its crookedness really is subtle, but now that he's pointed it out, I can't unsee it.

"You don't want to know," he replies, then glances at his watch. "Hey, we should probably get started, yeah?"

We head up to the Zen Zone, a gently sloped area of the mountain where beginners (and people like me) can practice skiing without fearing for their lives. Turns out my helmet isn't all I forgot—I accidentally left my poles at the café—but Tyler did have some adult-sized extras of those on hand.

"I've never actually done this before on any of my ski trips," I admit as we carefully make our way out into the snow.

"What? A private lesson?"

"*Any* sort of lesson," I say. "Ski school. The Zen Zone. My brother taught me how to ski when we were kids."

Admittedly, it was years before I tried to ski parallel and not just in wedge formation—Ian used to be so patient with me while I figured things out.

If only that had carried over into adulthood.

"Your brother's the daredevil of the family, then?"

I snort. "When we were kids, yeah. Now he's an accountant

who goes on the same vacation every year and never orders anything new when he eats at a restaurant."

Ian is predictable and safe and logical and firmly convinced his opinions are the best opinions—now, anyway. He wasn't always like that.

"What about you?" I ask. "Any siblings?"

"I—Oh, hang on a second," he says, twisting his wrist to check a message on his watch. He taps it and hits the tiny microphone icon. "Yes, comma, confirmed for seven this evening, period."

"Do you always voice text with perfect punctuation?" I ask, impressed, though it's not lost on me that he's deflected yet another personal question.

"Doesn't everyone?"

I laugh. "I try to . . . but that's just because I'm a writer."

His face lights up. "Maybe *that's* why you look familiar! Have you written any books I might know?"

I stop in my tracks. "I look familiar?"

Now it's his turn to blush. "Just a little. But I can't place you."

Interesting.

"You're a reader, then?" I ask.

"I love spy thrillers. Bonus points if they're in really epic settings—my favorite one is set in Prague. Have you written anything like that?"

"I've never written a novel before," I say. "But that's actually why I'm here, to work on a book. Ghostwriting a memoir."

"Isn't that an oxymoron?" he asks. "Ghostwriting . . . a memoir?"

I laugh. "You would think so."

"That's amazing," he says. "Anyone I've heard of?"

"The whole world has heard of him, so probably. I'm not really allowed to say more."

"So how'd you get hired to ghostwrite a memoir if you've never written a book before?"

"I'm a writer in my day job, just not a novelist," I say, weighing just how specific to get—I've probably already said more than I should. "My sister moved in a month and a half ago and wrecked my writing schedule. I couldn't get anything done at home, so they sent me here instead."

"Must be a big deal for them to hook you up like that," he says, impressed. "Be glad you weren't here a couple weeks ago for Presidents' Day—this place was as crowded as I've ever seen it."

He grins, gesturing to the wide-open expanse of snow before us. We're far from the only ones out here, but the space is so vast we might as well be. I turn to glance behind me, trying to see what he sees, but it throws my balance off for a second—he's quick to steady me, catching me with one strong arm around my waist before I turn into a total disaster.

His hand feels so *there*—the sort of strong-but-tender touch I haven't felt in years, if ever. Whenever Blake put his arm around me like that, it always felt . . . so . . . possessive.

"When's the last time you skied, again?" he asks, still steadying me.

"Six years ago, with some friends from college."

"And you went pretty often before that?"

"Almost every year with my family until I turned twelve, yeah—sometimes twice a year."

But then Lauren came along and we never went again.

"Okay, so let's just spend today getting you used to being on skis again—we can do a few practice runs here in the Zen Zone, and if you're feeling good, we can try something a little more difficult tomorrow."

"You're pretty confident I'll *want* to come back tomorrow."

"I'm pretty confident you'll want to come back every day, honestly."

"You're so cocky," I laugh.

"Just speaking from experience," he says smoothly, as if nothing has fazed him at all. "Everyone books me again."

"Maybe I'll be the first who doesn't."

"Maybe I'll make it so good you can't refuse." He raises those thick, dark eyebrows.

"You're ridiculous," I tease, rolling my eyes for effect even though I feel my cheeks heating up. "Maybe we should actually *start* the lesson now?"

We head over to something called the "magic carpet"—a conveyor-belt-like ski lift that will carry us up the bunny slope.

"Since you learned from your brother, I'm guessing you've never used one of these before?" Tyler asks as he demonstrates how to step onto it.

I shake my head, following his lead.

The magic carpet deposits us at the top of the hill. Even though it didn't look terribly steep from the base, we're definitely higher than I expected—I take out my phone to snap a photo for Chloe.

"My best friend will never believe I got out on the mountain unless she sees proof," I explain. I fumble for half a second before remembering I'm not wearing the sort of gloves that are compatible with phone screens. I tug one off just long enough to open the camera app.

"Want me to get a video of the run for your friend?" he offers.

It's not the worst idea.

I hand over my phone. Our gloves brush in the transfer, making me wish we were somewhere warmer, no thick fabric between us, like in front of a fireplace, maybe—curled up under a flannel blanket—hot chocolate in hand, or maybe some apple cider—

"Let's check your form first," he directs, pulling me out of my head and back to this cold, cold mountain. "Before I risk my life skiing down the hill with no helmet while making my cinematography debut, I just want to make sure I'm not going to capture a video of you crashing to your death."

"Wow, you really know how to motivate a girl, Tyler."

He laughs.

I show him my form, which—unsurprisingly—is a little rusty.

"Keep your shins tilted forward," he says. "And make sure your weight is centered over your feet as you move with your skis."

I thought I was doing those things already, but he closes the gap between us.

"Is it okay if . . . ?" he asks, gesturing toward my legs as if asking permission to touch them.

"Oh, yeah," I say. "Fix whatever you think will keep me from crashing into a tree."

He laughs again, tucking my phone into his pocket.

"You've almost got it—but—"

Tyler touches the backs of my knees lightly until I've bent them in just the right way, then straightens to correct my posture, one hand at my hip and another on my upper back. He's utterly professional, entirely respectful, yet it still sends shivers coursing through me.

"How does that feel?" he asks.

It takes a second too long for me to realize he's asking about my ski stance and not his hands on me.

"Good," I blurt out too emphatically.

"Good," he echoes, the corner of his mouth quirking up.

"Very helpful, thank you," I say, trying to recover before I die of embarrassment.

"Show me," he says, mercifully not lingering on what we both know I was thinking. He nods at my skis, then at a section of the hill that's more or less level.

I glide forward, steady and balanced, keeping my form exactly as he instructed.

"Better, yes—like that. Your technique isn't terrible."

"Like I said, you really know how to motivate a girl."

"You'd be surprised how many people say they can ski but are atrocious at it. It's a safety thing," he adds, shrugging. "No one will book another lesson if they break their neck on the first day—it's best for everyone if I'm honest."

He makes a few more minor adjustments until he's satisfied: a featherlight touch on my thigh, and another at my elbows to further reinforce my balance.

I could do this all day.

"Ready to head down?" he finally says.

I nod. "Ready to risk your life just so my best friend will believe this ski lesson actually happened?"

He holds up my phone; I'd almost forgotten I'd given it to him already.

"You've got a text," he says. "From Chloe?"

"Of course I do."

I can only imagine what she's written. Hopefully it isn't too mortifying—or worse, confidential. Too late, it occurs to me that *anything* could pop up in an email or text notification. What if Sebastian texts me and Tyler sees it?

We'd better get this over with, and quickly.

"Ready when you are!" I call out.

"Let's do this!" he replies, my phone's camera poised and ready.

I start down the hill, keeping my skis pointed inward so I don't go too fast too soon. Even at this slow pace, the wind stings my cheeks.

"Hi, Chloe," I hear Tyler say from behind me. "I'd like to state for the record that Alix did indeed show up for her ski lesson today—and that I offered her another slot for tomorrow. Here's proof!"

I laugh, tempted to let him have it for getting Chloe's hopes up that I might have another lesson so soon—she'll hold me to it for *sure*—but my slight dip in focus throws my balance off a bit, enough that I flail unattractively for a few seconds before regaining my composure. Two more bobbles (and two more recoveries) later, I make it to the bottom of the hill, proud to still be upright. Tyler skis around to face me, his movements smooth and easy.

"As you can see," he goes on, still recording, "she definitely needs to come back tomorrow."

He grins at me, then lowers the phone.

"I'm going to kill you," I say.

"Sounds like a plan," he says, still grinning as he hands my phone over. "Can you do four o'clock tomorrow? For my murder, to be clear."

I can't help but laugh. "Fine," I agree. "But only if I get enough work done."

This guy is something else, and his smile is next-level perfection.

"I'll put it on my schedule," he says. "Four o'clock murder with Alix *if* she gets enough work done."

I'm going to have an incredibly productive day tomorrow, no *if* about it. This lesson has been the most fun I've had in ages.

Of course, I will definitely not be admitting that to Tyler—or Chloe, for that matter.

He gestures to the magic carpet. "We've got time for a few more runs, if you want?"

I grin. "Let's go."

File: sebgreen_king of the world.mp3
Date Recorded: February 7, 2025

SG:

The first time I ever flew on a plane was for my meeting with
Jason out in LA.

Which isn't to say I'd never traveled before—my mom drove me
halfway across the country for an audition one time, all the way
up to New York from Nowheresville, Missouri. We used to spend
days in the car traveling to auditions that wouldn't even last an
entire afternoon, and we spent so many nights in the most run-
down motels you've ever seen in your life.

The label flew me out to meet with Jason and the others that first
day, and they kept flying me out until they officially relocated
us to a small house near the studio. I turned eighteen while we
were recording demos, before I was ever in the band, so I didn't
technically *need* my mom there after that. They let her keep the
house anyway.

I didn't pay for a single flight for years after that. Anywhere
I needed to go, the label flew us by private jet. Tours, press,

weekend getaways—pretty sure I spent more time in the sky one year than I did on land.

When the band broke up, I started chartering jets on my own. I got antsy if I stayed in one place for too long and had spent so much of my life chasing sunsets around the world that it felt wrong to suddenly see them from the same place every day. Yeah, I know it's controversial—high carbon footprint and all that, I've seen the lists I'm on. I tried to quit one time, I really did. Bought a house and managed to stay there for six months straight.

But then I bought another house. And a few more. And some others.

And I figured, well, it's kind of a waste for them to just sit there unused, yeah? How ungrateful and entitled would *that* be, to buy houses just to visit them only once a year?

I spent the first half of my life trapped in a car like a caged bird. Even when I was in the band, I was a different sort of trapped. Yeah, I got to do some amazing stuff—but none of it was *my* choice, you know? I went wherever they wanted me to, did whatever they paid me to. It might have looked like freedom, but it was just a different sort of cage.

I ripped right on out of there once that cage door opened—spread my wings to fly and never looked back.

6

I've been back at the penthouse for a couple of hours now, enough
time to thaw out in a hot shower and change into something comfortable for my evening work session: my favorite highlighter-yellow yoga
shorts and an oversized black hoodie cropped right above my navel.

I still haven't heard back from Sebastian about when I might be
able to ask him a few questions—I sent him another text as soon as
I got to the penthouse, but my phone has remained maddeningly
silent.

Instead, I listened to another voice memo and am now flipping
through one of the books I brought along for research, published
nine years ago at the height of the True North frenzy. It's full of old
photographs from their early days in the studio and on tour, along
with even older photographs from each of the members' childhood
days.

My phone buzzes on my desk. Finally.

But it's still not Sebastian—it's Chloe, just now replying to my
video.

SO, SO PROUD 👏 Sorry for the delay, btw, had a client meeting

It was fun, I write back.

Resisting the urge to say I told you so. ALSO. ALIX. Your ski instructor sounds hotttt

I can't help the smile that creeps onto my face. It's a very good thing she can't see me right now.

It was a good lesson.

Aaaaaaaaand? she replies.

And it was not the worst way to spend an afternoon, I admit, because it's the most neutral-sounding version of the truth I can find.

The actual truth: I can't stop thinking about him.

She sends back a long string of exclamation points. What's his name?

Tyler, I type back. Tyler Last Name Unknown. We scheduled another lesson for tomorrow . . .

Alix! I'm so proud of you for making time for yourself

I can only go if I get a ton of work done between now and then, I type back.

Which would be a lot easier if Sebastian would stop leaving me on read, I don't add.

Wish I could come write the book for you, Chloe replies. At least the skiing will be good for your deadline stress. I think Tyler Last Name Unknown will also be good for you. he sounds like a nice guy

It's not lost on me that Tyler could be on the other side of the wall right this very minute. I haven't heard his door—not that I've been listening for it—but that doesn't necessarily mean anything. Maybe he's just a quiet person. He could be making dinner, or listening to a podcast, or taking a shower—

Puffin head-butts my ankle, his fur soft against my skin.

"Okay, buddy," I say, reaching down to pet him. "We can get you some food."

I shut the book I was flipping through, set it aside for later. Puffin trots happily ahead of me, tail high, like we've lived here a year. We've been here one day and he already knows where I've hidden his food supply.

Every part of my body aches as I bend down to the bowl—muscles I didn't even know I *had* are aching. My hot shower clearly wasn't enough; I'm going to need an Epsom salt bath to recover from my lesson after I finish a little more work. I'm a fairly active person, but I guess I haven't done much outside of my running routine in a while. I'd forgotten how many parts of the body get a workout while skiing, especially when you're just getting back into it: my core and butt and quads and hamstrings and calves are *sore*.

A fleeting thought—*Tyler must be absolutely ripped*—careens recklessly through my head, and suddenly it's all I can think about. I do my best to stop it before my imagination gets too far ahead of me, with limited success.

I'm not thinking about Tyler while I make myself a light snack (oatmeal topped with some of the locally sourced maple syrup that was waiting for me in the kitchen upon arrival).

I'm not thinking about Tyler while I power through two more Sebastian voice memos—I definitely don't have to rewind them due to daydreaming. No more than twice, anyway.

I'm also not thinking about him while drawing my bath, or when I distractedly pour double the amount of lavender-scented Epsom salt into the water as is strictly necessary.

And when the sun has set and I've stripped all the way down, ready to soak my soreness away for a bit, I'm most definitely not thinking about his smile, and how—even in the short time I've known him—he's made me laugh more times than I can count.

At the precise moment I dip a toe into the water, there's a knock at my front door, its echo so loud in the colossal space that I hear it clearly from the master bathroom.

I completely forgot about dinner delivery—the person who dropped off my breakfast this morning took my order and promised to drop it off between eight and nine. (I requested it on the later side, as I'm a night owl and plan to work until midnight.) I throw on the closest thing I can find, a sage-green guest robe made of the softest satin, and scamper across the penthouse, careful not to slip on the polished concrete floor in my bare feet.

"Thank you so much!" I say, whipping the door open—only to find Tyler himself, in the flesh.

"You're not the room service guy."

His eyebrows rise. "And you're, uh—you might want to—"

Tyler gestures vaguely toward the knotted belt of my robe, averts his gaze to the heavens.

I glance down: *oh*. The soft satin is gaping all the way from my chest to my navel. One quick adjustment later, I'm no longer giving a minor peep show to my ski instructor–slash–next-door neighbor.

"I was just about to take a salt bath," I explain.

"With . . . your dinner?"

"My dinner?" I'm momentarily clueless. "*Oh*, because I thought you were the room service guy? No. I just forgot he was coming. I don't normally eat dinner in the bathtub."

My cheeks grow hot, and he grins.

"No?" he says, eyes twinkling as he leans against the doorframe. "Filet mignon and bubble baths aren't your ideal pairing?"

"Okay, first of all, I would eat filet mignon pretty much anywhere, no questions asked. But alas, I'm expecting rigatoni arrabbiata—and it's not a bubble bath. Can I help you?"

He shifts, the soft fabric of his mint-green tee rising just enough for me to catch a glimpse of his stomach.

It is very much as I suspected.

"One of my clients asked if I could fit her in tomorrow," he says, pulling me back to the conversation. "Would you be able to do your lesson at five instead?"

"Five works," I say, willing my eyes to stay trained on his face and not his perfect abs. "I'll bring my own helmet this time—don't want to press our luck with the whole you-not-breaking-your-face thing."

"Oh, totally," he says, nodding. "Now that you've seen the Zen Zone for yourself, you know exactly how treacherous it is."

I laugh. "Hey, the Zen Zone is no freaking joke—I'm sore *everywhere*."

"Hence the bath?" he says.

"Hence the bath."

His gaze flickers down to my robe, to the triangle of bare skin peeking out just above where I've pulled it tight, and then back up to my face.

"I guess you should probably go get in before the water gets cold."

"Probably, yeah."

His eyes linger on mine just a bit longer.

"See you at five tomorrow," I say with a wave.

When he nods, his wavy hair falls around his face like a curtain, and I melt a little. He tucks it behind his ear and smiles. "See you then."

My phone buzzes on the bathroom counter, just once: a text.

Please be Sebastian. *Please.*

I've been soaking for so long my hot water is verging on lukewarm, thanks to how totally and completely absorbed I got in the novel I brought with me. It's a rom-com, a grumpy-sunshine set in summer, in Venice, and I've just reached the part where the love interest finally shows the first hint of vulnerability.

I toss the book over onto the fluffy white bathmat by the sink, safe from any water I might splash on the way out, and towel off before tugging on my softest joggers and a longline bralette.

I take one look at my phone and groan.

It's Lauren.

SOS, ALIX! CALL MEEEEE

Honestly, I can't believe it's taken her this long—Lauren is not the most self-sufficient person in the world, to put it kindly. It started the day she was born and never really changed: she arrived several weeks early and the entire vibe in our family for the next few years was *Lauren is fragile*. Everything revolved around her, and everyone just got used to everything revolving around her, even after she left those years behind.

Once Ian and I were in college, Lauren really was the center of my parents' universe. You can't entirely blame her for expecting the world to revolve around her given how consistently it has for her entire life. You also can't blame her for not knowing how to deal with her problems on her own—my parents fought every battle for her. I'm sure they thought they were doing her a favor.

I am the black sheep in so many ways, not least in that I refuse to treat Lauren like the fragile little kid she once was. She's an adult now, and from our countless conversations over the last several weeks, I suspect there are good instincts buried under her insecurities—I just wish she'd learn to trust them.

I wait a few minutes, long enough to communicate that she can't just snap her fingers and expect me to drop everything to be her therapist, and then call her back.

She picks up on the first ring.

"This has been the *worst* day, Alix, you will not even believe it."

No *hello*, no *how are you?*—just the beginning of what is certain to be a half-hour monologue about the drama du jour at the museum.

I put her on speakerphone and listen as well as I can. In her defense, it really does sound like a terrible day: coworker drama with someone she considered a friend, impossible expectations from one of her bosses, and a guy who tried to feel her up on the subway.

"Lauren," I say when I'm finally able to get a word in. "It's going to be okay. *You* are going to be okay. Okay?"

Part of me is tempted to try and fix everything for her like my parents do—I'm not heartless. I just believe it'll be better for her in the long run if she can learn how to navigate her problems on her own.

"What do I *do*, Alix?"

"What do *you* think you should do?" I hate how patronizing my voice sounds, but thankfully, she doesn't seem to notice.

She lets out a long, dramatic sigh. "Give up and move to Antarctica where there are no other humans to deal with?"

"First of all, there *are* humans who live in Antarctica," I reply. "But I've heard the penguins are pretty cliquey—and you hate snow, remember?"

She laughs: mission accomplished.

I give in. I can at least try to point her in the right direction. "Have you talked with any of them about this stuff? Your friends—your boss?"

I already know the answer—Lauren is the most conflict-averse person I've ever met in my life—but I had to ask.

"Ugh, no."

"Well, I'd start there."

She starts to protest, but I'm too distracted to hear what she says: a message notification dips down from the top of my screen.

Sebastian. Finally.

in tahiti right now, time zones are brutal, major jet leg. i'll call u in an hour

His use of the letter *u* stabs me in the eye, but I remind myself that's one reason *I'm* writing his book and not him. I'm just glad to finally have confirmation that he's still alive and still planning to contribute to the project.

"Alix?" Lauren says on the other end of the line.

"Oh, sorry—I'm here. But I actually have to go get ready for a work call."

"A work call this late at night?"

"Time zone struggles," I say. I don't blame her for being confused.

Fortunately, she's too caught up in her own life to ask any more questions about mine.

I drop my phone on the bed after we end the call, and it sinks into the snowy-white comforter. My stomach growls—and that's when I realize I never got my room service delivery. The bedside clock reads 9:07.

Welp. Guess I'm going out tonight.

As long as I'm quick, I should be able to get back with plenty of time to collect myself before Sebastian calls. My list of questions is pretty thorough already, so I don't have that much preparation to do, but I won't be able to focus if I don't get food first.

I throw on a thick hoodie and my yellow hat with the pouf, then tug on my UGG boots. It's not *the* warmest outfit a girl could throw together, but I'll be fine. It's not like I'll be running a marathon in subzero temps, just taking a quick walk over to the main building, where I'll hopefully be able to warm up by a fire before walking back with my to-go order.

Two steps out my front door, I realize I've made a grave mistake: my phone is still on the bed. In its case are my debit and credit cards—and my room key.

I'm a split second too late to catch the door before it clicks shut.

BEFORE

Storms on the Horizon
for True North?

By Leif Mortensen // Starslinger Daily, *Staff Writer,*
Arts & Entertainment

It's another sunny day in Los Angeles—for everyone but Sebastian Green and Jett Beckett, that is. The infamous pair was spotted at Venice Beach's Tipsy Elephant for a private happy hour.

Jon*, a bartender who worked the coinciding shift, reported the meeting between Green and Beckett was anything but happy.

"It was rare to see them out together without the rest of the band," Jon said, "especially since they're, you know, rivals. I don't really follow them, but I don't live under a rock; I knew enough to know who they were. I didn't even recognize them at first, to be honest—they had an intense vibe, but it wasn't as contentious as I expected. Not until later. At first, they just sat there talking, debating something. They were too far away for me to make it all out. Only thing I heard clearly was right before they left—well, right before *Jett* left. I have no idea what the context was, but all I heard

---

* *Name has been changed so as not to jeopardize the bartender's employment*

was Jett say the phrase 'such a f—king puppet' before storming out. Sebastian apologized to all of us who were working and left a five-hundred-dollar tip."

It's no secret that Sebastian Green and Jett Beckett have had bad blood between them for a while, but it sounds like things took a turn for the even worse this afternoon. We hope they'll sort out their differences in time for their upcoming tour, which sold out within an hour of tickets going on sale. The tour will kick off early next year on the East Coast.

I try the door handle even though I'm certain it's locked.

How could I have been so careless? This isn't like me at all: I'm the girl who's always prepared. I've never locked myself out of anywhere, not once in my life.

I guess there's a first time for everything.

The guy who dropped me off yesterday mentioned an intercom system, but I was so confident I wouldn't need it that I didn't pay attention to where it was located.

If I at least had my phone, I could call the concierge and ask for help—

Or.

Maybe Tyler's home. If so, I bet I could use *his* phone to call the concierge.

I knock on his door before I lose my nerve.

It whips open only a moment later, and there's Tyler—

There's *a lot* of Tyler. Shirtless Tyler, with a light sheen of sweat, like I've caught him near the beginning of a workout.

I blink, force myself to look at his face and not, say, his washboard abs, or the line where skin meets fabric, his thick gray sweatpants hanging low on his hips.

He grins, amused. I've definitely been caught.

"Couldn't wait until tomorrow's lesson?" he says, and—I'm out of practice—but I would dare to describe it as *flirtily*.

Heaven help me.

"I was on my way to get dinner, and I locked myself out. Any chance I could use your phone?"

"Thought you were waiting on room service?"

"So did I," I say. "It never came."

His brow furrows. "You must be *starving*."

"I've literally only eaten an oatmeal snack and some maple candies from the café since breakfast."

He steps back from the door, gestures for me to come inside. "I can make you something, if you want? It'll probably take them a while to get over here to let you back in."

"Are you sure? Don't you have, like . . . ski work to do?"

Ski work.

Ski work.

"Promise you're not interrupting anything," he says, grinning. "Ski work's all done for the day. How do you feel about salmon?"

"I feel *very good* about salmon."

He leads me inside, and I take a seat on one of the barstools at his kitchen island.

"Be right back," he says, then disappears around the corner.

At a glance, his penthouse has the same layout as mine, only flipped—and the decor is opposite, too. Whereas mine is all white walls and warm wood, his is charcoal everything: charcoal floor tiles, charcoal walls, Edison bulbs inside geometric charcoal-gray fixtures. He's got potted plants, too—a trio of herbs right here on the island, and farther into the living room, a couple of monsteras. It's all very masculine, the entire space extremely well curated.

When Tyler returns, he has a shirt on, a fresh cotton V-neck in lilac. I can't help but picture him without it, the image of his carved stomach permanently impressed on my memory.

"Here you go," he says, sliding his phone across the island. "I pulled the number up for you."

"This says I'm calling someone named Julie."

He shrugs. "That's the concierge."

"You're on a first-name basis with the concierge?"

"Lived here a long time," he says. "It would be weird if I wasn't."

Fair enough. "Thanks again," I say, then put the call through.

Tyler pulls something out of his fridge—a piece of fresh fish still wrapped in paper from the market.

"You're *making me dinner?*" I say, still waiting for Julie to pick up. "I thought you had leftovers— Oh, hello!"

"You're not Tyler," a woman's voice says on the other end.

"I'm not," I say. "This is Alix Morgan—I met you yesterday when I checked in, I'm staying in the penthouse next door to Tyler's—"

"Let me guess, you locked yourself out?"

I blush. "I was wondering if you could send someone up with a new key, or maybe I could come down and get one?"

Across the island, Tyler brushes a maple syrup glaze onto the salmon while the oven preheats. I don't even see a cookbook.

"I'll send someone up," Julie assures me, sounding confident and professional and very kind to not give me a hard time about my mistake. "Don't worry—Tyler's locked himself out at *least* ten times."

"No wonder he has you saved in his phone!"

She laughs. "We go back a lot longer than that," she says. "But yes, I'm sure it didn't hurt."

Julie promises someone will be up in the next half hour. I'll be cutting it close for my call with Sebastian, but as long as maintenance arrives on time, I should still be able to make it. I slide the phone back across the island just as Tyler puts the salmon into the oven. He's wearing bright red oven mitts, reminiscent of lobster claws.

"Oven mitts? Even though the pan isn't hot?"

He grins. "Spoken by someone who's never burned herself on a preheated oven rack."

"Touché," I say. "So you and Julie—she said you go way back?"

He sets the oven timer, then leans back against the counter. "Known her since I was a kid, yeah."

"Did you ever date?"

"Definitely not—she's like a sister to me."

"So you grew up around here, then?"

"I did," he says simply, then takes a sudden interest in rummaging around his refrigerator drawers. "Sorry, I forgot to ask what you want *with* your salmon. I've got some salad greens—but no dressing."

"What kind of monster doesn't have salad dressing?"

"The kind that doesn't *like* salad dressing."

"What do you, like . . . put on the salad, though?"

"Fruit, nuts, seeds, goat cheese," he says. "Whatever I have on hand."

"Well, I'll eat whatever your favorite combo is," I say, because fruit and goat cheese does sound pretty good. "Surprise me."

Ten minutes later, the salmon is done and there's a bowl full of greens, goat cheese, apple slices, and walnuts in front of me. Tyler cracks a bit of fresh pepper over the top, and I have to admit, it looks great. I take a bite of salmon, and it's even more amazing than it looks.

"I think you might be in the wrong profession—not that you're a bad ski instructor," I quickly amend. "Do you do this for all the girls who lock themselves out?"

"Oh, yeah," he replies, not missing a beat. "One hundred percent of the time."

"Let me guess, I'm the only one who's done it?"

He grins, tucks that stray piece of hair that doesn't want to stay put behind his ear. "Don't get many people staying up here, to be honest. I can't remember the last time I saw anyone else on this floor."

"Probably because it costs a bajillion dollars a night to stay here," I say. I don't even want to do the math on how much it'll cost for the entire month.

"Writing must be pretty lucrative," he says, and I laugh so hard I nearly spit out my spinach, especially because I don't think he meant it as a joke.

"I could say the same for ski instructing. I'm only here because someone else is paying."

Now it's his turn to laugh. "Yeah, my job doesn't pay that well, either. Julie's family owns the resort—she took over when her dad died a while back. I get a friends-and-family discount."

So *that's* how he affords this penthouse. I'm hit with a surprising sense of relief: that he's not just some rich guy, obsessed with money—and obsessed with everyone *knowing* he has money—like Blake was.

"How long have you lived here?"

"I moved in not long after she inherited, actually. It turned out to be good timing—she was in over her head. That year was kind of complicated." He grimaces. "Also, please never tell her I said that. She'd resent the idea that I thought she needed help."

The phone buzzes on the counter between us.

"Excuse me for just a sec," he tells me, taking the phone into the next room.

"Yeah," I hear him say. "Yeah, the one from next door—yeah. She locked herself out."

Is it eavesdropping if the other person has simply moved around the corner? It's not like there's any music to drown out the conversation, and it's not like he's keeping his voice down.

"I know," Tyler says. "C'mon, man—you know I can't."

Can't *what*?

I wait for more, but he's quiet, listening. I definitely can't make out the voice on the other end.

"I mean, I know. We've been over this." A pause. "Can I call you back in thirty? Yeah, talk to you then."

I stuff a gigantic forkful of spinach in my mouth and hope it looks like I'm so enraptured with it that I've blocked out the rest of the world, especially the phone call I was absolutely not listening to.

"Sorry about that," Tyler says when he joins me again at the kitchen island, then smirks when he notices my face: I've bitten off more than I can chew, literally, and it must be a *look*.

"Enjoying the salad?"

I nod—with *enthusiasm*—since I cannot in good conscience try to speak. My ratio of greens to good stuff is very much not ideal; I think I only got a single walnut in this bite, and it's bitter without the other stuff to balance it.

"Need some water?"

He fills a tumbler with cold, filtered refrigerator water and slides it over. It's a lifesaver.

Naked spinach: not for me.

"Everything okay?" I say, nodding to the phone.

"Oh, yeah. My best friend—Julie's brother. Just giving me a hard time because *someone* told him I had a woman over."

I might be imagining it, but I think his cheeks are turning slightly pink.

"And that's unusual? Having a woman over?"

"Yeah," he says, meeting my gaze. "It is."

I study his eyes, his *gorgeous* eyes, wondering how it's possible that this guy doesn't have a girlfriend—how it's possible he doesn't have a woman over every single weekend. He could. I've seen what's under that T-shirt, and yeah, he most definitely could.

You know I can't, he told his best friend on the phone.

Ski Instructor Tyler is a mystery to me, one I want to unravel.

A knock sounds at the door, three sharp raps in quick succession.

"Maintenance!" a man calls from the other side.

And not a moment too soon—I've been here for almost *fifty* minutes, I realize when I glance at the clock. Sebastian will be calling any second now. How could I have lost track of time like this?

When Tyler opens the door, there's a man with a walkie-talkie clipped to his belt, his polo shirt and puffy coat both boasting the Black Maple Lodge logo.

"New key card for a Ms. Morgan? I appreciate your patience, we had some technical difficulties."

"That'd be me," I say, and he hands it over with a nod. "Thank you."

He gives a little salute and heads off to deal with whatever else needs fixing.

Tyler follows me out onto the elevator landing, propping his door open with the dead bolt so the maintenance guy doesn't have to come right back up.

"Thank you so much for making me dinner," I say. "It was amazing. Even the salad." I pause. "Mostly the apples and the goat cheese—but those made up for the spinach."

He laughs, and I like the way his eyes crinkle at the corners. "Come back again sometime and I'll make my famous brussels sprouts!"

I scrunch up my face.

"I'm not even kidding. They've won awards—not to mention there's bacon involved."

Now I'm laughing, too. "I would *try* them. I can't promise I'll like them."

I tap my key against the sensor on my door, and the lock slides open.

"All good," I say.

There's a beat there—a moment hanging in the air between us—and then he gives a little wave.

"See you on the slopes," he says.

I wave back and slip inside my own temporary home, the place where I'm meant to hole up and focus for a month. Focused is the last thing I feel: right now, I'm a mess of fizzy and reckless and fascinated.

Puffin rubs against my ankles, his fur soft.

"I know, buddy," I say.

I'm in trouble.

File: sebgreen_tipsy elephant.mp3
Date Recorded: February 13, 2025

SG:

Do you want to know what the number one question is that people ask whenever they meet me on the street?

It's not about my music, or my tour schedule, or that reality show I did. It's not about me at all.

Every single time—and I mean *every* time—it's: *Do you know what really happened to Jett Beckett?*

Maybe that sounds bitter of me to say. Maybe I *am* bitter. I've been in this industry for more than a decade now. When I got into it, I kinda hoped my legacy would be my own, you know? That they'd ask questions about me, not the same question over and over again about the guy I had to share the spotlight with.

And people never like my answer. I have no idea what happened to him, and that's the honest truth.

All I know is, as much as I hate to admit it, my career has been defined by Jett Beckett. I would've had a solo career from the start if not for him and the way Jason pulled us both into the band. If I'd somehow ended up in a boy band without Jett, I would've had the spotlight to myself, and that would have been different in so many ways. And when we woke up one morning and found out he'd just up and vanished overnight, he defined my career yet again, even in his absence. That was the beginning of the end for the band, and it was like a bolt of lightning shocking me out of the haze I'd been living in for . . . well. For a long time, I think.

Jett tried to convince me to quit True North one time—that *both* of us should quit, not just me—that night over drinks at the Tipsy Elephant. I thought he was full of it, trying to sabotage me somehow. I never considered that maybe he was serious.

People searched, people cried, people mourned. Even if he wasn't dead, he might as well have been—I knew in my gut that I'd never see him again, and I was right.

Here's a secret I've never told anyone, not ever.

Jett Beckett's disappearance was one of the best things that ever happened to me.

Sebastian never called.

He didn't call while I was locked out, and he didn't answer when I gave up waiting and tried calling him myself. I left two voicemails before finally going to bed, one embarrassingly long, the other stilted and short. He had hours to call back overnight while I was asleep—even a text would have been fine.

This silence is maddening.

Does he not care about his own book? Does he not want it to be complex and groundbreaking and *real*? That can't happen unless I know the whole story. I get that he's in Tahiti right now, but some of us are on deadline. He'd better have a good excuse.

Back to voice memo land I go, I guess.

My penthouse feels suffocatingly stagnant this morning. I try to work in three different locations before realizing I'm just too anxious to sit still—I need movement, maybe a change of scenery. Usually, the quiet would be a good thing. Today, it only amplifies my awareness of how silent my phone is.

I decide to head down to the coffee shop instead. It's snowing lightly, and I'm up so early it's still dark outside; I pull on the warmest jacket I can find and triple-check that my phone, wallet, and penthouse key are all safely tucked in my laptop tote before heading out.

Makenna is there when I arrive.

"Honey nut latte for here?" she asks, eyeing my tote.

"Sounds amazing. Can you make it a triple?"

I set up shop at a big table by the window. I'm the only customer in here, so of course I've picked the very best spot, one with a cushy single-sided booth made of blue velvet that has a full view of the glorious mountain.

Or, at least, it will once the sun is up.

"How'd your lesson go yesterday?" Makenna asks, setting my honey nut latte down on the table along with an almond croissant I didn't order. "On the house—they're fresh out of the oven, and you've *got* to try one."

"Ooh, thanks! And it went really well, actually. Better than expected after so many years."

"And Tyler?"

Tyler Fox, according to the ski school pamphlet I read from cover to cover before I went to bed. His name takes me right back to last night: shirtless Tyler and his superhero stomach—the way his eyes crinkle at the corners when he laughs—his amazing hair, and the way that one piece of it is always falling out of place. How he made me an *entire dinner* when I swooped into his penthouse without warning.

I shrug, like his name means nothing. Nothing more than *Ski Instructor Tyler*.

"He's nice. A good teacher."

"Mmm-hmm," Makenna says, like she can read every single thing I'm trying not to show. "Going back today?"

"I haven't skied in years," I say, busying myself with arranging my workspace in just the right way. "It would be irresponsible of me *not* to go back, right?"

Makenna laughs. "*So* irresponsible."

"Have you ever taken a lesson with him?"

"It's best for everyone if I stay off the mountain—one hundred percent, I'd end up breaking both wrists, possibly even my neck. Hard to make coffee with broken wrists."

"Hard to do *anything* with a broken neck!"

"You see my point," she says with mock solemnity.

Makenna heads back over to her station at the coffee bar, and I settle in to work. I catch a glimpse of golden light as the sun peeks through the clouds, a sliver of the sunrise radiating from the snow-covered mountains. It's still snowing outside, delicate little flakes: the perfect writing weather.

I pick up where I left off yesterday—I flagged one of Sebastian's voice memos to listen to after stumbling on an article about an argument he had with Jett Beckett. The title of this voice memo is the name of the bar mentioned in the article, so I'm hoping it will shed some light on what they were actually arguing about.

I open to a fresh page in my journal and hit play.

This is one of the lengthier voice memos, more than two hours long, but so far it's not at all what I thought it would be. Instead of juicy details about his heated exchange with Jett, the first half is all about his experience on a reality dating show he starred in a few years ago called *The Stag*.

I'm interested in that, too, of course—it was a huge scandal at the time, one of the most-watched finales in reality dating show history, in which Sebastian was famously rejected by both women at his final choosing ceremony. According to Sebastian, the double dumping was entirely staged: he claims he never intended to continue a relationship with any of the contestants outside the show. He even refused to sign the contract until the producers agreed to his idea of the perfect finale (i.e., one in which Sebastian ended up alone while simultaneously sparking a viral publicity moment for himself *and* the show).

From there, he talks at length about his public image—how the show affected it for better and for worse, how his solo album didn't quite land in the way he'd always hoped it would.

I write a question in my journal: Was Sebastian still represented by Jason Saenz-Barlowe when he agreed to that reality show? Was he pressured into doing it somehow, or was he just desperate to stay in the public spotlight at any cost? Was the twist ending really his own idea? If so, he's smarter than I've given him credit for.

I'm still making notes when something Sebastian says snags my attention: *Do you want to know what the number one question is that people ask whenever they meet me on the street?*

Yes, Sebastian. I do.

I hang on his every word, scribble out these revelations like they'll evanesce into nothing if I don't capture them:

As much as I hate to admit it, my career has been defined by Jett Beckett.

Jett tried to convince me to quit True North one time. I thought he was full of it, trying to sabotage me somehow.

Here's a secret I've never told anyone, not ever.

Jett Beckett's disappearance was one of the best things that ever happened to me.

And that's it: the end of the recording.

These are the kind of statements that will sell a billion books.

I close my eyes, pinch the bridge of my nose. When the conspiracy theorists get hold of this, they'll have an absolute field day. Sebastian's alibi was rock solid, and the investigators repeatedly emphasized that there was zero reason to think foul play was involved in Jett's disappearance—yet a small but vocal subset of the fandom refuses to accept that the case is closed, forever insisting there's more to the story. This new revelation about thinking Jett was trying to sabotage him, though . . . some might see it as motive.

I believe Sebastian when he says he has no idea what happened to Jett Beckett, but he isn't doing himself any favors with that final comment. I need to know what's behind it so I can make sure he comes off in a way that won't turn the entire fandom against him.

Would it be excessive for me to leave a third voicemail? At what point do I need to let Maribel, my editor, know I'm having a hard time getting Sebastian on a call and it's slowing down my progress? Maybe his service is just super spotty in Tahiti.

I take out my earbuds and close my journal.

The sunlight has shifted, and so have the shadows. It must have stopped snowing at some point—and I'm *starving*. I check the time: it's been almost three hours since I made a new home for myself here on this blue velvet bench. Three hours since I devoured my (incredible) almond croissant, and my honey nut latte is long gone.

Makenna is gone, too, replaced by a guy whose height and limbs can only be described as *adolescent giraffe*. Not that he's an adolescent—he's probably in his early twenties—but he's lanky, towering high above the espresso machine.

I take my phone off focus mode; I tweaked my settings last night to allow Sebastian's number to break through at any time, even while I'm asleep, but everyone else stays muted until I turn it off. I'm relieved to see I've only missed one text all morning, and it's from Chloe.

Hope you're not working too hard! Can't wait to hear how today's ski lesson goes 👀

Working a very appropriate level of hard, thank you, I write back. Otherwise I won't have time to hang out when you come visit in a couple weeks!

In that case, ignore everything I said and get back to work! TWELVE HOUR DAYS FROM NOW ON! (But I hereby give you permission—nay, ORDERS—to make time for ski school with Tyler Last Name Unknown!)

Tyler Fox, I reply. Found that out last night!

Ohmygosh Alix! she writes, followed by a GIF of some adorable baby foxes playing in the snow.

"Excuse me, but are you Alix?"

I look up to see the adolescent giraffe towering over my table.

"Um . . . yes?"

He slides a napkin onto the table in front of me. "This is for you."

There's a note scrawled on it in black Sharpie.

You looked really focused—didn't want to interrupt. Hope the book is going well! See you tonight. PS: Feel free to text at 555-253-9009

And then, the signature: Tyler :)

All the butterflies I tried to hide earlier, while talking with Makenna, come back in full force. I wasn't supposed to meet anyone who made me feel this way—now is *so* not the time for distractions.

I feel a little fluttery over the gesture, not to mention impressed that he was thoughtful enough not to interrupt my work.

Maybe it isn't such a bad idea, letting myself feel again. Chloe would certainly encourage it. I'm only here for a month—how serious could it get?

It's been a long time since I let myself just have fun.

Can't wait! I text back to him, triple-checking that I've typed his phone number in correctly. Thanks for your note ... see you in a little while.

I debate the punctuation for entirely too long, then ultimately just add a smile to match the one on his note.

Five o'clock can't come soon enough.

BEFORE

Dewdrops • /TrueNorth

#delirium #razorwings #mashup #fanedit #truenorth

u/TruestNortherner

12:03AM • October 17, 2016

Okay, y'all, hear me out: How absolutely *sick* would it be for True North to put out a remix/ mashup of "Delirium" and "Razor Wings"???? It'd be such an unexpected pairing but ahhhhhhhhh

COMMENTS

TOP **u/lizzyloveslove**

DELETE THIS RIGHT NOW YOU HAVE NO RIGHT TO GET OUR HOPES UP WHEN WE ALL KNOW JETT BECKETT AND SEBASTIAN GREEN WOULD NEVER

↳ **u/zebrastripes**

THIS. As much as we NEED this mashup, can you imagine the fight they'd have over which bridge to use? Both are iconic and I kinda feel like only one of the guys would make it out of the studio alive

↳ **u/jettbeckettconspiracytheorist**

oof, this thread is like six months old but it did NOT age well—did you see that Jett Beckett went missing last night?

9

Tyler greets me outside the ski school with the widest smile, eyes crinkling at the corners. Just past him, I notice a helmet and an extra set of poles leaning against the A-frame's front window.

"It's almost like you're expecting someone to forget their equipment," I say, making a show of tightening the strap on my helmet.

"Don't know why it seemed like a good idea to be prepared, just in case," he replies, matching my flirty tone. "Couldn't possibly be because someone forgot their equipment yesterday. Or locked herself out of her place while in pajamas."

"Those were not pajamas, number one." He doesn't need to know how right he is. "And number two, I am usually the most prepared person wherever I go."

"I guess I'll have to gather a little more evidence," he says, grinning. He tugs on his goggles, tightens his helmet, and we start off toward the Zen Zone. "I'll believe you—for now—but only because your entire life was spread out on that table at the café."

Heat rushes to my cheeks. I must have been seriously focused to not notice him.

"Not my entire life, Tyler. I left my cat back in the penthouse."

He glances over his shoulder, puts his finger to his lips. "Around here," he says in a mock-hushed tone, "we don't *advertise* that we live in penthouses. Also—you've got a cat?"

"Do I not seem like a cat person?"

"I'm just surprised they let you bring one," he says. "They've got a pretty strict no-pet policy. People kept bringing their dogs, and the snow—let's just say we had a vibrant yellow section at one point."

I scrunch my nose. "Ew."

"Hence," he says, "my surprise."

"Well, Puffin is an indoor cat, so maybe they were confident he wouldn't use the mountain as his own personal litter box."

"Maybe so," Tyler says, but then he goes quiet.

I can't begin to guess what he's thinking.

"So I guess you don't have any pets, then?"

He grins. "Actually, I do. His name is Pete. As previously discussed, he's not strictly allowed."

"And . . . what . . . *is* . . . Pete?" I ask as we board the magic carpet conveyor belt, beginning our ascent up the Zen Zone's gentle slope.

"Pete is a goldfish."

I burst out laughing, I can't help it. "A *goldfish*? They won't even let you have a goldfish?"

"Aquariums can do a surprising amount of damage—but it's not like I smuggled him in. Not really." He's quiet again, weighing how much to tell me. "Let's just say Julie gave me special permission since he's only in a small fishbowl, and I don't make a habit of letting anyone know about him."

"And his name is Pete," I say. A statement, not a question.

"What's wrong with Pete?"

"I don't know, it's a bit . . . human?"

"Says the girl who named her cat after an entirely different species."

"*Exactly*," I say, laughing. "It works."

"Once you meet him, you'll agree that he's totally a Pete," Tyler says. "But just out of curiosity, let's hear your better suggestions."

"Mongoose," I pull from absolutely nowhere. "Axolotl. Sandhill Crane."

"You think I should name a goldfish *Sandhill Crane*."

I shrug. "I don't think it's any worse than Pete."

Now we're both laughing, and I slip ever so slightly on my skis. He steadies me, one strong hand secure on my upper arm and the other at my lower back.

"Pete would be pretty upset if he learned the very mention of his name had sent a woman crashing to her death," Tyler says in a low, faux-stern voice, flirty eyes locked with mine.

His actual words barely register—but *how* he says them stirs something in me. I swear this guy could read his to-do list to me and I would find it steamier than a sauna.

We go over everything he taught me yesterday. He checks my form; it's possible I get it slightly wrong on purpose just so he can correct me. I can't get enough of how confident he is, but also how careful—his corrections are firm but fleeting, and even though I gave him permission to put his hands on me yesterday, he asks again today.

Finally, we head down the mountain for our first run. We're still in the Zen Zone, so it's not too steep, but my skis are closer to parallel than they were before—compared to yesterday, it almost feels like we're flying.

We ski down the mountain, then head back up again, over and over, until my muscle memory from years ago finally starts to kick in. All that's missing is my daredevil brother, Ian. I've been missing him for a long time, though.

Ugh, *Ian*.

Just the thought of him makes me tense up, and before I know it, my right ski is slipping, skidding out of control.

"It's okay!" Tyler calls out. "Bend your knees—and try to square up!"

I manage to regain my balance, avoiding a fall. It's a good thing this slope is relatively gradual: *transform self into crumpled pile of skin and broken bones* is very much not on my list of goals for this month.

"Nice recovery," he says once we make it to the bottom, grinning.

"Thank you," I say, trying to figure out exactly how ridiculous I looked, flailing down the mountainside.

I can't quite see his eyes through his Oakley goggles, a single reflective lens that reminds me of a fiery sunset, but I'd put money on it that they're doing that cute crinkly thing right now.

"Probably should've gone over this yesterday, but—"

A split second later, Tyler slumps over, falling sideways into the snow. It's so shocking, so fast, and I kneel down as gracefully as I can in my snow gear to check on him.

"Tyler! Tyler?"

I put a hand on his shoulder—his *thick* shoulder, muscles clearly defined even under his ski clothes—and that's when I realize he's shaking.

With *laughter*.

He rolls over, and I playfully swat his chest.

"You nearly gave me a *heart attack*. What was that?!"

"Just showing you how to fall if you have to."

"With exaggerated drama?"

"To the *side*," he says. "You're less likely to break or twist something if you fall sideways instead of backward."

"Yeah, see, all I got out of that was 'Top Ten Ways to Terrify Someone.'"

"Sweet of you to worry," he says, still laughing.

"What kind of person would I be if I didn't?"

"I'm glad I don't have to find out." Tyler sits up, and now we're face-to-face. The snow is cold under my knees, even through my thick ski pants, but the look he gives me is hot, hot, hot. "Any chance you'd let me take you out to dinner tonight to make up for scaring you?"

Dinner is harmless. I have to eat, right? And eating *with* someone beats eating alone. Not me crashing his place unannounced because I've locked myself out—but us going somewhere together, on purpose.

The thought of going out to dinner with Tyler is . . . yes. He's funny, he's thoughtful, he's kind. He's patient and considerate—the sort of guy any girl would be lucky to spend time with, romantically or not.

"Only if there's no naked spinach involved," I reply, downplaying my excitement.

"I'll make sure any spinach we encounter is completely, decadently clothed," he says, and suddenly all I can focus on is his mouth, full and tempting in its playful smirk. "I promise."

"Okay, then," I say. "It's a date."

After my lesson ends, Tyler walks with me back to our building so we can both freshen up for tonight. The clouds have edged out the sun for the first time since this morning, and it looks like snow might not be out of the question.

Tyler offered to store my ski gear with his at the ski school so I won't have to keep hauling it back and forth, and it's amazing how much more pleasant this walk is now that I don't have to juggle it all. Quicker, too—and with infinitely more opportunities for his hand to brush against mine (*three* times, so far!). He's giving me a mini tour along the way, pointing out notable spots in the ski village, all of them picture-perfect and straight out of a travel magazine.

We wind down the path, passing the ice-skating rink and the café and all the other village shops, as well as the place where another path splits off toward the main lodge. It's getting darker by the minute. Between the fiery lanterns and the globe string lights everywhere and the way all of it makes the snow sparkle, this place feels incredibly magical: the perfect setting for a first date.

A date, I mean.

His hand brushes against mine again, and he's so close now that our arms brush, too.

What have I done?

I told myself I would take the Chloe approach to hanging out with Tyler—nothing too serious—but the more time I spend with him, the more I wonder if I'm capable of Chloe's level of chill. Maybe it would be possible to keep my heart out of it if Tyler were less handsome, less thoughtful—if he never made me laugh, never put me at ease.

But then again, without those things, I wouldn't be so drawn to him in the first place.

By the time we make it to our elevator, he's quiet. The lighting inside is rich and warm, a cozy contrast to the outside world. We're standing close together, closer than two people alone in an elevator really need to be. His body heat radiates between us, and I'm tempted to get even closer—tempted to break the silence, too. But the longer it goes on, the more of a bubble it is.

When the doors open to our shared floor, the bubble finally pops.

"Meet you here in an hour?" he says, eyes bright.

They're so familiar and so new all at once.

"See you then," I reply.

I have a *date*.

To: Sebastian Green (seabass_the_mighty@sebastiangreen.com); Alix Morgan (alix.morgan@amorganwrites.com); Evan Wright (e.wright@wrightwayliterary.com)

From: Maribel Tovar (m.tovar@mcclendonmurphy.com)

Subject: Congratulations!

Hi Team,

Wanted to drop a quick note your way about our early preorder numbers: THE GRASS IS ALWAYS GREENER is already breaking records, and not just here at McClendon & Murphy. Within the first hour of announcing, it shot straight to the #1 spot—in *all* books—and has held steady ever since.

We appreciate your efforts to spread the word online, Sebastian and Evan—and Alix, we hope the writing is going smoothly! I'll reach out with next steps when the time comes. Congratulations on what is already on track to be the biggest book of the year!

Best,
Maribel

10

I'm seven minutes late, but when I walk out my front door, Tyler's not there.

My mind skips straight to the possibility that maybe he changed his mind—it wouldn't be the first time a date has bailed on me without warning, and it happens to Chloe on a semi-regular basis.

I'm just about to text him when his door opens. I smell him before I see him—in a good way, a *very* good way. Whatever he's wearing smells spicy, masculine, expensive.

The sight of him is even better.

Tyler's legs look even longer than usual in those navy pants, fitted but not too tight, tapered at the ankle just above his white sneakers. He has a lightweight cream-colored sweater underneath an unbuttoned khaki button-down, sleeves pushed up to reveal his rather glorious forearms—an unusual combo, but it definitely works. The whole look is put together in a way that makes me wonder where his personal stylist is hiding.

He gives me a little wave, holding up his phone.

Sorry, he mouths.

"Yeah," he says to whoever's on the call. "We'll be there in ten." A pause. "I'm not sure yet—be ready for either, I think?" Another pause, and then, "Thanks, tell Julie I owe her."

When he pockets his phone, his eyes go wide like he's seeing me for the first time.

"You look great," he says, tucking that piece of hair behind his ear again. Does he *know* how hot he looks when he does that? Did someone tell him?

"You look pretty great yourself," I reply. "And thank you."

I make a mental note to thank Chloe, too—we did a quick FaceTime when I realized I'd brought absolutely nothing that would work for a date. My current look is what I'd call a Lululemon miracle: black leggings that accentuate all the right places, some shiny black Ralph Lauren ankle boots that are *technically* classified as rain gear, an oversized black cable-knit sweater that pairs perfectly with the leggings, and a simple necklace that pulls it all together (and makes it look less like bank robber–chic). I spent a little extra time on my hair and makeup to compensate—beach waves for my sandy-blond bob and a rosy glow that's meant to look like it took no effort at all.

"So where are we going?" I ask as we step into the elevator.

This close, it's impossible to ignore how incredible he smells.

"I can tell you everything—or you can wait and be surprised."

"Okay, well, now I'm intrigued." I would almost always pick *tell me the plan*, but there's a playfulness to his voice that makes me think he's really excited to surprise me. "I think I'll wait and see?"

"*Excellent.* You're gonna love it."

"You're pretty confident, as usual." I nudge him with my elbow, feel the warmth radiating between us.

He grins. "If you don't like it, I'll make you dinner again instead—but you're gonna love it."

We take the path back down toward the village, but this time, we continue toward the main lodge instead of the ski school. It's snowing, just enough to be magical. The lodge gives off a warm glow; somewhere in the distance, I hear the faint sound of live music.

"Turn here," Tyler directs as we approach the main building.

A white neon sign boasts the words HONEY & THYME. Beside the hostess stand waits a petite Asian woman whose name tag reads JULIE—I recognize her from the concierge desk when I checked in. She's beautiful, and the very definition of professional.

"Jules, this is Alix. Alix, Jules."

She smiles and gives my hand a firm shake. "So lovely to officially meet you, Alix."

"Thanks for pulling this together," Tyler says.

"You're lucky I was still here," she replies with a playful smirk.

"When are you *not* here?"

"Fair point." Julie glances at me, then says, "Follow me."

She leads us inside. I remember reading about this place in the welcome brochure—it was described as a lounge, and that feels accurate. Lots of buttery leather couches and warm lighting, numerous servers buzzing around with drink trays. It's fairly crowded but not overly loud.

Julie leads us all the way to the back of the place. We veer toward a set of double doors, breezing right past a RESERVED sign and onto the patio.

Did he—did he reserve this *entire patio*?

Two couples were waiting near the hostess stand, and several more groups were just inside. This patio could easily seat twenty.

There's only one table.

It's a table for two, set up elegantly with a simple black cloth and sparkling dinnerware, right near the patio's focal point: a large fire-pit, a lively fire blazing inside. I can feel its warmth even from here.

Julie leads us over, gestures for us to have a seat. "Hannah will be taking care of you tonight—she'll get you started with drinks."

"Thanks again, Jules."

She gives him a firm side-hug, one that fits the *she's like a sister to me* vibe he told me about last night.

"It looks like this place only does drinks?" I say when it's just us again, giving the cocktail menu a once-over.

"That's part of the surprise," he says, fire twinkling in his eyes. "Okay. So. One of the restaurants here at the lodge is a pretty big deal in the culinary world—they've got two Michelin stars. Even with Jules's help, it's impossible to get a same-day reservation. So . . . they're bringing the restaurant to *us*."

"Julie must really love you," I tease.

"She's very protective of me," he says. "Her younger brother and I must have annoyed the shit out of her on a regular basis, and we fought like I was part of the family, but she's always had my back. I think I told you she inherited Black Maple Lodge when her father passed away—she was only twenty-four. She's been pulling strings around here for a lot longer than that, though."

"And you're still friends with her brother?" I ask, remembering the phone call he took last night while I was over at his place.

Tyler averts his eyes to the menu, studying the cocktails.

"We don't get to hang out much anymore," he finally says. "But yeah, we talk almost every day."

There's a story there, and I want to ask about it—but is it too soon for questions like that? Blake never had boundaries when it came to the details of his personal life; his favorite subject was himself. Tyler seems more guarded, though. Less self-obsessed, too.

"Sounds complicated," I say, an invitation for him to go deeper if he wants.

"It is."

For a second, it looks like he's about to say more—an expression passes over his face that I can't quite read—but then he holds up the drink menu instead.

"They're known for this one," he says, pointing to one called the Honeybee that involves gin, lavender honey, a squeeze of lemon, and sliced serrano peppers. "If you're not into spice, you can order it 'without the sting.'"

He makes air quotes around "without the sting," and it's maybe the most adorable thing I've ever seen.

"Oh, I'm into spice," I say, rolling with the subject change—I can keep it light, keep it fun. "But I'm totally tempted to order it plain for the *sole* purpose of saying 'without the sting.'"

He laughs. "I'm sure you wouldn't be the first!"

A few minutes later, our server comes over to take our drink order. "Still need some time, or do you know what you'd like?"

We order a pair of stingless Honeybees with lavender sugar on the rim, and she promises to be right back with them.

"We're not in any hurry," Tyler says smoothly. When she's gone, he says, "So, for dinner, we have options. The restaurant specializes in steak and sushi, and I'm not exaggerating when I say they've perfected the art of making every sort of potato."

"*Every* sort of potato? Even lefse?"

His thick brows furrow, somehow making him even hotter. "What's that?"

"It's Norwegian," I explain. "One of our family traditions at the holidays—it's like a tortilla, but the dough is mostly made of mashed potatoes. It can be really, really sticky if you don't know how to do it right."

"Okay, so maybe not *every* sort of potato. But that sounds amazing."

"You eat it with butter and sugar and—*ohmygahhhhhhhh*—sorry, now that's all I'll be able to think about until I get one at Thanksgiving."

"For eight months?"

"It's going to be a problem for me," I deadpan. "But please, tell me more about the potatoes they *do* make."

He laughs. "Since you like spice, I'd say go with the horseradish mashed potatoes. Those and a filet mignon—medium—might even make you forget about your holiday potato tortillas."

"*Lefse*," I say, laughing. "For real, though, literally everything you just mentioned sounds amazing."

"So I can confirm you don't need to see a menu?" Tyler asks. "Jules kept saying I shouldn't assume, so she texted it to me just in case."

"Yeah, no. I'm good. It sounds—really good."

His eyes hold mine for longer than is strictly necessary, making me temporarily forget everything else. It's just Tyler and me and the sound of the flickering fire, embers and ashes and sparks flying.

The moment hangs between us until Hannah brings over our drinks. We give her our dinner order, and she slips away.

"How's the writing going?" Tyler asks, sipping his stingless Honeybee; a bit of lavender sugar catches on his lower lip and I have the sudden urge to lick it off.

"The writing?" I say, forcing my eyes away from the sugar. "It's good. Slower than it should be—but good."

I put in so many hours today, but my word count still came up short. I'll just have to trust that I'll write *more* than my goal one of these days. It can be tricky to figure out the exact right way to put someone else's story down on paper—especially when the subject of said story still hasn't called you back.

"I know you can't talk about the project itself," Tyler says, "but I've always wondered about how it works when someone else writes a memoir about a person they've never met."

"How do you know I've never met hi—the person—I'm writing about?"

He shrugs. "I guess I don't. Have you met them?"

"I have not. Not in person, at least."

Something in my tone makes him laugh, and now I'm laughing, too. "What?"

Tyler shakes his head. "I just—"

He cuts himself off, his eyes locking on mine again with an intensity that burns a hole straight through me.

"It's just that I haven't met anyone who makes me laugh like you do in a really long time," he says. "Not everyone is so easy to talk to."

"Not even your client who asked to switch times with me today?"

"Brenda is seventy-three years old, has four dachshunds and a doctorate in statistics, and recently made a bucket list for herself that includes 'ski a double black diamond' and 'skydive in Indonesia,' among other things. She's fascinating—but no. None of my other clients are like you."

I sip my Honeybee (it's halfway gone already—I guess it's a house favorite for a reason), unable to hide my smile. Tyler's known me for two days, but I'd be lying if I said he didn't make me feel the same way. I knew Blake for years, dated him for half that time, and things never felt this relaxed, this easy. I never felt like anything but an accessory with Blake—and Blake had *endless* accessories, replacing me in less than a month after I broke things off.

With Tyler . . . Tyler looks at me, and I feel seen.

"Is Indonesia a popular skydiving destination?" I ask, still processing everything he just said.

"No idea," he says, laughing. "But she's already booked her flights."

"That's amazing." I take another sip, catching a bit of lavender sugar on my tongue.

His gaze flicks down to my mouth for a split second, then back up again. "It is."

The intensity of his eyes, the way they linger on me—it suddenly feels like maybe we're not talking about Brenda and her bucket list anymore. I'm about to tell him I feel the same way, that it's been entirely refreshing and unexpected to meet someone who puts me so at ease, but then he leans in like he's got something else to say, something I most definitely want to hear.

"Sorry for the tangent," he says. "I never let you finish. What's the writing process like?"

"It's, like, ninety percent staring off into space, two percent snacks, and eight percent actual typing."

"It'd be at least five percent snacks if it were me."

"Two percent might be an underestimate, honestly," I say. "But one percent is also just me banging my head on the table."

"That bad?"

I shrug. "Only sometimes. The guy I'm writing about—he's been kind of difficult so far." Quickly I add, "But I didn't say that."

Tyler laughs, even though I really shouldn't have said it. Anyone famous enough to have a ghostwriter writing their memoir is probably difficult to work with to some degree.

"Difficult how?"

"Oh, mostly just impossible to get in touch with. He blew off a call we were supposed to have and still hasn't returned any of my messages."

"Wow," he says.

"Yeah."

"And that's why you've been banging your head on the table?"

"No one likes to be ghosted," I say with a shrug. "But also, there are some things in his voice memos that I really need to ask him about—things that could damage his whole reputation if he actually means them the way they come across in the recording."

Tyler's eyes grow wide.

"That sounds . . . bad, yeah."

"Right? So I might need to do damage control to soften it all up," I say. "I'm hoping there's just some context missing that'll make it better somehow."

"It's not, like—something that makes him dangerous to society or anything, though, I hope?"

"Thankfully, no." *That* would put me in a seriously uncomfortable position; I suppose the situation could always be worse. "He just made a comment that makes him sound pretty heartless, like, that a thing a lot of people were sad about was basically the best thing to ever happen to him."

Not to mention how some people might take his *other* comment the wrong way—how he thought Jett was trying to sabotage him by getting him to quit the band—but that is one detail I should most definitely not share.

"Okay, yeah, he sounds like a piece of work—I'm so sorry you have to deal with that, and that he won't return your calls."

Tyler looks so sincere, so invested in how this situation is affecting my progress on the project. I mentally add *empathetic listener* to the growing list of his attractive qualities.

"Thank you," I say. "Hopefully there's a good explanation."

Hannah returns a few minutes later to deliver our food, and we dive in. It's *heavenly*. I want to eat this filet mignon for every meal, forever. I want to swim in these mashed potatoes. The zing of horseradish on my tongue feels like an electric current, sharpening my focus—perfection.

And at the center of that focus: Tyler.

His smile. His eyes. His thick eyebrows, distinctive and expressive. His laugh, and how rare it apparently is for someone to bring it out of him—how *I* bring it out of him. That piece of hair that just won't stay put; the place where his nose was broken once upon a time.

There's still something so familiar about him, like I've known him forever—I think he just has one of those faces. An REI model with a Whole Foods glow, outdoorsy and athletic and strong, the type who could build you a campfire, make dinner over it, and then curl up with you under a thick flannel blanket (s'mores optional).

Okay, so that's a bit specific. But the point is, Tyler is simultaneously like no one I've ever known and like everything I never knew I might want. He's the farthest thing imaginable from Blake's Wall Street crowd.

"Have you ever gone ice skating before?" Tyler asks once we're done with dinner.

"Only long enough for my brother to trip and fall and get his left pinkie skated over. I was eight."

Tyler grimaces. "Gruesome. Well. I promise nothing like *that* will happen, because I'm not going to let you fall."

The idea of him breaking my fall—those lean, muscular forearms and his (for lack of a better word) *capable*-looking hands—makes me feel all sparkly inside.

It's almost enough to make a girl want to fall on purpose.

"I always did harbor secret dreams of winning Olympic gold," I say as we head down the path in the direction of the rink. "You don't happen to *also* coach figure skating in your spare time, do you?"

"Depends on how you define 'figure skating,'" he replies, grinning. "Can I help someone learn how to skate a giant loop around the rink without falling? Possibly."

"No death spirals, then?"

"Most definitely not."

"No triple Axels either?"

"Not even a *single* Axel, I'm afraid." He laughs. "If you actually want a lesson, I bet Jules could teach you some stuff—she used to skate competitively when she was younger."

"Seriously? That's incredible! Does she still skate?"

"She likes to pretend she doesn't," he says. "But I've seen her out here at dawn a few times when she thinks she's alone."

We head up to the skate rental counter inside a little hut just off the rink.

"My usual, please," Tyler says. "And for the other pair, we'll need a—"

"Size eight," I fill in.

From a distance, I've always gotten the impression the skating rink would be beautiful, but it's even more charming up close: the ice shimmers under all the twinkling globe lights overhead, countless rows of them zigzagging from one side to the other. Fir trees line the far edge of the rink, densely packed with snow clinging to their needles. On this end, a snack bar sells only two items: hot cocoa and soft pretzels, both of which smell *amazing*.

Everything but the ice itself—the rink railings, the skate rental hut, the snack bar, and all the benches in between—is made of smooth pine. Tyler and I sit on one of the benches, change into our skates. At the rink where Ian got hurt, we were given generic worn, brown skates; these, though, are pristine white leather, and the white laces are flecked with sparkly silver thread. Tyler's are solid black suede, different from mine and all the others I see waiting behind the counter.

"Tell me those aren't your own personal skates," I say, growing more confident with every second that they very much are.

"Okay," he says, playing along. "They're not my own personal skates."

"*Liar*," I tease. "I thought you said you weren't really a skater?"

"Never said that. I only said I couldn't do any Axels."

We ease out toward the ice, and it takes more effort than I expect to keep my ankles from wobbling.

"So now I need to know," I say. "On a scale from total beginner to Nathan Chen, where do you fall?"

"Somewhere in the middle," he admits. "I never took any formal lessons, but when your best friend is on the ice every afternoon as a kid, you kind of have to pick it up if you want to hang out."

"You picked it up for Julie?" I ask, suddenly intrigued.

He shakes his head. "Jules skated pairs with her brother," he explains. "My best friend."

Tyler steps confidently onto the ice, holding his hand out to me as I follow him through the gate. I take it, steadying myself, and by some miracle do not fall the instant I leave the walkway.

His grip is firm—or maybe it's just that I'm holding on for dear life—and warm, even through our gloves.

"You've got it," he says, sounding more like Ski Instructor Tyler than Date Night Tyler. "If you think too much about falling, it's more likely that you will."

"Don't become a self-fulfilling prophecy," I reply. "Noted."

Slowly, we make our way around the rink. He doesn't let go of my hand, not even when I start to get the hang of it. At some point, it becomes less me holding on for dear life and more just holding on to *him*.

Tyler is steady and confident, skating elegantly like he was born with blades on his feet. My skating, by comparison, can only be described as aspirational. Despite my early Olympic ambitions, I'll never understand how anyone could feel comfortable enough to propel themselves up into all those triple Axels and quad Salchows and toe loops they do for *fun*—I'm perfectly content to skate in a giant circle, thank you very much. Perfectly content to keep all my bones in working order.

We skate and skate. At the far end of the rink, where it's just us and the snowcapped fir trees and the occasional skater who whizzes past in a flurry, Tyler slows us down. I follow his lead, and the next thing I know, he's turned around and we're face-to-face.

Well. More like face to chest, since he's quite a bit taller than I am.

He looks down at me, straight into my eyes, and—oh no.

Up close, his eyes look almost unnatural, surprising flecks of blue amid varying shades of brown. I was totally and completely mistaken if I thought I could keep myself from feeling all the *feelings*.

The corner of his mouth quirks up. He pulls me in closer, then settles his hands on my hips; I reach up and wrap my arms around him loosely, like we're dancing.

"Is this okay?" he murmurs, even though there's no one else around to hear.

"Very okay," I reply.

"And this?" His fingers brush lightly across my temple as he tucks my hair behind my ear, the soft leather of his gloves so smooth I almost ask him to do it again.

"It is."

He traces my jawline, tilting my face up to his until there's barely any space between us. "What about this?"

His lips are dangerously close to mine, his breath hot amid the chilly breeze.

"Mmm-hmm," I answer, closing the gap between us. "It's good," I manage to get out just before his lips meet mine.

The kiss is *everything*. It's steamy and slow and perfect, just hungry enough, and it's like time stops. His tongue flicks lightly against mine, lighting me on fire from the inside out.

I return the favor and feel his fingers press more firmly against my hips. I press back, too, and he kisses me harder, deeper. This is a man who knows what he's doing: a little bit teasing, entirely fun, never crossing the line into *too much*.

I could live in this kiss.

Only when it starts snowing again—giant puffy flakes that get caught in my hair and Tyler's—do I realize it ever stopped in the first place.

"I've got an idea," Tyler says, pulling back just far enough to get the words out. "How do you feel about soft pretzels?"

I burst out laughing—it's that alluring tone, those unexpected words, the straight-faced delivery.

"I feel very, very good about soft pretzels. Right up there with mashed potatoes, if I'm being honest."

His entire face lights up when he smiles, one more thing that makes me want to stop time and stay inside this moment forever. When he takes my hand in his, we skate back toward the snack bar. I'm cool and collected on the outside, but just under my skin, my thick layers of ice have started to melt.

This, I can't help but think, is how avalanches start.

BEFORE

True North Snub Leads
to Fan Outrage

By Alix Morgan // Starslinger Daily, *Staff Writer,*
Arts & Entertainment

It's Grammy nominations week! We're thrilled to see so many talented artists on this year's shortlists, both established and up-and-coming—but there's a gaping void this year, with True North absent from every category they're eligible for. Naturally, the internet is supremely unhappy about it.

This has undoubtedly been a breakout year for boy band True North, with hit after hit taking top spots on every chart out there. Their music videos, too, have even received <u>praise from one of Hollywood's most decorated directors</u>.

Why, then, have they been unilaterally excluded from this year's awards?

Fans have already been vocal about their outrage, arguing that the band should have been included in the mix for Album of the Year and Best Music Video at the very least. Some speculate that bad blood between the band's manager, Jason Saenz-Barlowe, and an influential someone in the Recording Academy could have led to the snub.

Whatever the reason, True North is clearly still winning in all other ways—with fans in their corner and numerous hits dominating top-ten lists, it's safe to say they're not going away anytime soon.

I wake up in a tangle of sheets, too-bright light streaming in through the windows. There's a faint buzzing on the bedside table—I peer over the cloudlike comforter just in time to see my phone vibrate itself right onto the floor. The alarm clock reads 11:37.

I rarely sleep past seven thirty these days—can't even remember the last time I slept through an alarm, especially when I have a ton of work on my plate. I also never forget to close the curtains, but apparently a single (incredible) kiss and the best soft pretzel I've ever eaten were enough to turn me into an entirely different person overnight.

By the time I get to my phone, it's stopped ringing.

No, no, no—

It was a video call from Sebastian. Because of course.

I sit up, rub my eyes. It's too bright in here.

After a quick once-over in the mirror, I head to the living room and call him back. I grab my notebook as the phone rings, flop down on the couch near the window.

Surprise, surprise: he doesn't answer.

I groan so loudly Puffin perks up.

"It's okay, buddy," I tell him, even though it's not. Sebastian literally *just* called me—but he doesn't pick up when I call him back two minutes later?

I open my notebook and scan my list of questions. If I ever do get Sebastian on the phone, I have no idea how long I'll be able to *keep* him on the phone, so I go down the list and put asterisks beside the most pressing ones.

At the moment, my list looks like this:

- Manager manipulation: When did Sebastian and Jett realize their manager had fed them the exact same promises, the exact same lies?
- Sebastian's solo album: Was Jason his manager then?
- TIPSY ELEPHANT FIGHT: Can he tell me more about his argument with Jett?*
- Potentially controversial comment about how Jett's disappearance was the best thing that ever happened to Sebastian—can he clarify?*

I'm still thinking through how to word everything when—miracle of miracles—Sebastian calls me back.

"Hiiii," I say as cheerily as possible, since I probably shouldn't greet him with my first choice of *Well, look who's alive!* "Wow, where are you?"

Behind him is the most unreal sight I've ever seen: an unbroken stretch of crystal-blue water below an infinite, cloudless sky.

Sebastian laughs. "Still in Tahiti."

He looks like he's just rolled out of bed.

"Sorry I couldn't call before—I dropped my phone in the ocean, and it took a while to get another one." He laughs again, probably at the obvious look of relief written all over my face. "What—you thought I'd ghosted you on *purpose*?"

My cheeks go hot; the thumbnail image of my face confirms that I'm blushing, and not in a subtle way.

Take a breath, Alix.

I've had countless celebrity interactions, extensive media training. I don't make a habit of insulting famous people—of insulting *anyone*, for the record—or insinuating they're in the wrong in any way. Only once was I pushed past my breaking point into borderline unprofessional territory; coincidentally, that was the time I interviewed Jett Beckett.

"Of course not," I reply as smoothly as possible. "And I'm sorry I missed you earlier."

"It's all good."

"I don't want to take too much of your time, but I have a few questions."

"Hit me," he says with the sort of cocky casualness only an ex–boy band pop star could get away with. He *winks*.

"I've been working through your voice memos," I begin. "And a lot of my questions are about the dynamics involving your manager, Jason, as well as Jett Beckett."

I pause, trying to gauge his reaction when I say Jett's name, but his expression is unreadable.

"Understanding those dynamics will help me share your story in the most accurate and powerful way possible," I go on. "So to start, I was wondering if you could tell me more about how Jason manipulated you both into joining the band—when did you realize Jett had been promised the exact same things as you?"

Sebastian shakes his head. If I had to describe the look on his face, it would be wounded puppy with a dash of rage.

"Man, where do I even start with Jason?"

He considers it for a moment, biting his lip.

"Jason was an asshole, but he hid it well—always gave the impression that he was on your side," he finally says. "For maybe three months, I thought Jett was like the others, handpicked just for the band. It wasn't until Jett made a comment in the studio one night—how Jason was all lies, that we shouldn't trust him, and *why*—that he and I realized we'd been made the exact same promises. That Jason had strung us both along, fed us both the same hope about how huge our solo careers could be. It explained so much, especially why Jett had such an attitude all the time."

"But it didn't bring you closer? Finding out you'd been through the same thing?"

Sebastian looks away.

"It did not," he says, his voice hardening.

I wait for him to go on. A seagull swoops over the ocean behind him, in the frame and then gone again.

"Finding out Jason was even more of an asshole than he thought only made Jett angrier," he finally says. "Jett really wanted a solo career, was never passionate about being in a boy band. He wanted to make his own music."

"And you didn't relate to that?"

Sebastian shrugs.

"It's not that I didn't relate. But we had a good thing going with the band—quick success, lots of fans. Money pouring in. I guess I was just more patient, figured all of that would only help when I—or we—eventually broke off and went solo."

I glance at my notes.

"It seems like you weren't just willing to be more patient with Jason, but also more forgiving, even after he manipulated you both—but in your voice memos, it sounds like your feelings about

Jason and the whole situation changed at some point. When was that, and what caused it?"

"Now *that's* a loaded question."

He runs a hand over his five-o'clock shadow, which barely even qualifies as a shadow since it's blond and only visible when the sunlight hits it in just the right way.

"It . . . it took way too long to sever ties with Jason," he says. "I should have done it a lot earlier. Jett tried to get me to do it sooner—"

He breaks off and looks away.

"We met up one time, just Jett and me, and he pitched this idea—he wanted us to, like, go on strike, refuse to play Jason's games anymore. Refuse to record, refuse to perform, stuff like that. Said it would only work if both of us did it together, which was probably true since none of the other guys could carry the lead vocals. He didn't say so, but I'm sure he thought it would get under Jason's skin if I suddenly started putting my foot down about stuff—Jason played favorites, and I was his favorite because I never made trouble or asked too many questions."

"And Jett did?"

"Oh, all the time. And he hated that I went along with everything Jason wanted, called me a puppet or something stupid like that. Jett and I were never on good terms, so I was suspicious of the whole thing from the minute he asked me to go get drinks. I thought maybe he was just trying to pull me down so he wouldn't be the only one on Jason's bad side."

"So you said no," I say, "because you were happy enough as it was and because you didn't want to burn bridges with Jason?"

He nods. "Didn't realize until later that bridges aren't worth keeping if they lead straight to snake pits."

I scribble that line down word for word—that's definitely going in the book.

"When was that?" I ask. "The 'later,' I mean, when you finally came to that realization?"

His jaw tenses as he looks off into the distance.

"When Jett disappeared and Jason found a replacement by the next weekend."

Wow. *Wow.*

I had no idea he'd been replaced *that* quickly—their PR team must have buried that detail somehow. They definitely didn't announce the new guy until some time had passed. I remember because I wrote one of the "breaking news" articles that went viral. The band didn't last much longer after that, though, so the replacement—Adrian Silva—didn't make a lasting impression on most of the fandom.

"I don't think it really hit me until then how right Jett was about Jason, or that he'd been sincere when pitching the idea to strike all those months earlier. It sounded ludicrous, honestly—we were all under contract, you know? It's not like we could just say no to stuff. It's not like we could just walk away from any of it. When Jett disappeared, though—"

He cuts himself off.

"When he disappeared," Sebastian starts again, "I felt really, really sick. Like maybe if I'd gone along with his idea, maybe things—maybe he wouldn't have—"

He closes his eyes.

"Maybe he'd still be here."

His words hang between us, even across the ocean and the internet.

As if he realizes how heavy it sounded, he adds, "I mean, he has to be out there somewhere, right?" What he doesn't say is that eight years is a long time to stay that far under the radar. "But whatever happened to him . . . it could've been different."

108

This is it, I think—this is my opening. Now or never.

"In one of your recordings, you said that his disappearance was one of the best things that ever happened to you," I say. "What, exactly, did you mean by that?"

His eyes flicker downward, then back up to the camera.

"It was the thing that finally made me wake up and muster the guts to cut ties with Jason. Best career choice I ever made."

He pauses, bites his lip.

"I hate that it took Jett disappearing for me to do it, though. And sometimes—"

His brows knit together. Gone is the shiny veneer he shows to every camera and anyone else who'll look: this is the real Sebastian. I didn't truly believe he had this level of vulnerability in him.

"Sometimes I can't sleep because I feel so guilty about it. How much better my life is now that Jason doesn't have a hold on me anymore—how I have the life Jett always wanted, but it took him disappearing for me to get it. Was he, like, rotting in a ditch somewhere while my own life got better? Sorry, I know that's graphic."

Sebastian has *survivor's guilt.*

This I can write about. I hate it for him—but people won't hate him for it.

I try not to show how reassured I am by his confession. I definitely don't want to tell him I was worried he was a heartless egomaniac there for a bit, especially not when he's given me such a raw, honest look inside who he really is.

"That all sounds really complicated," I say. "Totally understandable, though, all of it."

I jot down a couple of quick notes before I forget them. Sebastian's quiet on the other end.

"I've got one more quick follow-up question, if that's okay?"

He nods.

"Was there ever a part of you that felt relief that your biggest rival was gone? It had to have created a wide-open lane for you when you launched your solo career."

"I mean, who wouldn't be at least a little relieved?" he says evenly. "But it felt like bad luck to think that way, you know?"

"Hey, Seb," a woman says from somewhere off-screen. "Can we go get breakfast now? I'm starving!"

He glances past his phone's camera at what is probably a gorgeous woman in a tiny string bikini, if she's wearing anything at all—it could be either, judging by how he's looking at her right now.

"Yeah, almost done here." Sebastian looks back to me. "Sorry, Alix, gotta go."

And just like that, his pop star façade takes over again, pushing out all hints of his former vulnerability.

I have more questions, but this is plenty to work with for now.

"Sounds good," I say. "Thank you for—"

He ends the call before I finish my sentence.

"Your time," I say to no one.

Forgot to mention, I text Sebastian a little while later, let me know when might work well for us to meet up in person here in Vermont?

No surprise: it goes unanswered.

I indulge in room service for my extremely late brunch, take it and my laptop out to the expansive balcony off the living room to get started on writing while our call is fresh on my mind. I may or may not have picked this particular balcony because it's the one that borders Tyler's, the two separated by a waist-high railing—but if I do happen to see him this morning, I'll most definitely say I chose it for the mountain view.

I certainly didn't choose it for its warmth. Thankfully, the heater is easy to figure out, and so effective I have to move farther away from it only a few minutes after I sit down. The outdoor couch is incredibly comfortable, too—my only fear is that I'll spill coffee or the raspberry compote from my granola yogurt all over its plush white cushions.

I get to work crafting Sebastian's relationship with Jason into a narrative that roughly reflects the conversation we just had, typing furiously until the chapter starts to take shape. This revelation—survivor's guilt—will make Sebastian seem like an extremely sympathetic character to the reader, especially given how public his rivalry with Jett was and what a contrast these lingering feelings are to all of that.

I write about the hold Jason had over him, and how it took Jett's disappearance to break the spell. I try to fill in the gaps I didn't get to ask about—the timeline of his eventual solo album makes me think he'd ditched Jason by that time, and a quick internet search tells me I'm right.

I'm not sure I've ever listened to that solo album all the way through, now that I'm thinking about it. I pull it up on Spotify. The first track is just as mediocre as I remember: though catchy, it's nothing groundbreaking. The second track is similar but with better lyrics, and the third track is somewhat forgettable.

All of this gives me a false sense of security, because I am not prepared for the fourth track. Track four is almost unlistenable—I think Sebastian was going for sexy, but it's more reminiscent of a cat in heat. A *wounded* cat in heat, maybe?

I can't yank my earbuds out fast enough.

"Must've been a terrible song," a familiar voice says as I throw my AirPods on the table.

I whip my head up and see Tyler, mug of steaming coffee in hand, standing at the railing of his own balcony.

He is, once again, shirtless. Flawless.

It can't be more than forty degrees out here.

"How are you not freezing?" I ask, shutting my laptop. I could use a little break.

Tyler shrugs, and I force my eyes up to his face.

The face that was so close to mine last night. The lips I kissed—and that most definitely kissed me back.

"You get used to it. I like to come out here first thing in the morning with my coffee to help me wake up."

"It's hardly first thing in the morning," I reply.

Understatement: it's well past noon.

"Not the first time I've been out here today," he says, grinning, a reminder that not all of us overslept this morning.

"Do you have a lot of private lessons to give later?"

"I've got three this afternoon," he says. "But I've got time for another five o'clock if you want it?"

I'm still sore from all the skiing I've done this week, and probably from the ice skating, too—but it's too tempting. Especially since I now know, thanks to the deep dive I did on the ski school pamphlet, that he technically doesn't advertise five o'clock slots since it's borderline too dark at that time.

He's made exceptions to spend time with me this week, and I can't fully process it without a blush creeping into my cheeks.

"Sounds perfect," I say.

Tyler nods toward my table full of books. "Those for your project?"

"Research, yeah," I say.

Casually, I shift my laptop on top of them so he won't be able to tell what they are—a trio of coffee table books about True North. The spines aren't facing him, so I doubt he saw too much. But still.

"Did the guy you're writing about ever call you back?"

"Finally, yes." I make a face. "Turns out his phone was dead because he dropped it in the ocean."

Tyler cracks up, eyes crinkling at the corners. "He did not."

"If he didn't, he's a pretty convincing liar," I say.

"Or a pretty creative one, at least." He gestures to my laptop. "Is it hard not to talk about the book?"

"Not as hard as you'd think," I reply. "I mean, this guy's life is living rent-free in my head right now—but that also means I want to *stop* thinking about it whenever I'm not working."

"I bet you wish you could talk about whatever it was that inspired such violence against your earbuds."

I shudder, wishing I could unhear Sebastian's melismatic journey through an unholy number of octaves.

"Be glad I can't inflict it upon you," I say.

I'm dead serious, but he laughs.

"Well, good luck with all of that." He raises his coffee mug in a toast. "And hey, I just wanted to tell you . . . last night was a lot of fun. I'd love to take you out again."

The memory of last night—his hands on my hips, his lips hot against mine—

Fire and ice and *magic*—

All of it comes crashing back.

"Something more than this, right here, now?" I say, playing down how into the idea I am.

"Something with a little less patio railing in the way," he replies, grinning. "I can't do dinner tonight, but if you're free after that, I have something perfect in mind."

"I'm intrigued," I say, and not just by the mystery of it all: he doesn't seem to get out much, so I'm fascinated by the idea that he might have plans outside his own penthouse that don't involve ski lessons.

"Oh, you'll love it," he says, eyes sparkling in the sunlight.

"You're confident," I reply. "As always."

"Have I been wrong yet?"

He hasn't, and he knows it.

I don't admit it.

"Where and when?" I say instead.

"Meet me at the ice rink at ten—but we're not skating tonight. And you should wear something warm."

REVIEW:
Sebastian Green's Solo Effort, *Daydreamz*
(C-)

By Zeke Xanderfeld // Writer & Critic, Moondazzle.com

Two years after boy band True North officially split up, former frontman Sebastian Green has finally dropped a long-rumored solo album, *Daydreamz*.

It's the first time Green has stepped out on his own without his bandmates, and the results, we feel, are hazy. *Daydreamz* boasts neither the magnetic charisma nor the catchy melodies fans grew to expect from True North; instead, the album meanders from shallow lyric to shallow lyric, bathing its listeners in lukewarm, lackluster ambient tracks with nary a discernable beat.

That said, fans are undeniably obsessed with the album, praising Green for reinventing himself as a solo artist. Indeed, the limited-edition vinyl record sold out the night it was announced, and two of the tracks that immediately landed in top-twenty spots on various streaming services continue to have staying power.

We miss the electric energy of Sebastian Green's tension-charged dynamics with his bandmates, especially once-rival Jett Beckett; his debut as a solo artist can only be described as a serviceable effort with few standout tracks.

<u>The Verdict:</u> For all but Green's most devoted fans, *Daydreamz* is a snoozefest—don't expect anything revelatory.

12

I migrate to the café midafternoon for a change of scenery. I've made good progress today, knocked out another entire chapter—a fluffy one about Sebastian's time on the reality dating show—but I'm in desperate need of a break.

Makenna's just clocking out when I get there.

"Honey nut latte," she tells the other barista before I've even had a chance to order it. "Unless you want to try something else this time?"

"No, that sounds great. Done for the day?"

"Done *here*," she says. "I picked up a bartending shift over at the lounge tonight, but I've got a couple of hours to kill. You?"

"Taking a minute before getting back to my project."

She straightens a few syrup bottles on the counter, then glances up at me.

"I saw you together last night," she says, eyes sparkling. "Skating."

My cheeks burn. Did she see us *skating*—or did she catch that moment when time stood still, when we kissed, the fact that we were on skates a mere technicality?

"It was a really fun time," I say evenly, unable to conceal my smile.

"I bet it was. I've never seen Tyler out there with anyone," she says.

"Yeah, I get the impression he doesn't get out much."

Makenna snorts. "An understatement! And such a waste. You don't see a lot of guys who are that hot *and* that kind. Not in my experience, anyway."

Not in my experience, either, but I keep that to myself—if I say anything at all, I risk revealing just *how* hot I find him, just *how* kind.

"Honey nut latte!" the other barista calls out, sliding my drink across the bar. It's beautiful, but so, so full—one wrong move and it'll be everywhere.

Makenna wishes me good luck with my work before heading out, and I ease my way over to my favorite spot by the window.

My phone buzzes violently on the table as soon as I sit down. Chloe's face lights up the screen, a black-and-white photo from when we grabbed ice cream one day last summer: in it, she's mid–brain freeze, caught in a moment of joy that lives on every time she calls.

"Tell me *everything*," Chloe greets me. "Everything!"

"You waited long enough to call," I tease. "Did someone steal your phone this morning?" It's nearly four in the afternoon, the longest she's ever taken to touch base.

"Lots of work drama today." Her tone drips with resentment. "But I didn't want to call too early and *interrupt* anything, if you know what I mean."

"I know exactly what you mean, and I'm sorry to inform you that there was nothing to interrupt."

"Nooooo!" she says. "The date wasn't good?"

"Oh, it was good."

I can still feel hands on me, his fingertips, his kiss like fire—

"But it didn't go anywhere?" she asks.

"Not all of us spend the night on a first date, Chlo."

So many times throughout our friendship, I've wished I were the sort of person who didn't take everything so seriously—the sort of person who could let go and have fun, who doesn't need every hookup to mean something. Chloe has perfected the art of having fun and then moving on before anyone has a chance to get hurt.

I'm not sure I'm capable of that kind of no-strings fun.

"But you wanted to?"

She would kick me in the shin if she could see the smile creeping onto my face right now.

"The only thing that kept me from inviting him in was that I'd left my project all over the kitchen island, all the True North books and everything," I admit. "At best, I'd look like a boy band stalker."

Chloe howls. "If he only knew! You are the least starstruck human I've ever met in my life."

"They're just people," I say. "Sometimes they're *awful* people."

"But they're loaded most of the time, and they all have ten beach houses and cars that cost more than I make in three years. And they're *gorgeous* and can take you to gorgeous places. I bet they have the best stories."

I snort. "Yeah, you say that now, but ninety percent of what they talk about is themselves."

"You're just saying that because you've spent too much time listening to Sebastian for your book—that's different! Your job is literally to listen to his life story and write it down."

She does have a point.

"I'd totally let Sebastian Green take me to one of his beach houses,"

Chloe says, and I laugh. "So tell me about last night? Where did Tyler take you on your date?"

"Dinner, then ice-skating under the stars—it honestly felt like something you'd see in a movie."

Chloe squeals on the other end. "Alix! Stop it. That sounds like the most romantic date ever!"

I can't help it, I smile. "It really was."

"*And*?" she prompts, like she can sense my smile even over the phone.

"And he kissed me," I say in a rush.

"Ahhhh, I knew it! I knew it. When are you seeing him again?"

"I have another ski lesson at five, but we're also meeting up later tonight—he told me to wear something warm."

"To do what?"

"I have no idea—it's a surprise. But last night was, too, and he was just . . . really thoughtful."

She sighs dreamily. "He sounds amazing, Alix, really. I can't wait to meet him when I come visit!"

My stomach flips. Not that he isn't introduction-worthy—he totally is.

But that's what's scary.

Right now, it feels like Tyler and I exist in a beautiful, sparkly snow globe. If our world were to tip upside down, it would only make things *more* beautiful, because that's part of the design. I can't bring my real life inside its safe glass wall without breaking it, though—and that could get messy, even painful.

"I promise I won't say anything embarrassing!" Chloe goes on, misreading my silence.

"You'd better not," I say, going along with it so I don't have to admit the truth about how much it scares me to think about my worlds colliding.

She tells me a little more about the drama she's having at work and about how she's interviewing for a promotion tomorrow. Her work rival is also up for the promotion, but Chloe feels confident she has it in the bag—her boss specifically encouraged her to apply for the new position, which seems promising.

When we're finally off the phone, I crack open my laptop to read over the chapters I wrote after talking to Sebastian.

In the process, my arm knocks into my honey nut latte, and not gently.

It's a slow-motion disaster: what's left of my latte sloshes right out of its mug, all over me—all down the front of my favorite long-sleeved fuchsia running shirt, even up into my hair—and all over my laptop's keyboard. I didn't think there was much honey nut latte left, but apparently I was wrong. It's *everywhere*.

"No," I say urgently, under my breath. "No, no, no, *noooo*."

As if telling it to stop will magically keep it from seeping into every crevice.

I can't afford a new laptop right now.

And I can't afford *not* to have one.

Frantically, I rush to back up my work in case it—I don't know—short-circuits on me? My old boss ruined a computer like this once. His shut off immediately and wasn't salvageable, but hopefully there've been some technological advancements in the last ten years.

I'm trying to minimize the damage with half a tree's worth of napkins when something sizzles and the screen goes black. It's a hopeless, sticky mess. I'm not getting any more work done today. I'll be lucky if I get any more work done this *week*.

And I'm supposed to meet Tyler at the ski school in an hour—there's no way. There's just no way. Even if I were somehow able to forget about this long enough to relax, there's still the inconvenient matter of my soaked, stained outfit. I love the smell of honey nut latte and all, but it's not exactly my go-to scent—and it's dripping from the tips of my hair.

I need a shower. I need a lot of things.

So, so sorry, I type out, but I'm going to have to cancel my lesson today. Work emergency.

Tyler doesn't reply immediately—he's probably on the mountain with his elderly client who has all the dachshunds, making sure she doesn't break a hip or tear any important tendons.

Sure enough, when I've just gotten back to my penthouse, smelling of sickly sweet old coffee and more than ready to wash this day off my skin, he writes back: Oh, no . . . sorry to hear that. We'll make it up another day. :) Still on for tonight at 10 or better to cancel that, too?

His reply brings tears to my eyes. No guilt trip, no pressure to rehash what happened, no indication that I've offended him by canceling at the last second.

It's refreshing, and so different from how Blake would have reacted. Blake would have asked a million questions until I ultimately gave in and went along with the original plan.

What does it say about the men in my life—specifically my ex and my brother—that such a simple message makes me feel so seen?

Puffin rubs up against my ankle, purring. I kneel down to pet him, but he backs away when he smells my coffee-soaked sleeve.

Wouldn't miss it, I finally write back. See you then :)

Q how to fix|

Q **how to fix** a broken heart

Q **how to fix** the heat when you're renting an apartment

Q **how to fix** a ruined laptop

13

I arrive at the ice-skating rink five minutes early. At ten on the dot, Tyler comes into view, headed my way on the path from the main lodge. He looks even more like an REI model than usual—dark jeans, red flannel shirt, leather-and-shearling bomber jacket, wavy hair peeking out from under a charcoal-gray beanie, forest-green backpack.

Honestly, he could pass for a *model* model right now—like full-on Paris runway, if you swapped out his woodsy chic for high fashion. I'm trying to pinpoint exactly what it is that feels different, and I land on his beanie: something about it accentuates his cheekbones, making them look more chiseled than usual. Maybe it's just the lighting.

As soon as he spots me under the lamppost where I'm waiting, his face splits into a huge grin.

"Hey," he says when he gets closer.

It's a single, simple syllable, but it's the way he says it that gets me—soft and low, like a secret.

"Hey," I reply. "Sorry I had to cancel earlier."

He waves it off. "It happens. Need to talk about it?"

"Maybe. Not now, though. Right now I want to forget work even exists."

Tyler grins. "*That* I can help with. But first—"

He gestures for me to follow him, so I do. Instead of taking one of the paths away from the skating rink, though, he leads me closer to the entrance to the ice.

"I thought you said we weren't skating tonight?"

"We're not. But we *are* in need of some cozy snacks," he says. "I have it on good authority that you like the soft pretzels around here."

Flashback to me devouring more than my half last night when we split one, and the way his gaze lingered just a little too long on the salt on my lips.

"Not sure what gave you that impression," I say, straight-faced. "But if you insist, I guess we can get one."

"Oh, we're not getting only *one* this time—we're getting a half dozen!"

"A half dozen? Are we building a tiny pretzel fort for some lucky squirrel?"

He laughs. I love that I can make him laugh, even with what might have been the dumbest joke anyone has ever dared to tell.

"One for you, one for me," he replies, "and a few for me to eat tomorrow morning for breakfast."

He really does order a half dozen, and the girl behind the counter doesn't even blink. We also get a pair of hot cocoas to go—marshmallows on mine, whipped cream on his. The cup is delightfully warm in my hands; I didn't realize I'd forgotten my gloves until it was too late.

"The best way to eat these," he says, setting his cocoa down on the smooth pine railing, "is like this."

I watch as he carefully removes the lid, then—horror of horrors—*tears off a piece of his pretzel and dips it into his cocoa.* When he pulls it out, it's soggy, brown, and streaked with whipped cream. He devours the whole piece in a single bite.

I blink.

"What. Just happened."

Amused, he replies, "It's salty. It's sweet. It's perfection."

"It looks disgusting."

"Haven't you ever heard that you shouldn't judge a book by its cover, Alix?"

"First of all, that's no book. And second, if it were and it looked like that, I would absolutely judge it because *clearly* no one loved it enough to keep it from drowning in a muddy swamp."

His smile is contagious as he tears off another piece, dips it in, and holds it out to me.

"C'mon, you should try it. Just a bite."

He's looking at me with those gorgeous eyes, grinning like he knows there's no way I could possibly say no.

"Okay, fine. But if I hate it, I'm holding you personally responsible."

And if that's not an empty threat, I don't know what is, but I take the soggy pretzel piece and try it.

"*Mmmmmphhhhkgh,*" I mumble, in undeniable culinary heaven.

"That good?" he says with a playful smirk.

I close my eyes, finish the bite.

"You have ruined me for all other pretzels for the rest of my life."

"When I say something's good," he says, with a pointed look that heats me up from the inside out, "you can trust me."

The thing is, I really feel like I can.

A few more bites of cocoa pretzels later, and he turns to me, eyes full of stars.

"Ready?"

"Are you sure that wasn't the main event?" I ask. "Because it could've been."

He grins. "Follow me."

We turn down a path I haven't taken before, one that leads away from the lodge and the village and toward the mountain. The slopes closed hours ago, so I have no idea where he could possibly be taking me.

I'm even more confused when we arrive at one of the gondola landings.

It looks very, very closed.

As in, the only light on—other than the lampposts on the path we took to get here—is a small, red emergency button.

"I know what you're thinking, but trust me. This is going to be *so* worth it."

He pulls a key card from his back pocket, holds it up to the sensor beside the control booth door. There's a hum as the lock releases, but I just stare.

"You've got a key—to the gondola lift?"

He grins. "I've got a key to *everywhere*."

An all-access key to the entire lodge? To the entire *mountain*? Julie must have a lot of faith in him.

"And Julie's okay with you just, like—using the lift after hours?"

"Julie's the one who *taught* me how to use the lift after hours," he says, grinning. "Jules and her brother and I used to hang out up at the scenic point all the time. The stars are next-level up there."

He pulls out his phone, opens a text thread with Julie.

TYLER

Meteor shower tonight, okay if I
take someone up to watch?

JULES

Who are you, and what have you done
with my reclusive friend??? Of course
it's okay. I'll let security know.

I'm buzzing with anticipation. I can't remember the last time anyone put Tyler's level of thoughtfulness into their dates.

"Sounds amazing," I say. "Let's do it."

Halfway up the mountain, I look out the gondola window and take in everything around us.

The snow that blankets the slopes below is so thick and smooth it reminds me of an impeccably decorated wedding cake, like if I took a treacherous leap from this gondola it would turn out just fine, because I'd land in a sea of buttercream frosting. And then I'd take a big scoop of it in my fingers to taste it—and it would be sweet, and perfect—but I'd smell like sugar for days.

Down in the valley, lamplight and string lights and flickering flames in their firepits give the whole place a warm, cozy glow. The village—and the lodge behind it, and our building just down the path—looks like something straight out of a postcard.

It's a clear night: only a waning crescent moon slices through the black, velvety sky, and the stars—the *stars*! Just imagine someone took a whole bowl of silver glitter and flung it up to the heavens and somehow it stuck. That's what it's like. More stars than I've ever seen, more stars than I even realized *could* be seen with the naked eye, sparkling and wonderful. It's gorgeous.

"Beautiful, right?"

His voice cuts through the silence.

"I've never seen anything like it," I say.

"Just wait 'til we're at the top," he replies, eyes twinkling like all the glitter in the sky.

But nothing could have prepared me for the feeling that slams into me when we reach the scenic point landing: pure, awestruck wonder.

"This—this is—"

The words get stuck in my throat.

There really aren't words for it anyway. Nothing I can think to say feels big enough. Good enough. *Enough* enough. It feels like we're giants on top of the whole world, yet infinitesimally small under the multitude of stars.

"I know," Tyler says, his voice quiet, smile soft. "This is where I go when I need to clear my head. There's nowhere else like it."

He sets his backpack down on a nearby bench, pulls out a fleece blanket and wraps it around my shoulders. I look like a blanket princess, my nearly empty cup of cocoa my scepter, this entire mountain my kingdom.

Even with the blanket, it's freezing.

Tyler notices I'm still shivering, then leads me by the hand to the bench. We sit, and he pulls me in close. I won't be cold for long, not with his arm around me—and most definitely not with my back pressed up against his chest, which feels even more solid than it looks. Heat radiates between us.

"I've got these, too," he says, shifting slightly to pull something out of his backpack.

He passes me a rechargeable hand warmer, fingertips brushing against my skin as he settles it into my palm. It's smooth and heavy as a river stone, already toasty to the touch, like it came straight from a hot spring.

"Feels good, right?" he says.

I can hear the smile in his voice, feel the barely there graze of his lips against my temple.

Everything feels good, I want to tell him.

"It does," I reply.

We settle into the most electric silence I've ever experienced, the two of us keeping each other warm on top of a mountain, with all the stars in the universe looking down on us. His message to Julie mentioned a meteor shower, but I have yet to see any shooting stars. It's a good thing we're not facing each other, or else I wouldn't know there were any stars up there at all.

I could sit up here all night, honestly.

I most definitely do not feel cold anymore.

He's still holding me tight, firm but tender. Neither of us has acknowledged the way his fingers have found my hair, the way his knuckles brush up against my jawline every now and then, the way the memory of this moment will forever be entangled with the night sky: expansive and sparkly and unforgettable.

"It must be amazing to have this kind of view in your backyard all year long," I say quietly.

Not once have I missed my apartment in Brooklyn since arriving here. I don't miss my loud neighbors, the unreliable heat, the uninspiring view, the never-ending construction across the street. I don't miss Lauren making the place feel even smaller than it already is. I've always considered myself a city girl at heart—but maybe that's because I only ever wanted to get out of the small town where I grew up.

"I love it," he says. "Some people up here . . . I think they stop seeing the world around them after a while and forget how incredible it is."

"But not you?"

He's quiet again, and I feel the rise and fall of his chest with every breath. I think back to last night at dinner, how he changed the subject when we delved too deeply into his life. Is he about to share something real now? Something more than the fact that he took up ice-skating because his best friends were training for it, I mean. Something more than his odd (but admittedly respectable) preference for dipping soft pretzels into hot cocoa.

Finally, he says, "I left this place behind for a while. I had a job opportunity that paid well and took me all over the world."

It's like he's poked a hole in the sky—the barest pinprick of blazing light, hinting at everything still hidden behind that thick velvet curtain—and now I want to rip clean through it. I wish he'd let me see all the things he so clearly feels he needs to keep to himself.

Maybe if I don't push, if I just let him give, he will.

"But you came back here to be with your friends," I say, because it's a fact—because it focuses on where he ran to and not what he ran from.

"I did." He takes another deep breath, sighs it out in a long exhale. "You travel the world long enough, you leave a little bit of yourself every place you go, and after a while, you start to forget who you are—especially when the people who are supposed to have your back turn out to be snakes."

Suddenly all I can think of is Sebastian Green, of everything he went through with his manager and how perfect his life looked on the surface. I guess you can never truly know what someone is going through.

I stare up at the sky, wondering just how awful a person would have to be for someone as great as Tyler to refer to them as a snake.

"It makes it hard to know who to trust when that happens," he goes on. "When you're not even sure who you are anymore, so you question your own judgment, and it just makes you more and more paranoid, but also more reluctant to listen to your own instincts because you aren't sure what's real."

I stay quiet, give him space to continue.

When he doesn't, I say, "I'm so sorry anyone made you feel that way."

I want to say I can't even imagine it happening.

"It wasn't just someone," he says. "It was pretty much everyone."

It's hard to imagine Tyler outside of the context of this ski resort, as some sort of fancy businessman traveling the world, surrounded by people who ended up breaking his trust—it's starting to make a lot more sense why he came back to his roots. To Julie, to his best friend, to the peace and quiet and serenity of the mountain. Maybe he doesn't *want* to be a recluse so much as he's afraid not to be.

I'm weighing how—*if*—I could ask more about what happened, since he's trusted me enough to crack the door open and let me peek into his past.

But then he says, "It was a long time ago. I want to hear about *you.*"

And just like that, he closes the door.

I watch the sky. Still no sign of shooting stars.

"What do you want to know?" I ask.

"Well, I know you're a writer," he says. "And I know you're writing a book. And I know you can't talk about the book. But the first day we met, you told me the subject matter was in your field and that's how you got the job. What do you normally write about?"

Never in my life have I had to think before answering that question—but now that Sebastian's book is in the mix, it gives me pause. Tyler doesn't at all seem like the type who cares one bit about entertainment journalism: if I had to guess, he's the type who curls up in a worn leather armchair, reading his spy thriller novels until well after midnight, not a smartphone in sight.

He's given me more than I expected—it's only right that I give him something real, too.

"I'm in entertainment," I say. "Pop music, reality shows, royal weddings. Stuff like that." It's a vague enough answer: maybe I'm writing a book about a prince!

Still leaning against him, though, I feel his muscles tense. But as quickly as I felt it, he relaxes.

Maybe this was a mistake—maybe he's like my brother and thinks entertainment journalism is a complete waste of time. A complete waste of my *life*. Maybe—

"How long have you been doing that?" he asks.

Relief floods through me. There's no trace of Ian-like disdain in his voice at all.

"A little over a decade now. It started as a side gig my freshman year of college but turned into my actual job somewhere along the way."

"Do you ever get to interview famous people?"

"I've interviewed more famous people than I can count," I reply. "It's not as great as everyone thinks. Most of them act like they're some superhuman gift to the planet, and like all the rest of us were put here to worship them. It used to make me feel small. Then it made me feel angry. And now—now I'm mostly indifferent."

There's an edge to my voice I didn't mean to let in, at odds with this crystal-clear, delicate night.

Tyler is quiet behind me, taking in my words, my sharp tone.

He wraps his arm tighter around me, pulls me in closer. I lean my head back and breathe him in. It's instant comfort.

"I can't imagine anyone ever *meant* to make you feel that way," he finally says.

"Oh, I think some of them definitely did mean to." The Jett Beckett interview comes to mind, and I shove the memory back down into the putrid cesspool from which it came. "Pretty sure most of them were too wrapped up in themselves to consider anyone else might have feelings, though."

He reaches down, finds my hand, and intertwines his fingers with mine. In this moment, it feels as intimate as a kiss, this purposeful connection from someone who's done everything he can to disconnect from the world—a way to say *I see you* now that he knows I've spent far too many years feeling unseen.

"I've never understood why the world glorifies celebrities," he says softly, "when it's only luck and timing that put them under a magnifying glass instead of someone else."

I think again of Sebastian: how luck and timing changed his life, how a single powerful someone happened to see him performing in a high school musical and brought him out to LA for that fateful first meeting at the record studio. It could have happened to anyone—anyone who had just the right mix of talent and charisma and a cocktail of blessed genes.

"Alix," Tyler says suddenly. "*Look.*"

I follow his gaze just in time to see a shooting star streaking across the sky, here and then gone.

Fame is like that, I think.

So are some moments. Like if you were to blink, you might

miss your chance—might not know it ever existed in the first place.

Still wrapped in the blanket and his arms, I twist around to face him. I could kiss him right now, we're that close. All it would take is an inch, maybe half, to close the gap between us.

"That was beautiful," I say.

My voice is so quiet I wonder if he might ask me to repeat myself.

"We might see more," he replies, "if we keep watching."

But he doesn't turn to look at the stars, and neither do I.

His lips find mine, there in near darkness, soft and slow and tender. He doesn't hurry, he doesn't press for more than I might want to give—but that only makes me want to kiss him harder, more fervently. I don't—

Not yet.

With every lingering kiss, every second I resist the urge to take this fire up one notch, the flames feel hotter all on their own. I can tell he's holding back, too, relishing the tension as it builds. And it does build—I feel it in how he touches me, one hand in my hair and the other at my low back, firm but gentle, like it's taking all his restraint to keep himself under control.

Until finally—*finally*—the tension breaks.

I'm the first to give in.

I kiss him harder, deeper. Like I can't get enough, like this moment might be every bit as fleeting as fame and shooting stars, like this night will slip away if I don't stay as present as possible in the here and now.

I take it all in: the hint of pretzel salt and sweet cocoa on his tongue; the scent of him, fancy cologne and fresh soap and fabric softener; the silence and stillness on this incredible mountaintop; the chill I would feel in my bones if he weren't here, burning me up from the inside out.

Unfortunately, it isn't long before the temperature drops and reality sinks in—that it *is* actually very cold out here, that I am currently shivering.

"We could go somewhere warmer?" Tyler suggests.

"Warmer sounds good," I say, pulling the blanket tighter around me. It doesn't do a thing.

I don't want this perfect night to end.

As we make our way back toward the gondola lift, I glance up and see a pair of shooting stars glittering across the sky. I stop dead in my tracks to watch—but Tyler doesn't see me, doesn't realize I've paused until he barrels right into me. I lose my balance, step right onto a slick patch of ice, and the next thing I know, I'm on the ground staring up at the entire night sky.

My wrist *hurts*.

BEFORE

BREAKDOWN:
Epic Jett Beckett/Sebastian Green
Backstage Fight

By Aria Statler // Pop Culture Blogger, LifeLoveLattes.com

Hi, everyone, and welcome to Breakdown, where we take an in-depth look at the day's viral news. Tonight we're talking about <u>this video</u> of Jett Beckett and Sebastian Green—a stealthy observer captured the backstage drama after tonight's True North show in Boston, and it's already gotten more than a million views in the half hour since it showed up online. Let's break it down!

First: note the body language. The video picks up mid-fight, so we don't know what started it. But it's clear that Jett is absolutely livid—his aggressive stance is like that of a lion, though it's tough to say whether he's the aggressor or simply defending his territory. Sebastian, usually the easygoing one, is equally on edge.

Next: the fight itself. Again, it's unclear who started it—but what *is* clear is that this tension has been building under the surface for quite some time. Sebastian, mere inches from Jett's face, loudly accuses him of being a "self-centered asshole" who "never puts the band first." This lights an emotional fuse in Jett, who further escalates the situation with accusations of his own: that Sebastian is a "narcissistic sellout" who "know[s] nothing about what [Jett has] been through." River rushes to intervene, moving between them—and thank goodness he did, or else the intense altercation almost certainly would have turned physical.

River makes eye contact with whoever's filming, and the video abruptly cuts off. From start to finish, the video is just shy of twenty seconds long—not long enough to give context for the drama but more than enough time to give viewers an ugly peek behind the True North curtain.

[UPDATE, 5:42 p.m.—Due to this afternoon's breaking news that Jett Beckett has been missing since late last night, we have turned off the comments in the interest of limiting insensitive speculation regarding all band members involved.]

14

"I am *so* sorry, Alix," Tyler says for what has to be the tenth time since the accident.

"Please don't apologize. It's my own fault for stopping so suddenly—or maybe we should blame the meteor shower."

He laughs. "Still," he says. "Here, let me get the door."

He pulls out his key card, and I wince thinking about how painful it would be if I were to try the same movement right now. When Tyler suggested going "somewhere warmer," he most certainly did not mean the resort's twenty-four-hour medical center, but the twenty minutes we spent there did the trick. Now we're back at our building with a few more bruises than when we left.

The doctor wrapped my wrist in an ACE bandage and told me I'd been lucky to fall in a pile of relatively fresh snow—I've got a light sprain that could have been much worse if I'd fallen elsewhere. It hurts, but it should heal in less than a week as long as I rest and ice it.

Which means no ski lessons for a few days. And I probably *shouldn't* type with it, but I have a deadline.

"This day," I mutter as we wait on our elevator. "You were definitely the best part of it."

"Given that I took you on a date that ended at the medical center, it must have been pretty bad before that."

Between my laptop that smells hopelessly like honey nut latte and the throbbing pain in my wrist, today has not been my favorite.

Outside my penthouse door, I attempt to extract my key card from my wallet using only my good hand—which is, fortunately, my dominant hand—but the zipper is a struggle.

Tyler gestures to it. "I can—if you want?"

I hand it over, and of course he has immediate success.

"Do you want to come in?" I ask.

He follows me inside.

Puffin greets us at the door, rubbing his head on my legs as always. He trills out a tiny meow—his *treat, please* meow—and trots hopefully toward the kitchen.

"He acts sweet," I tell Tyler, "but he turns into a total drama queen if he doesn't get his midnight snack."

Tyler laughs. "I mean, same, honestly." He holds up the bag of leftover soft pretzels. "Want me to heat one up?"

"One for us to split, or one for each of us?"

"Yes," he says. "Whatever you want."

When we get to the kitchen, the smell of honey nut latte is strong. It's more like *burnt* honey nut latte—and fried electrical parts.

"*Oh*," Tyler says, eyeing my kitchen island.

Like some sort of monument, my laptop is positioned in an upside-down V, precisely as the internet advised. There's a small puddle of brown liquid underneath it, and all I can think is: this is basically the electronics version of a horror film.

I'm fairly certain it's deader than dead.

Electrocuted—then exsanguinated.

"Not ideal while trying to hit a deadline," I say.

"Not ideal *ever*," Tyler counters. "Any chance it might still work?"

I sigh. "I think it's fried. It *sizzled*."

"Sizzling's no good."

Puffin meows again, more insistently this time. I manage to get the container of treats off the shelf, but the screw-top lid proves tricky with just one hand—that's what I get for going the environmentally friendly route and packing his treats in an old jelly jar.

Without me even having to ask, Tyler's by my side in a heartbeat. I hand over the jar, and he opens it easily before pouring *five* treats into Puffin's food dish.

"You're going to be his new favorite person," I say. "I usually only give him one or two at a time."

Puffin practically inhales them—predictably—then starts rubbing on Tyler's leg.

"See, Tyler? He loves you already."

"What can I say? I'm good with pets."

"Says the guy whose pet is a goldfish," I tease.

"Hey, Pete's nearly eight years old! He hasn't died from malnourishment yet, nor has he slammed himself up against the glass to put himself out of his own misery."

"Give this man a trophy," I announce to the kitchen appliances. "His goldfish is content to live another day!"

Tyler grins, his eyes crinkling at the corners, and nudges me playfully in the (uninjured) arm.

"I, on the other hand, might not live another day if we don't have our midnight snack." He pulls two giant soft pretzels out from our to-go bag.

Ten minutes later, we're settled on the living room floor near the fireplace, a plate full of reheated pretzels between us on the woven rug. Tyler lit a fire for us—something I had no clue how to do—after pointing out that my clothes were still a bit damp from falling into the snow. In my bedroom, I peeled off everything that was even a little wet and changed into black yoga pants and a thick lavender hoodie.

And now, we feast.

"What are you going to do about your laptop?" Tyler asks, mid-bite.

"Other than begging someone at the Apple Store to make another one magically appear on my doorstep?" I sigh. "Probably wait a couple of days to see if it comes back from the dead, then order a new one if it doesn't."

I *could* spend some of my book deal money to buy a new one—but that's just one more expense standing in the way of me eventually finding a bigger, better, warmer, quieter apartment.

"You'll be losing work time, though, right?" Tyler asks.

"I'll probably be able to make it up later as long as I pull some late nights," I say. "But yeah, honestly, I can't really afford to lose even a day or two. Maybe I can try to write by hand?"

Tyler's quiet. He pops the last bite of his pretzel in his mouth, and a single fleck of salt clings to his lower lip for a half second before he licks it away.

"You should borrow mine," he says, looking up at me with those gorgeous brown eyes. "My laptop."

I blink. "You . . . won't need it?"

He shrugs. "I'm a ski instructor. I use my laptop to catch up on world news and take care of scheduling, all of which I can do from my phone."

"That would be amazing, if you're sure it won't be too much trouble?"

"Really, it's no trouble at all."

Chloe will be proud of me, accepting help like this—let's just say I have a pattern of doing things the hard way just so I don't inconvenience anyone.

I think what makes this feel different is that I can tell Tyler truly won't mind being inconvenienced if it makes things easier for me.

"Okay," I say. "Thank you."

He holds up a finger, like *be right back*, and I hear my front door click shut on his way out. As soon as he's gone, it feels entirely too quiet in here: it's just Puffin and me and the flickering fire.

I take a quick glance at my phone, notice I've missed numerous texts and a call from Lauren.

Call meeeeeeeeeeeeeeeee

Alix

ALIX

Locked myself out and can't remember who I should call for your spare key???

One of your neighbors just hit on me, ew

WHERE IS THE LOCKSMITH

WHERE ARE YOUUUU

Back inside. Sorry for freaking out but ughhhhhh 😭😭😭 Had plans to go out this weekend but now I can't bc it cost more than $200 to unlock the door

My stomach drops.

So, so sorry I missed all this, I type out frantically. Glad you're back inside . . . Chloe has my spare key if you ever need it again, she's only a few blocks away

I take a deep breath. Lauren can come off as self-centered at times without meaning to—I honestly think she relies on me so much because she's not quite sure yet how to be an adult herself. I'm trying my best not to be irritated over the fact that she expected me to text back immediately even though it's well after midnight.

I shut off my phone and set it on the floor—right beside my stack of True North research books, which I absentmindedly dropped off when I came inside from the balcony earlier.

They are *right* where Tyler was sitting. As in, if he'd turned his head to the right, he would've been up close and personal with three thick spines, all of them betraying the fact that I'm most definitely writing a book about a boy band—a *specific* boy band.

Did he see them? My heart's in my throat just thinking about it.

I remind myself that he has no reason to blast my news all over the internet, no social media followers to blast my news *to*. And it's not like he has that many people to tell in person, either. Just Julie, as far as I know, and maybe the best friend he keeps up with over the phone.

Still. I should've been more careful.

I should probably move them before he gets back, just to be safe.

When I try to lift the stack, a shock of pain shoots through my injured wrist—the books are too heavy, and I drop them immediately. They fall to the floor, each landing with a resounding thud.

I'm scrambling to straighten them when Tyler knocks on my front door, his muffled voice saying, "Forgot to prop it open!"

"Be there in a second!" I call out, stacking them one by one behind the big leather armchair, spines hidden from view. I flip the top book upside down to hide its cover—that'll have to be good enough.

When I open the door, I do a double take.

Not only has Tyler changed clothes—thick sweatpants in dark charcoal gray, light-green cotton V-neck, wavy hair loose and no longer confined under a hat—but he's also added a pair of black-framed glasses that somehow make him look even hotter. Maybe it's the intimacy of it: knowing this isn't his usual look, that it's rare for someone else to see him like this.

I have the sudden urge to take it all off—his glasses, his V-neck, his everything else—to get as close as I possibly can, to tangle my fingers in his hair.

Heaven help me.

"You said you were going to get your laptop," I say as casually as possible, "not that you'd be transforming into a totally different person."

Tyler laughs. "I *did* get my laptop."

He holds up a worn leather satchel that looks entirely at odds with his loungewear. It's even monogrammed: *TJB*.

"We're not going to talk about your pajamas?"

"We're not going to talk about *yours*?" he counters.

Never mind the fact that neither of us is actually wearing anything particularly risqué—we could both go jogging in public and no one would bat an eyelash.

"I live here, and it's nearly one in the morning," I reply, committed to giving him a hard time. "Pajamas are standard."

"It's nearly one in the morning and my place is so close to yours we could practically be roommates," he says, grinning.

"Except for two crucial details: those extremely lockable front doors we both have, and the fact that I would never in a million years move in with someone I've known for less than a week."

That's a bit of a white lie, as I actually did have a college roommate I moved in with on a whim—great location, even better rent thanks to her family's connection to the landlord—but four months of living with her is *why* I would never move in with a stranger again.

"I can go change back into my date clothes? Or maybe a Halloween costume?"

"Hey, I never said I was *complaining* about your pajamas—but I'm intrigued by the costume."

"Let's just say you'd never look at velociraptors the same way again."

"Which is how, exactly?"

He laughs. "Oh, you know. You'd be more likely to run straight into their tiny arms than to run away screaming in terror."

"Because I see *so* many velociraptors on a regular basis," I say, and now I'm laughing, too. "And aren't T. rexes the ones with tiny arms?"

"You and your details," he says, waving it off. "Where should I put this?"

His biceps flex as he holds up his laptop satchel, and it's all I can do to keep from staring.

"How about here?"

Tyler follows me over to the armchair where my stack of boy band books sits gloriously incognito. I've been working all around the penthouse over the past few days—maybe I'll just stay in this room tomorrow. It would certainly be easier than relocating all the books.

"Thank you again," I say.

"Use it for as long as you need to."

His smile is soft, sincere. This close, something feels a little different about him—it's probably just that I'm not used to seeing him in glasses.

"I might need it for a while if mine really is dead, just warning you."

"It's more necessary for your work right now than mine," he says. "Promise."

He puts one hand on the small of my back, and I inch closer, closer, until there's no space between my body and his.

"Text me if there's anything you need, even if it's six in the morning," he says. "Puffin seems like an early riser. And I can bring you breakfast, or coffee, or . . . anything."

That's just the beginning of the list of things that might be painful and/or difficult to do one-handed.

"You're the best," I say, tilting my head up to his. "And you're right, Puffin *is* an early riser."

My smile is contagious, and I'm not prepared for how radiant his looks up close. I'm still smiling when he leans in and presses one perfect, warm kiss onto my lips.

"I'd better get to bed, then," he says. "Sounds like I'm going to need my energy tomorrow."

I give him one more kiss to match the first, tempted to tell him not to go home at all, that he can stay right here—we are, after all, practically roommates.

But he tells me good night, and then he's gone.

As soon as he leaves, I want him to come back.

I'm in bed, almost asleep, when I suddenly realize what seemed different about him. It wasn't just his glasses—I was so distracted by the fact that he was wearing them at all that I didn't fully register what had changed beneath them.

Behind his lenses, his irises were a deep, striking blue.

15

Not brown with subtle blue flecks—not brown at all.

Tyler's eyes are cobalt blue, each with a starburst of gorgeous Caribbean teal: unnaturally beautiful, a color I've rarely seen on another person.

But I have seen it before, I'm sure of it.

I'm just not sure where.

16

I hardly sleep.

My mind races with questions: Why would Tyler opt for brown contacts when his actual eye color is so beautiful? Did he think I wouldn't notice they'd changed—or is his nighttime routine so deeply engrained that he didn't think about it at all?

On top of that, my wrist hurts. Like, *hurts*. I keep accidentally rolling over on it in my sleep.

At five o'clock, I give up.

Even though I'd planned to write first thing this morning, it seems best to throw some ice on my wrist and rest it instead.

I know Tyler said I could text him if I need anything, but five in the morning seems a little *too* extreme—surely I can make a fresh ice pack all on my own. The doctor gave me a reusable one last night, but like Puffin's treat jar, it has a screw-on cap. I rummage around in one of the cabinets, find some Ziploc freezer bags: perfect. Between this and the automatic ice dispenser in the fridge, I'm good to go.

I settle onto the armchair where I left my work supplies last night, shifting Tyler's laptop bag to the floor. I'll write later, but for now, I figure I might as well flip through one of my True North research books.

This particular book was published nine years ago at the height of the True North frenzy and is full of old photographs from their early days in the studio and on tour, along with even older photographs from each of the members' childhood days.

Sebastian's eighteen-year-old face stares up at me from one of the recording studio photos, bright-eyed and laughing, and in the blurry background, there's the barest glimpse of his long-lost bandmate, Jett Beckett. Must be one from the early days when the band was flying high on the promise of their potential, before all the envy and resentment and rivalry grew into tangled roots between them.

I make my way through the Sebastian pages, which run the gamut from his talent shows to his infamous high school musical performance to album covers and tour shots. There's even one serious throwback—a Christmas morning photo of him as a toddler, hugging a guitar that's bigger than he is.

I flip through the bulk of the book, scanning the other band members' sections for any additional places where Sebastian might come up. I start with River Wu's section.

River was always one of the most low-key members of the band. His signature haircut was cut short in the back, but with unruly bangs in the front—I always wondered what he was really thinking behind that hair, behind those kind eyes. He hung out often with Jett and Sebastian but rarely with both of them at the same time.

I've seen River hundreds of times in photos, but now it's like I'm seeing him for the first time: he's taller and more muscular, but his face—something about the light or the angle makes it feel like I've met him for real. I wrack my brain. Was it one of the Wall Street bros? One of Lauren's museum friends? The guy who unloaded my bags when I first arrived here at the lodge?

Or, wait, no—maybe it wasn't a guy at all, though I do think it was here at the lodge.

And then it hits me: he looks like Julie, so much so that they could be twins.

Julie, the concierge at this very resort—

Julie, whose brother is Tyler's best friend.

My heart rate picks up.

I turn the page, looking for any sign of a sister. While I don't find any mention of siblings one way or the other, I do see another photo that feels like I've just discovered a hidden key: it's a picture of eleven-year-old River and a friend about the same age, bundled up in ski gear.

The mountain looks familiar. And there's an ice rink in the background.

I take a closer look at the caption off to the side: *River Wu (age 11) and Jett Beckett (age 11) prepare to carve the slopes in Stowe, Vermont.*

Stowe, Vermont: that can't be a coincidence.

In the photo, Jett Beckett is wearing a mint-green helmet.

I think of the one Tyler loaned me at my first lesson. *Limited edition*, he told me that day. *Super rare.*

I flip a few pages over, find the section devoted to Jett, and scan through until I find a picture from his later days in the band—nine years ago. I gasp.

If you were to break that perfect nose—

And cover up that flawless complexion with a five-o'clock shadow that's grown out for a few days—

And turn the clock forward by nearly a decade—cheekbones

and jawline more defined, smile lines at the corners of his eyes—a transformation from polished pop star to rugged outdoorsman—

And add some brown contacts to those piercing blue eyes—

And let those eyebrows do their own thing—

And grow that short, bleach-blond hair out into long, dark waves—

And hide it all under helmets and goggles and ski gear for extra measure—

You'd get Tyler.

Title: 💀💀💀

Metadata: jettbeckett_interview.mp3

Duration: 0:09:24

Date: March 29, 2017

Alix: Hi, Jett—my name is Alix Morgan, and I write for *Starslinger Daily*. Thanks so much for meeting with me today. I wanted to state that we've started the audio recording. This is my assistant, Bridget, who's going to listen in.

Jett: [inaudible]

Alix: I'm sorry, could you please repeat that?

Jett: No one told me this was on the agenda. How long will this take?

Alix: Oh, I'm so sorry to hear that—we've had it scheduled for months. Your manager, Jason, cleared it with us back in January?

Jett: Jason. [laughs] The guy thinks he owns us. Don't print that.

Alix: Don't worry. Not everything you tell me will end up in the article. I'm just recording so I don't misquote you.

Jett: That's a relief.

Alix: Okay, I only have a few questions—

Jett: Get me some water, love?

Alix: Excuse me?

Jett: Some water. I need some.

Alix: I—um. Bridget? Could you please go find some bottled water?

Bridget: On it.

Jett: Make it cold. No ice, though. Limes would be great, too. But no wedges—make them sliced.

Alix: I'm sorry, but I don't think we have any sliced limes. I'm not sure we have any limes at all, actually.

Jett: I've been on tour for weeks. My voice is tired. I *need* some limes.

Alix: And here I was, believing the gossip bloggers who accuse you all of lip-synching everything.

Jett: [laughs] Only River lip-synchs. The rest of us sing live.

Alix: Now we're getting somewhere. Mind if I ask you some questions while we wait on your water?

Jett: If that means this will be over sooner, go ahead.

Alix: I'm sorry—is there anything else I can do to make you more comfortable?

Jett: *Ha*. No.

Alix: You seem to hate your job. This part of it, anyway.

Jett: That was on your list of questions, or did you come up with it all by yourself?

[0:08 silence]

Jett: There are parts I like.

Alix: Like the privilege of having people bring you fancy water whenever you want it?

Jett: Even that gets old.

Alix: So what *do* you like?

[0:15 silence]

Jett: I like that my best friend and I get to tour together.

Alix: I'm guessing you mean River, and not Sebastian.

Jett: Is that supposed to be a joke? [incredulous laugh] Sebastian—of course I mean River.

Alix: So the rumors are true? There's tension there? Between you and Sebastian, I mean.

Jett: Do I really need to confirm that? I thought it was obvious.

Alix: I like to give the benefit of the doubt.

Jett: Let me make it very clear. Sebastian Green is cancer to the band. You can quote me on that.

Alix: I, um. I'm not sure this is exactly the sort of interview Jason had in mind to promote your tour?

Jett: All publicity is good publicity, right?

[0:05 silence]

Alix: With all due respect—if you're that unhappy, why don't you walk away? Go solo, start your own thing?

Jett: With all due respect, mind your own [microphone malfunction] business. No one walks away from the sort of life I have. Why shouldn't *he* be the one to leave?

The book is still open to old photos of Tyler—of *Jett*—when a text vibrates my phone.

I hope you're still asleep, but just wanted to let you know I'm up and can help with Puffin or breakfast or whatever, he's written, along with a yellow cat emoji.

An hour ago, I would have turned to a puddle of heart-eyed goo at it.

Now, I cannot for the life of me reconcile the fact that Tyler—who absolutely would punctuate his texts with adorable emojis—is one and the same as Jett Beckett.

Jett Beckett was notorious for many things, none of them adorable.

If I had to describe how those of us in entertainment journalism perceived him back then, the words that come to mind are *on edge*. My entire job the year I spoke to him was to cover True North, as their tour was so massive—my coworkers usually complained about how lucky I was, how fun my assignments always were.

No one—and I mean *no one*—envied my task of interviewing Jett Beckett.

The day of the interview, they got me a gigantic bouquet of black roses along with a gift card to the wine bar down the street. "For later," my boss said morosely as he handed it to me.

I gave everyone in the office a hard time, told them surely Jett Beckett couldn't be that bad.

He was that bad.

It wasn't just me, though I'm not sure that makes it any better. That was just how he was. With *everyone*.

Rumor had it that the smallest things would set him off. Changes in the set list, changes to his daily agenda—anything Sebastian did. Where Sebastian thrived on the band's collective fame, Jett warped under the spotlight they shared. Their manager had given them both front man status, and for better or worse, their loathing chemistry worked: Sebastian was the golden boy, and Jett the shadowy rebel. It was good publicity, *great* publicity. Everyone loved to pick sides—it was a whole thing. I would go so far as to say their electric rivalry was one of the essential elements that propelled them to the level of fame they ultimately achieved.

Until Jett disappeared and it all came crashing down.

How did I not realize it was him sooner?

Some of it has to be contextual: take the famous skateboarder who never gets recognized in plain clothes at the airport (or anywhere), for example—you don't necessarily expect to see a megastar in the aisle of your neighborhood drug store, or on your daily jogging route, or while on vacation. Maybe they're dressed differently—or maybe they've purposefully altered their entire look to make themselves utterly unrecognizable.

You certainly don't expect to see someone who's been missing for more than eight years . . . just . . . casually teaching ski lessons at a posh resort. Especially not when his onstage persona was the polar opposite of an outdoor adventurer.

You don't put it together that this daydream of a human who makes you dinner when you're locked out—who takes you on the most creative, magical dates—who offers to feed your cat at five in the morning—could possibly be one and the same as the nightmare who so condescendingly commanded, mid-interview: *Bring me some water, love.*

As if I were some sort of servant, not a member of the press trying to give his band publicity during their tour.

And I cannot emphasize enough how Tyler really does not exude boy band energy anymore. How he is the very definition of hiding in plain sight—he pulls it off because he's done everything in his power to blend in. Whereas Sebastian is a walking trend, committed to reminding the world that they should want his autograph, his very presence shouting *I am THE Sebastian Green!* everywhere he goes, Tyler couldn't be further from that.

If you'd asked me to describe Jett Beckett in a single word after my experience sitting down with him for an interview all those years ago, the word would've been *ego.*

Now, though, after getting to know him here at the lodge, I have to wonder if I was wrong—if maybe I caught him on an exceptionally bad day.

I suddenly feel compelled to go back and listen to the recording of that interview; I'm sure I have it saved somewhere. I've changed phones since then but specifically remember wanting to delete it and deciding not to. It was his disappearance that kept me from doing so: my interview was the last he gave before that pivotal moment in pop culture history, and that seemed important.

Did I ever want to actually listen to it again?

Decidedly not.

Now I'm glad I kept it. I scroll deep into my iPhone's voice memo history, down into all the tracks that have made the leap with me through at least three new phone upgrades.

There it is—March 29, eight years ago. I titled it, very eloquently, with a series of skull emojis.

I press play, wishing I could whisper in Past Alix's ear that her bright-eyed optimism is not going to age well.

The contrast between our voices is even more stark than I remember. Mine is patient, professional, borderline chipper (I hate the way I sound in recordings), while his is . . . the opposite. His tone is gritty, hurried, bitter with cynicism. Demanding. Condescending.

Underneath it all, I regret to admit, I hear undeniable shades of Tyler in Jett's voice. It's like when your favorite audiobook narrator pivots from villain to romantic love interest in unrelated books— voice actors are chameleons.

Maybe pop stars are, too.

My own voice pulls me out of my head and back to the interview as I hear myself say, *"With all due respect—if you're that unhappy, why don't you walk away? Go solo, start your own thing?"*

And then his sarcastic drawl, replying, *"With all due respect, mind your own f—eeeeeee—cking business."* There's feedback on his mic, a side-effect of him twisting around and trying to rip it off. *"No one walks away from the sort of life I have. Why shouldn't* he *be the one to leave?"*

He, meaning Sebastian.

I'm stunned.

In all my rage, I had completely forgotten that I'd suggested he walk away from the band—I remember feeling hung up on the way he'd cursed at me, how he'd ripped his mic off and thrown it on the floor, how my assistant had finally returned with his chilled lime water only to find me staring at an empty director's chair.

No one walks away from the sort of life I have.

But two days after that interview, he did.

Twenty minutes later, I'm still lost in thought about the whole thing, but am pulled rudely back to reality when Puffin leaps up onto my lap, his back paws landing on my injured wrist.

Pain zings through me as he stretches up to rub his soft gray face against mine, totally oblivious. His large green eyes say, *Breakfast?*

I should probably text Tyler back.

I don't know how not to be weird about it, though.

There's just no great way to casually say, *Hey, I know you made yourself disappear, but I've figured out who you are.* It will have to be a Big Conversation, one in which I'm more sure of how I feel—and I'm not sure yet about so many things.

I came to this resort to write a book, not meet a guy—especially not a world-famous one. Part of what attracted me to Tyler in the first place was how opposite he seemed from the self-obsessed Wall Street bros of my past. Tyler's never come across as someone with a massive ego, and—unlike Blake—he's never seemed to think of women as mere accessories to his own privileged existence.

Jett Beckett, though: he had all that in common with Blake and more. That's how it came across from the outside looking in, anyway. It's no exaggeration to say that the man I interviewed all those years ago singlehandedly soured me on all future interactions with celebrities.

I don't know how to reconcile the infamous Jett Beckett with the man I've met here at the resort.

Tyler, who made me feel more comfortable being myself than

anyone—even Chloe—has made me feel in years. Tyler, who is funny and patient and thoughtful, creative and kind. I want so badly for Tyler to be real: for his current persona to be the true one.

Still, even if this is the real him, what he said in that interview struck a nerve: *No one walks away from the sort of life I have.*

Millions of dollars. Opportunities so many others give blood, sweat, and tears to have—to have even a *chance* at. Fame, even if he was painted as the rebel of the group. Access to the most luxurious locations in the world—weekend getaways, private jets. Relationships, surely, with people who legitimately cared for him.

And he gave it all up.

Part of me understands—based on my limited knowledge of how toxic their manager was—how making himself disappear might have felt like his only option.

But the other part of me? The other part of me doesn't take professional opportunities for granted—because I need to pay rent on my tiny, frustrating apartment with the terrible heat and the terrible neighbors. Because I need to *eat*. Because Puffin also needs to eat.

Puffin, who's now curled into a bagel on top of the True North book that's still open in my lap, purring loudly, probably still starving.

I sigh, pick up my phone.

There's a new text from Lauren.

Ughhhhhhhh, it says, along with a preview of an image.

I slide open the notification and see a handwritten note from the landlord affixed to my front door. I skim it and my heart sinks: in short, Lauren apparently had some loud friends with her late last night while waiting for the locksmith, and they caused three separate noise complaints. Technically, she's not even supposed to be living with me—so this could get dicey in a hurry if we're not careful. This is just a warning, thankfully. If she gets another one, however, I could be in danger of eviction.

My building is pretty strict about quiet hours, I reply.

Yeah, I noticed 😬

If you're going to have people over, please please please make sure they're quiet, I write back. I can't afford to get evicted.

My apartment might be tiny and frustrating, but the rent is fantastic for the location—the only reason I've been able to live there as long as I have. I also don't want to have to explain a move; our parents have never quite understood my choice to work in entertainment journalism. Even though I'm making it from month to month and have a nice little savings cushion from the book deal, I don't want to give them any more reason to gossip with my siblings behind my back about how they wish I'd picked something more lucrative, with more stability.

A fleeting, terrible thought crosses my mind: I could probably get a gigantic windfall of cash now that I've located the long-lost Jett Beckett—auction off the story to the highest bidder, telling the world how he's been living a secret life all these years as a ski instructor in Vermont. And not only a pile of cash . . . but a byline that would make my name instantly recognizable and guarantee work for the foreseeable future.

I squeeze my eyes shut, try to force the thought from my mind. Spilling Tyler's secret could change my life in unimaginable ways, but it would almost certainly ruin his.

What kind of person would that make me?

A smart one, maybe, my inner voice supplies.

Smart or not, I'm not sure I'm ruthless enough to take advantage of someone that way, even out of desperation. Especially not someone who sent me a cat emoji less than an hour ago—who offered to help with Puffin, with breakfast.

Guilt twists in my gut as I pick up my phone to reply.

Hiiiii, I write back to Tyler.

I'm choosing to continue thinking of him as Tyler, since a) that's the name he's chosen for who he is *now*, and b) I'd erase all memory of my interaction with him as Jett if I could. If I'd never met him as Tyler, I'd sell him out in a heartbeat—but the fact is, the guy I met on the mountain has been nothing but kind to me. Nothing but generous, gracious. Trusting.

The least I can do is let him explain himself.

You didn't wake me, I was just lost in work, I continue. I could use your help if you're still up for it? Puffin jumped on my wrist and it's not feeling great

His reply is immediate: Perfect. Went ahead and started on a batch of Belgian waffles ... could totally eat them all on my own ... would rather share if you want to come over :)

And then, in another bubble that quickly pops up, he says, I'll come feed Puffin first, though. Be right there

Our first day on the slopes, he said I looked familiar. Now I know why.

Has he put it together yet that I'm the same journalist who interviewed him years ago? The one who asked him *the* question about walking away? He must have met hundreds of girls back then. Thousands, maybe.

If he were to figure out where he recognizes me from, would he say anything? Or would he be too afraid to bring it up?

There's a knock at my door. Puffin lifts his head, ears perking up.

"Sorry, buddy," I tell him as I urge him gently off my lap.

I cannot let myself get any more invested in Tyler, I coach myself as I go to let him in.

Because what sort of future could there ever be for us, even if I ultimately decide to keep his secret for as long as I live?

For the first time, it occurs to me how incredibly lonely he must be after eight years of keeping himself hidden, and how hard it would be for him to resurface after all this time. No wonder he doesn't make a habit out of having women over—

And what does that say about the fact that he let me in?

I whip the door open, find him in those thick charcoal sweatpants and the same light-green V-neck from last night, slightly rumpled.

He smiles, and it's devastatingly beautiful.

And that's when I realize: once you start falling, it's nearly impossible to stop—you pick up speed, and you might flail a little to course-correct, but at the end of the day you find yourself in over your head.

"Hi," I say, a blush creeping into my cheeks despite myself. Despite *everything*. "Come on in."

True North:
Where Are They Now?

By Rylee Jay // Senior Editor, Moondazzle.com

In light of <u>recent news</u> about Sebastian Green's upcoming tell-all memoir *The Grass Is Always Greener*, it's only fitting that this week's edition of "Where Are They Now?" shines the spotlight on True North.

It's been eight years, give or take, since the band officially broke up. Some of the guys have continued to embrace the spotlight, some have pivoted in entirely new directions, and one is famously unaccounted for. Let's dig in!

Sebastian Green

Arguably the biggest star produced by True North's heyday, Sebastian Green has had staying power like no other. From boy band member to solo artist to an ill-advised stint as reality television star, Sebastian has kept himself firmly in the public eye—and in the hearts of his fans. If <u>social media</u> and book presales are any indication, Sebastian Green remains one of the most beloved pop stars of our generation.

Charly Johannsen

Like Sebastian Green, Charly Johannsen also explored a career as a solo artist, pivoting flawlessly from pop to folk in one of the most critically acclaimed albums of the year. His album, *Songbird,* snagged three Grammy Awards (reviving old rumors that Jason Saenz-Barlowe—former manager of True North, with whom Johannsen parted ways immediately after the band's dissolution—was partly responsible for the band's infamous Grammy snub during their breakout year). Having apparently achieved all he'd set out to do, Johannsen stepped back at the height of his solo career and now owns a quaint violin shop in his hometown in coastal Oregon. Fans continue to clamor for a follow-up album, though Johannsen <u>has expressed</u> that he's more than happy to have moved on from his life in the spotlight.

Ayo Okeke

Perhaps the most underrated star from the True North galaxy—no doubt thanks to his quiet, kind demeanor that allowed him to blend in while others in the group made concerted efforts to stand out—Ayo Okeke went on to cofound the beloved a cappella group Spidercrown, singing bass and giving the occasional (absolutely stellar) beatbox performance. When he's not touring with the group, Okeke can be found leading workshops for vocal groups at various universities in Texas, Kansas, and California.

River Wu

While most of the band (excluding the unaccounted-for Jett Beckett) went on to pursue music in the next iterations of their careers, River Wu stepped back from the pop star life entirely as soon as True North broke up. Having family ties to the luxury travel industry, Wu now leads a comparatively quiet life consulting for various resort properties around the world. Still, he's become somewhat of a legend among True Northerners—he had a significant surge in social media popularity over the last year after fans invaded one of his travel industry conferences, and has reluctantly embraced his status as an influencer.

Jett Beckett

Much to the dismay of all who loved—and loved to hate—Jett Beckett, his disappearance remains one of pop culture's biggest mysteries. Even the most casual observer has seen the theories, the rumors, and the primetime coverage that aired in the years that followed. Devoted fans and casual observers alike are split: some fear the worst, while others believe his disappearance was a voluntary (though brutal) step back from stardom. Whatever the case, his talent—and his talent for stirring up drama—has been sorely missed.

18

As soon as Tyler opens his own front door, I'm hit with the strong and delightful smell of breakfast heaven: waffles and powdered sugar and fresh coffee, citrus and bacon and butter.

"You didn't say you were hiding the resort's entire cooking staff in here, Tyler!"

I peer around the corner into his kitchen; not a soul in sight. It also looks cleaner than it would if I had attempted to make such a breakfast feast on my own—no spills or splatters, just a single dirty mixing bowl, a pile of orange carcasses on a cutting board beside an old-fashioned juicer, and a Belgian waffle maker out on the counter.

"I assume there's some actual food in here somewhere?" I say, and he laughs.

"Thought we'd eat somewhere with a slightly better view than my kitchen island this time." He grins, eyes sparkling.

Notably, they're back to brown this morning.

I follow him through the living room, which I'm reminded is

just a flipped layout of mine. My place feels breezy and bright, but
his—with its charcoal grays and Edison bulbs and potted plants—
feels cozy in a different way. I keep my eye out for any signs that
I am in the home of a long-lost world-famous pop star, but the
personal touches are few and far between.

There *are* a few, though: a pair of well-loved fleece-lined leather
slippers at the foot of his couch. A small hourglass on his mantel
that's the exact shade his irises would be without the contacts. A
bookshelf stuffed full with worn paperbacks he's probably read over
and over. A large goldfish bowl housing a bright orange fish that
can only be Pete.

And in the corner, a Taylor guitar.

That one is a bit of a surprise. None of the guys played instru-
ments while they were in the band—they were known for their
vocals, their harmonies, their synchronized choreography.

True North was not the sort of band where you could envision
any of its members being particularly invested in the lyrics—and
their backing tracks were always so synthy and produced, not a
traditional instrument in sight.

I knew he and Sebastian both started out with ambitions for
solo careers, but I guess I just imagined his would have looked
like Sebastian's—a watered-down version of the sort of music they
made with True North.

"You play guitar?" I can't help but ask.

I want to believe it's a sign that the man I've met here on the
mountain is the *real* one: that maybe it's a hint of who he really is—
who he *wanted* to be onstage—who he would have been if Jason
hadn't packaged and marketed him as something else entirely.

"Oh," he says as we pass into the next room, a single syllable
that feels weighty—like he's trying to decide how much to share.

"I do," he finally adds. "My grandfather taught me."

"Do you sing, too?"

I'm pressing my luck.

"Doesn't everybody?" he says, grinning, subtly redirecting like I've come too close to the truth about a past he'd rather not think about. "I bet you sing in the shower, put on shows for Puffin."

My eyes grow wide as I try to do mental calculations of just how thin these walls are, just how far my master bath is from Tyler's main living space.

"You didn't hear me—"

He raises his hands in defense. "I only heard a little. You're not bad, although I have to say I was surprised by the song choice."

I'm mortified.

"First of all, pardon me while I go hide in a cave somewhere," I say, laughing. I don't sing in public—ever—and with good reason: primarily, that I'm a horrible singer. "And second, 'Winter Won-derland' is a perfectly fitting choice for this particular resort."

"It's March," he replies.

"It's *snowy*," I counter. "Why confine such a perfect song to only December?"

We round one more corner and—wow.

"The way you casually told me you'd made waffles *really* didn't do this justice," I say, eyeing the full breakfast spread laid out on a dining table that, like the living room, overlooks the mountain. My penthouse has a pool table in this section of the house.

Tyler shrugs, and with a wry grin, says, "I was pretty confident I wouldn't be eating alone."

I shake my head. "That will go on your gravestone," I say. "'He was a pretty great guy until he died of overconfidence.'"

This really makes him laugh, and that smile—that *smile*—

It occurs to me that his smile is another reason it took me so long to realize who he really is: Jett Beckett was a *scowler*. He looked undoubtedly hot while scowling, sure. His smile is transformative, though, lighting up his face in a way that bears no resemblance to how he looked before.

We sit together at the table, and he peels back the kitchen towels he's draped over the hot dishes to keep them warm: a pile of Belgian waffles, pure Vermont maple syrup, a dish of powdered sugar, a bowl of strawberries, bacon that looks just crispy enough, a carafe of freshly squeezed orange juice, and a French press full of black coffee. The French press is wearing something I've never seen in my life—it's like a little cozy of some sort, chunky purple yarn knitted into a rectangle, wrapped around the French press and held in place by three yellow buttons that are shaped like stars.

He catches me staring at the French press sweater.

"Jules made that," he says. "I don't go through that much coffee very quickly on my own, so she gave it to me as a gift one time. Helps it stay warm."

It's a loaded thought, really, one that makes me feel secondhand loneliness: he hasn't had anyone to share his coffee with for eight years.

And then I remember that he chose this for himself. Thousands would have lined up for the chance to share any of this, all of it, with him. It didn't have to be this way.

What would he do if I just came right out and asked him about it?

I'm still debating whether I should bring it up when he holds a Belgian waffle out with a pair of tongs.

"One waffle or two?" he asks.

"One for now, thanks."

He loads it onto my plate, passes me the maple syrup and the butter. "So your wrist is still hurting pretty badly?"

"It's actually not too bad at the moment," I say, pleasantly surprised to realize I haven't really noticed it in at least ten minutes. "I slept on it funny, and then Puffin jumped on it, but I think my ice pack helped a lot this morning."

"Such a bummer you can't ski for a bit," he says, loading both of our plates with two long strips of bacon. "You were just about to level up, too."

"Guess the double blacks will have to wait until the weekend," I say with an exaggerated sigh for effect.

He laughs. "Yeah, it's really too bad—you were on track to compete with Olympians by the end of the month."

We devour our breakfast. The view is amazing, the food is even better, and it's simultaneously the loveliest and strangest breakfast I've ever had in my entire life. I sense that this is a big deal for him, inviting me into his private world like this, and then there's the additional layer of me knowing his most tightly kept secret—but he doesn't *know* that I know. I keep looking for cracks in Tyler, for any glimpse of Jett Beckett just beneath the surface, but the man at the table with me seems wholly sincere, entirely reborn from the ashes of the past he so thoroughly torched.

I want very badly to ask him about it.

I also don't want to ruin breakfast or make him completely shut down—or shut me out—by forcing him to talk about it before he's ready.

So I eat my waffle and drink my coffee and enjoy the view—not just the mountain, but Tyler himself, his smile and his laugh and his eyes that crinkle at the corners, and his rumpled shirt that makes me hope he'll have some sort of syrup malfunction that results in him taking it off so I can see what's underneath again. Those perfect abs, it occurs to me, must be the product not only of years on the slopes but also years on the stage and in the dance studio. Tyler was known more for his vocals than for his dancing, but it makes sense now that River was always the best dancer in the group, thanks to his years of pairs skating with Julie.

When we finish, Tyler walks me to the door.

"I'll miss giving you a lesson today," he says, taking my hand in his and pulling me into a big warm bear hug.

I rest my face against his strong chest, feel his heartbeat quicken just underneath. Mine picks up to match—

I could live in this hug.

He promises to come by later if I need anything, and I promise to not push my wrist too hard today while I'm working.

An hour later, I'm set up at the café for a change of scenery, and also because I won't have to make my own lunch or snacks. Makenna puts my honey nut latte in a to-go cup this time, even though I plan to sit here for hours.

"No laptop disasters today," she says, sliding it across the counter along with a bag of maple candies I didn't order.

When I question it, she waves it off and says, "On the house! How's your project going? Looks like your computer's okay?"

"Unfortunately, mine's a corpse now—this one's Tyler's."

Her brows shoot up, but mercifully, she doesn't comment.

She doesn't have to: it's written all over my face how far I've fallen for him. Which is a problem, because didn't I *just* establish that falling for Tyler is a very bad idea?

File: sebgreen_meetingtheband.mp3
Duration: 12:16
Date Recorded: February 7, 2025

SG:

I'll never forget our first day as a band: the five of us, together for the first time, and our manager. Jason. I loved him at the time— he was like a dad to me. I trusted him like a dad. I still believed he had my best interests in mind, even though the pivot from solo artist to boy band wasn't at all on my radar when we started working together.

I didn't know about Jett yet, before that first meeting. Didn't know Jason had fed him the same pile of lies he'd fed me, the same empty promises—I wouldn't learn that for a while.

Jason found us all in different ways.

Ayo had a video go viral where he'd layered his own vocals and beatboxing on top of each other, then danced along to the track. He knew a way to perform all the parts live at the same time, this pedal that would loop his parts back on themselves, but his gimmick got old fast. Really, his stuff worked better for a group—

he was the first to say yes when Jason eventually floated the idea of the band.

I was next. Jason and I had already started working on my studio album when he discovered Ayo, all those endless months out in LA listening to demos and recording countless songs that were supposedly in the running to be my first single. Jett was apparently doing the same thing at a studio down the street. Jason was working with both of us, even gave us some of the same songs to record. He and the label were never satisfied with any of our takes and ultimately didn't like either of us as individuals as much as they liked the idea of us in a group. Ayo said yes, and so did I. Jett was harder to convince.

The label needed more than two yeses and a maybe to make the band they had in mind, though, so Jason put out feelers to some of his contacts. Charly was from Orlando, grew up with four older sisters and had basically lived at the dance studio since before he could walk. Jason snapped him up immediately.

Jett was livid when Jason pulled the bait-and-switch on him after he'd spent all those months in the studio for his promised solo career, and even made noises about a potential lawsuit. We'd both signed management deals with Jason already, though—*sketchy* deals, we later realized—so he was locked in just like I was. He would've killed his career before it ever started if he'd walked away from it, and Jason knew it.

That didn't stop Jason from promising him the world to get him to say yes—to get him to keep quiet about how unhappy he was. Jason said yes to more money, more prominence, more everything. He even said yes to a whole other *person*.

Jett had a friend who could dance, he told Jason: his best friend, River, who'd spent years training as a figure skater. For whatever reason—probably just so he had someone on his side—Jett insisted he wouldn't say yes to the band unless Jason offered the fifth spot to River.

Everything is history from there.

Hearing that Jett wouldn't say yes unless his friend got to come along, that's the first time I knew we wouldn't mix. How do you consider saying no to an opportunity like that? Even if it wasn't what we'd originally planned, this guy was still making a huge investment in us, in our careers, and we were about to be the biggest thing on the planet. Sorry, but I would've given everything up. I *did* give everything up.

The last thing I needed was to have some bitter guy sharing my spotlight after he'd made it clear he could take the band or leave it.

Things were sour from the day we first met, and they never got better.

I—

There are a lot of things I would say to Jett Beckett now, if I could.

19

Sebastian's voice memo abruptly cuts off, my phone screen switching over to an incoming call.

It's Lauren.

I shut my eyes, count to three, and pick up.

"Aliiiiiix," she groans, sounding like the human equivalent of the distressed emoji.

"Good morning to you too."

"It's *not* a good morning. I'm just, like, a total distracted mess today—my boss has already yelled at me twice. And I spilled coffee all over my favorite white dress."

"Yelled? At the Met?"

"Well, it *felt* like she was yelling. She's really hard to please."

She pauses, like she has more to say but isn't quite sure how to say it—and then it all comes out in a rush. "But like I said, I'm just really distracted today. I need to tell you something. My coworker who was so loud while I was waiting on the locksmith—Veronica—the one who caused the noise complaints? She's, um,

178

kind of been living here, too. Will you really get evicted if we get another complaint? I told her to keep it down, but she just rolled her eyes. I'm worried she's going to get you in trouble and I don't know how to fix it."

I blink. That is . . . a lot.

"You didn't think you should ask me first about someone else living in my apartment? *You* aren't even supposed to be living there."

"I know. But I didn't know it was going to turn into this, I swear! We were watching a movie and then she, like, dumped all her roommate drama on me and asked if she could spend the night. I said sure, but then she just . . . didn't ever go home again. And now I don't know how to get her out."

"And this is someone you know through your internship?"

"Yeah. We work the same hours, so she keeps tagging along whenever I head home—I even tried to cut out early yesterday, but my boss was right there, so I couldn't get away. It's getting awkward."

I pinch the bridge of my nose.

"Have you tried talking to her about it?"

"I'm still working up the nerve . . ."

"So that's a no?"

Lauren sighs. "I've seen her get super petty with people at work when things don't go her way. And it's like she doesn't even hear me sometimes—I'll say I want Chinese for dinner, but she wants pizza, so we end up getting pizza. I'll say I need the shower, but then she sneaks in to use it while I'm grabbing a fresh towel."

I snort. "No wonder she's having roommate problems."

"Yeah."

"I know you hate confrontation," I say carefully. "But you really, really need to talk to her—and not just because she could get me evicted. She's walking all over you. *Using* you. You have every right to stand up for yourself."

Lauren goes quiet on the other end.

It's silent for so long I worry the call dropped somehow.

"Fine," she finally says, sighing. "I don't know if she'll listen, but I'll try."

"You can do this, Lauren. Don't let her steamroll you."

I hear another muffled voice in the background of the call.

"That was my boss," Lauren explains. "Break's over."

We hang up, but the conversation plays on a loop in my head. The more I think about it, the more anxious I feel: my good standing as a tenant is in the hands of my well-meaning sister who doesn't know how to put her foot down. Even if she musters the nerve to actually *have* the conversation, there's a real possibility that her presumptuous coworker won't take it seriously—and then what? More noise complaints could lead to my eviction, which would mean apartment hunting, then inevitable discouragement when there's nothing else in my neighborhood I can afford.

Again, the fleeting thought crosses my mind: I could sell Tyler out and have five digits—maybe even six—in my bank account in a heartbeat.

It's the easy answer.

It also makes me a little nauseated to think about.

If money were the most important thing to me, I'd still be with Blake—I would have contorted myself into someone who could deal with his toxic behavior just for the sake of being comfortable in material ways.

But money has never been the most important thing to me.

I chose a career I love because it makes me happy. I chose a life without Blake even though it meant I'd have to work so much harder.

I've never taken the easy way just because it's easy. And I'm certainly not feeling all that motivated to betray Tyler—who's been nothing but kind to me, nothing but generous—just because my sister's gotten herself into an uncomfortable situation.

Nope. Not feeling all that motivated at all.

My head hurts.

I try to focus on work instead, picking up with the voice memo I was listening to before she called.

"Things were tense between Jett and me right from the start," Sebastian says. *"He hardly said two words to me that entire first rehearsal, and he was so opinionated—it was like his ideas were the best ideas, end of story. It was always like that. Maybe he was trying to be such an ass that Jason would have no choice but to let him out of his contract? I don't know. It backfired if that's what he meant to do. All it did was put the rest of us on edge, and then Jason decided that worked for us—for me and Jett, specifically—and he started feeding it. Intentionally giving Jett his way just to piss me off, or giving me a solo Jett wanted to piss him off, things like that, all the time. I told Jett he was just paranoid and bitter when he tried to point out how Jason was fueling our rivalry, but eventually—after Jett was, uh, gone—I saw it. He was right."*

There's a long pause. I check to see if the audio is frozen, but it's still going.

"Everyone knew we had tension," he finally goes on. *"A lot of people assumed I had something to do with him going missing. I hated the guy most of the time, yeah—really publicly, unfortunately. But I just wanted him out of the band, not wiped off the face of the planet. He made life miserable for the rest of us, especially me, and I spent so much time resenting him for it. But I swear I have no idea what happened to him. I wish I knew. I hope he's out there somewhere, if only so people will stop giving me shit about how I must have driven him to . . . whatever happened . . . for the rest of my life."*

I rip out my AirPods.

What do I do with *that*?

I could make Sebastian's life easier in a heartbeat if I told the world the truth—but it would be at the expense of Tyler's peace, Tyler's privacy. Never in a million years did I imagine I would have more insight into Sebastian's life story than Sebastian himself. How am I supposed to convincingly ghostwrite his tell-all while holding on to a secret like *this*?

I blink, staring out at the mountain where Tyler's probably giving a ski lesson right this minute. Where he has been for years, hiding in plain sight.

And then I remember: I'm not the only one who knows he's here.

River knows. Julie knows. River could've let Sebastian in on the secret right from the start, but he didn't, and the logic feels obvious: there's no way the secret would have stayed secret.

River was loyal to Tyler. *Has* been loyal, keeping his secret for all these years. But Sebastian made the arrangements for me to stay here—not one of the countless vacation homes he owns. *Here.*

Why on earth would River—and Julie, for that matter—allow me to move in right next door to Tyler, knowing full well who I'm writing about?

Maybe it's the writer in me spinning up stories where there aren't any, but it almost feels like I've been set up. Do they *want* his secret to get out?

I take a deep breath.

Is there any scenario in which Tyler's secret *stays* secret?

CHLOE
3:33PM

HELP, your sister is texting me

ALIX
3:33PM

Please tell me she didn't lock herself out again

CHLOE
3:34PM

Worse . . .

ALIX
3:34PM

I hesitate to ask what could be worse

CHLOE
3:34PM

She's asking if some girl she knows from the
museum can move in with me. Until MAY.

ALIX
3:34PM
🙍🙍🙍

This girl has apparently been crashing
at my place for days, racking up noise
complaints—I told Lauren she needs to
talk to her about moving out. I did NOT tell
her to shove her onto someone else . . .

CHLOE
3:34PM
I don't know how to politely
tell her she's unhinged

ALIX
3:35PM
Oof. I'm so sorry. Tell her you're
coming to visit me soon and you're not
comfortable with a stranger staying in
your place while you aren't there?

CHLOE
3:35PM
Good idea. Also—you're still up for me coming
to visit, then? You're not too busy with work?

ALIX
3:37PM
I'm behind at the moment but let
me see how things go over the next
few days. Plan on it for now!

CHLOE
3:37PM

Perfect! Yeah, just keep me posted. FYI, I think I'm going to block your sister's number . . . she just texted again to see if I got her message 😬

ALIX
3:38PM

Wish I could do the same sometimes, honestly.

20

I spend the day engrossed in my work, camping out at the café for far longer than I mean to. Makenna brings me a fruit and cheese platter at one point, along with a flaky butter croissant.

I write and I write and I write, trying my very best to do justice to Sebastian's perspective without letting my own spill out onto the page.

I haven't heard from him since our video call—he never responded to my text asking when he might want to meet up here in Vermont.

Now, though, I'm thinking a face-to-face meeting might be a very bad idea.

What if he and Tyler see each other? Aside from the obvious, that their relationship was nothing but contentious, it would put me in an extremely awkward position: both of them would find out I've been keeping secrets.

That the book I'm writing is about Tyler's biggest rival and the band that made his life miserable.

That I know exactly where Jett Beckett ended up but haven't breathed a word about it to Sebastian, even though the mystery has tormented him for years.

That I would be inviting Sebastian straight to Tyler's doorstep, knowing full well how it could risk—could *ruin*—the privacy Tyler sacrificed his whole life for.

But.

A huge reason I'm here at all is so Sebastian and I have a private place to meet up in person. I feel professionally obligated to touch base with him, even if it's only to tell him I'm making good progress and that sticking to video calls is perfectly fine with me. And if he insists on coming? I have a feeling he won't—but at least I could plan around it, if so. Get Tyler to leave while he's here, make sure Chloe schedules her visit for some other time.

Hi, Sebastian, I type out. Wanted to check in and see if you've figured out yet when you might want to meet up here in Vermont? If you have too much going on, I think another video call or two would suffice . . . the book is coming along well!

Predictably, he does not write back right away.

I set my phone down and look up to find the sky has grown dark outside the panoramic window. There are no other customers in the café—I'm the only one spending her Saturday night on a date with her laptop, apparently.

My phone buzzes on the table. Could Sebastian really have written back so soon?

Of course not.

It's Tyler, and his text makes me smile.

Meant to check in much earlier, but I've been booked solid. How's the wrist?

My stomach growls so loudly he probably heard it all the way back at his penthouse. The cheese and fruit and croissant were lovely—but they were just enough to trick me into thinking I'd had an actual dinner and not just a glorified snack plate.

Also, it's past nine o'clock, and that snack was four hours ago.

The wrist is doing much better, thanks. I've been at the cafe for approx two million years

Sounds like a good work day, he writes back.

Productive day before I died of exhaustion, I reply.

His next message is a modified emoticon—:))))—like he doesn't know the emoji keyboard exists. I don't know why I find it so charming.

How about you? I write. Good day on the mountain?

I am also currently dead, he replies.

Didn't know ghosts could text 👻

I'm a ghost of many talents, Alix.

It was a pretty last day, at least

SO pretty, he replies. I lost count of how many runs I did this afternoon. Some double blacks, some regular blacks. Too many greens. One of my clients had a pretty bad fall today

😵 Hopefully your client was more graceful than I was last night . . .

I'm becoming a regular at the medical center for all the wrong reasons, he writes back. Doc gave me a hard time about it lmao

Are there ever any *good* reasons to become a regular in the medical center?

Very good point

So are they okay? Your client?

Torn ACL, he writes. Hate to see it. Especially because the guy insisted on trying a black, but he wasn't ready for it. Told him I didn't feel comfortable taking him up, so he went on his own after our lesson was over. Found him struggling at the bottom, he could hardly walk

Yikes, I reply. It reminds me of the guy I dated in college who tore his ACL under eerily similar circumstances.

Yeah :(

Sounds like a pretty good day otherwise with all the skiing, though? I've just been working

It was awesome otherwise, yeah, he writes. Super sore now, though

Wow, ski instructors get sore, too? I thought pros were immune to that sort of stuff

Shhhh, he replies. Don't tell anyone. It could ruin our image

Sounds like you need a massage

I've just hit send when I realize it sounds a lot like I'm offering to give him one rather than suggesting he go see someone at the resort's spa, which—

I mean—

I would.

Give him a massage, that is.

Wouldn't say no to that, he replies. But if your wrist hurts too much, no worries :)))

I blink at my phone screen.

It's an open invitation. The image of him shirtless flickers across my memory—taut muscles under smooth skin—and the idea of my hands, my hands *on him*—

My wrist still hurts if I twist it the wrong way, but it's been mostly good this afternoon.

The idea is too tempting to resist.

Let me pack up my work, I write back. I'll come over

The path back to our building is more crowded than usual: cozy couples walking hand in hand; a group of teenage girls who look

very copy/paste right down to their matching to-go cups of cocoa; the occasional resort staff member dressed in uniform. Saturday night is in full swing, and I suddenly find myself with plans just like everyone else.

I almost back out at least twice on my walk over.

When I'm talking with Tyler, or texting with him, it's easy to forget his past; his warmth is magnetic, and he makes me feel so comfortable in my own skin.

When the talking and texting ends, in the silence, I remember.

I remember all the things he ran from. All the people he left in the dark, worrying and wondering and making theories—making accusations. I don't entirely understand it, not yet.

But I want to.

Was it really his only option to make himself disappear like he did? Would he ever make himself disappear again if things got too hard?

Does he ever regret what he did?

I can tell myself all day long that it's a bad idea to get close to someone with a history like his—someone who chose to run, to leave everything behind—but what it comes down to is that I like him. I like him a *lot*.

Which is why, I've decided, I'm going to just come out and ask him about it.

I want to hear him defend it. *Need* to hear him defend it, especially if I intend to continue keeping his secret. I haven't entirely made up my mind yet on what to do about that—I could justify my decision either way—so this conversation will hopefully be the tipping point.

The elevator opens, and there he is, leaning against the wall outside my door, freshly showered and smelling like a dream of shampoo and soap and cologne. He's wearing a different pair of comfy pants this time—black joggers, thinner fabric than his thick charcoal ones—and a light gray V-neck.

"Hi," he says with the sort of shy smile that seems impossibly at odds with the fact that he's a world-famous pop star.

There's already a fire blazing in his living room fireplace, and the Edison bulbs give the place an extra-cozy feel. It's too warm in here for all the layers I'm wearing, so I tear off my cropped lavender hoodie and the long-sleeved base layer underneath it, leaving only a black tank top paired with dark teal yoga pants.

"Would you like a drink or anything?" he calls out from the kitchen as I check out his collection of novels on the bookshelf. He was not kidding about liking spy thrillers. "Wine or a cocktail?"

I join him in the kitchen, see an unopened sauvignon blanc he's clearly pulled straight from the fridge.

He notices me eyeing it. "That one's one of my favorites," he says, pulling two wineglasses down from a nearby cabinet.

A few minutes later, we're sitting together on his leather couch. The fire radiates heat, the wine is crisp and chilled, and we're also splitting some pita and hummus he had on hand since I sort of forgot to eat a real dinner.

Every sip of wine infuses me with more courage.

Unfortunately, every sip of wine also makes me want to forget talking altogether. I'm ready to get to the massage I promised—and maybe more—

But if I don't bring it up soon, I might never work up the nerve.

Maybe I should just do both at once. All intimidating conversations go down smoother with a side of massage—that's a saying, right?

In the end, I decide to just dive in before I change my mind.

"Your laptop bag is monogrammed," I say as casually as I can manage. *TJB*. "I realized earlier that you never told me your last name."

It's possible that I practiced this intro in my head on the walk over. I know what the ski school *says* his last name is . . . but he doesn't know that I know.

His gorgeous eyes meet mine, and everything moves in slow motion: the flicker of panic that's there and then gone—the muscle in his jaw that subtly twitches—the way he seems to be weighing his options.

Truth or lie.

Truth or dare.

What he does now will make or break any chance of a future with him. Will he lie to me? I've given him a wide-open door here, the perfect chance to confess his secrets before things go any further between us. If I had to guess, he's thinking about how his name on Black Maple Lodge's ski school pamphlet is Tyler Fox and how he probably wishes the *B* in the monogram looked just a little bit more worn so he could explain away the discrepancy.

"It was a gift from my mom when I was in high school, but someone screwed up the monogram," he finally says, and I'm sure—*sure*—he's about to lie to me until he glances down at the bag and then back up to me and says, "The *B* should be in the middle."

His eyes on me are intense.

Intensely honest.

Intensely intimate.

"Because your last name isn't Fox," I say quietly, daring him to look away.

Daring him to lie.

He knows I know. I can tell—he knows.

"I remember meeting you before," I add while I still have the nerve, direct but not unkind. "When you had another name."

I wait for him to deny it.

He doesn't.

I'm fairly certain he still hasn't placed me—the world really must have been a blur to him at the height of his fame—so I slip my phone out, scroll until I find the voice memo I saved all those years ago.

It only takes two seconds of playback for the recognition to hit.

"Shit, shit, holy shit. Alix. That was *you*?"

I'm stunned.

Not a single hint of denial—or explanation—but instead, concern for *me* is all over his face. His thick brows knit together. I've never seen him this serious, not as Tyler. And when he was this serious as Jett, he never seemed this sincere or this kind.

"I remember you too," he says. "You look a lot different now, though."

I laugh. "You're one to talk."

His eyes are still searching mine, scanning my face for hints that remind him of that day. But he's not the only one who's changed his look since then—I ditched my dark hair color eight years ago, ditched the blunt bangs a year after that. When it all grew out, I ditched my flat iron, too—or, at least, I stopped using it to straighten my hair. Now I use it to make my trademark beach waves instead.

"I've never forgotten that interview," he says slowly, carefully. "What you said to me."

His eyes gleam in the glow of the firelight, the Edison bulbs.

"It was the worst day. The worst *week* in the worst month. I was drowning—and I know that's no excuse for how I treated you—but the world felt heavy and twisted and nothing like anyone promised it would be. And then I remember you asking me something like, 'Why don't you just leave?'"

He blinks rapidly, like he's trying to clear his eyes—he's held so much in for so long—and then he looks straight at me.

"It was a lifeline."

His words are a whip, snapping the world into focus.

"It seemed so simple when you said it. 'Why don't you just leave?' Like it was easy. I remember feeling so alone in that moment—so angry, so trapped. It was the most ludicrous thing anyone could have suggested, especially in the middle of that tour, and the contract we had for three more albums and three more world tours, and the press commitments, and so many pointless dinners, and every single minute of every single day being scheduled out for the next five years."

His voice is a tightrope about to snap, his bitterness and resentment the most tenuous connection to the past. Still, there's a tenderness to his tone that tells me it isn't *me* making him feel bitter or resentful—it's the memory of everything he left behind.

"But to you, it was simple. 'Just leave.' I didn't think I should have to, obviously," he goes on. "I *knew* no one would want me to, that no one would ever allow it. Our manager, Jason—his wife had just left him because of the band, the person it had turned him into. None of us liked him much except Seb, but of course Seb liked him, because Jason played favorites and Seb was his. I hated that. The more I thought about it that night, the idea of just—just *leaving*—wouldn't leave me alone. It seemed impossible. I didn't see how it could ever work. And that made me want it more than anything."

His words are a flood, like he's actually *wanted* to talk about it all this time but never knew how to start.

"What I'm trying to say is—thank you." He looks down at his hands, and then back up at me. "Thank you for the question that saved my life, and for never releasing that interview even though

I was so rude to you. I'm so, so sorry, Alix. I hope you know I'm not the same person I was back then—I tried to leave behind more than just my name."

I don't know what to say, not to any of it.

He's basically just confirmed that it was *my* question that sparked his decision to disappear—when I listened back over that interview, I guess I just assumed the timing had been coincidental.

It's a lot to process.

"Tyler Jett Beckett," he says now, and I tuck it away like the secret it is. "That's what the monogram was meant to represent."

His gaze locks with mine.

"In eight years," he goes on, "you're the only person I've ever actually *told*. Riv and Jules know, of course—but they helped me get out, start over. They know because they lived it with me."

I set my wine on the side table, shift as close on the couch as I can get without sitting on top of him. I'm facing him, one knee tucked up to my chest. I could kiss him right now, easily—but there are still things left unsaid.

"Thank you for telling me," I say. "For *trusting* me."

He breathes out a little half laugh. "Of all the people in the world to figure it out," he says, shaking his head, "an *entertainment journalist*. Because of course."

I tense on instinct.

Can he tell that one of my first impulses when I realized the truth was to sell him out?

Honestly, if he'd lied to me tonight, I would have felt more inclined to do precisely what entertainment journalists do: send a splashy article out into the internet with the intent of making his incredibly juicy gossip go viral.

But the fact is, he told me the truth. He trusted me.

Which makes everything feel more complicated.

This man has trusted literally no one but his two best friends in the last eight *years*—but he let me in. And while some aspects of my life might be easier if I were to betray that trust, I can't help but wonder if I'd be happiest in the long run if I were to prove myself worthy of it instead.

"In all fairness," I say, "only an entertainment journalist in exactly this situation would have had all the pieces to put it together like I did. So if it hadn't been me, another one of us might have figured it out eventually."

His smile is soft, subdued. "I'm glad it was you."

"Me too," I say, and then I can't stop it—the force that pulls us together—and the next thing I know, his lips are on mine, and this kiss is full of more fire than any we've had yet, any I've had *ever*.

His hands find their way to my face, fingers tenderly tracing my jawline until they're buried in my hair. He kisses me harder, harder still when I wrap my arms around him and pull him in closer. Everywhere I touch is soft cotton over pure muscle—his strong upper back, the defined curve of his shoulders, the smooth skin of his biceps just below the hem of his sleeve.

He returns the favor, his strong hands tracing the lines of my racerback tank down to my waist, and then to my hips.

"This okay?" he murmurs between kisses.

"Definitely okay," I reply.

"And what about this?" he says, as he tugs me onto his lap so that I'm straddling him, my knees sinking into the soft leather couch, gravity pulling us even closer and reminding me there is very little fabric between us right now.

I nod, kiss him again. "Yeah," I say. "It's good."

Very good, actually, but neither of us says another word, and we get lost like this, lost in each other. He doesn't press for more than I'm ready to give—and as much as *more* would be fun (*fun* being the understatement of the century), I scrape together just enough self-control to stop before I get even more hopelessly entangled.

I want it. I want *him*.

But being worthy of his trust means his secret has to *stay* secret. I don't know how any of this can ever exist outside the bubble of this penthouse, this resort.

I pull back, surprised to find myself blinking away tears. I'm not quick enough to hide them.

"Do you want to talk about it?"

I'm still on his lap, sitting back now, arms loosely draped around his neck. "I want this," I say. "I want *you*. But . . . your life . . . we can't . . ."

Tyler nods, like he gets what I mean but haven't quite managed to say.

He presses his forehead against mine, his hands still resting lightly at my hips. I slide off his lap and tuck myself into his warm, strong body; he wraps an arm around me and pulls me even closer, his breath hot in my hair as I curl into him.

We stay like this, quiet, for a long time.

He never gives me an answer because there isn't one.

WJKS—
URGENT WEATHER ALERT

WINTER STORM WARNING FOR ENTIRE
VIEWING AREA

Residents of upstate Vermont should take special notice of what's shaping up to be a record-breaking snowstorm: all models agree that the sizable blizzard could dump as much as thirty inches of snow in some locations, which would shatter local records.

Friday currently looks like the most likely day for intensification, though one model predicts that the storm could ramp up as early as Thursday morning.

Please stay weather aware as you plan for this unprecedented winter storm event. Resources and more information regarding how to prepare can be found here.

21

For the next two days, all anyone can talk about is the weather. The local meteorologists have waited their entire careers for a storm like the one that's supposed to hit later this week, predicted to be *a blizzard to end all blizzards* and *an absolute monster*—which has led to people dubbing it the Yeti.

The Yeti is supposed to arrive on Thursday—three days from now—and they're saying it could drop as many as thirty, even *forty*, inches of snow here in our part of Vermont. I'm not a snow expert by any means, but even I know those are potentially record-breaking numbers.

I love a little snow . . . but not the kind that could keep Chloe from visiting. I'm hoping the Yeti will turn into a total nonevent, which is actually a possibility, according to a single hype-averse weatherman who insists it will bypass us entirely or fizzle to nothing. The forecast alone should be enough to keep Sebastian away for a bit longer, thankfully—not that I've heard from him. In a perfect world, this weekend would bring all the cozy vibes with none of the drama.

I haven't seen Tyler since Saturday night. He was already booked for most of Sunday with private lessons and ended up over at the main lodge until well past midnight last night, helping Julie take care of last-minute food and supply orders after one of her assistants had to fly home for a family emergency. If hundreds of guests get stranded here for days, myself among them, it's a relief to know the lodge is prepared to handle it.

I pull out my phone, type out a text to Chloe: Ugh . . . have you seen the forecast?

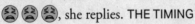, she replies. THE TIMING

Let's keep an eye on it. . . . I've gotten a lot done the last couple of days, so as long as the weather cooperates, I think this weekend will work for you to come visit!

BRB, currently googling snowshoes and how long it would take to walk to Vermont if everything shuts down

The image of Chloe in snowshoes—the same Chloe who insists we get delivery instead of going out anytime the temperature dips below thirty degrees—makes me burst out laughing.

(Conclusion: WAY TOO LONG!!!!), she types back before I can tell her I can't even picture her snowshoeing to the coffee shop at the end of her block.

Let's hope it doesn't come to that, then! I reply, then add a GIF of a bundled-up guy trudging through a heavy blizzard.

I spent all of yesterday inside my own penthouse, so this morning, I'm working at my favorite café booth again. My wrist feels almost normal after all the ice and rest I gave it over the weekend, so I'm planning to draft at least one entire chapter today, maybe even two.

I feel uneasy over keeping my own secret—that it's Sebastian's book I'm writing—when Tyler gave me the whole truth about his. I try to brush that feeling off since it's really not my place to tell, not my choice to keep quiet.

I'm convinced, after hearing Tyler's side of things, that his rivalry with Sebastian wasn't overblown by the media or just for show; that Tyler was absolutely *miserable* before he walked away from the band.

Now, listening to Sebastian get worked up about how moody Jett always was in rehearsals and how they could never agree on anything—which songs to record, which one of them would take lead vocals, and on and on—I feel a sort of defensiveness bubbling up in me. History *did* play out in Sebastian's favor, much more than he acknowledges or maybe even realizes.

The songs Sebastian wanted to record were given priority.

The songs Sebastian sang lead on became the band's singles.

The set lists for that final stretch of the last tour—now that I'm analyzing them—were weighted heavily with Sebastian songs at every single stop until the last one. Sebastian sang lead on twice as many songs as Jett, including at the now-iconic show where one of Sebastian's songs got cut for time due to Jett's insistence that they perform one of *his* songs instead—a twelve-minute version of "Que Será, Será," with the rest of the guys backing him up from the shadows. Everyone lost their minds over that performance, it was that good. *He* was that good.

No one knew it at the time, but that would be Jett's final show. And his fight backstage with Sebastian—the one that went viral—would be their final fight.

It's no wonder Sebastian took so much heat from the fandom when Jett disappeared. Everyone saw that fight, everyone heard the things they said to each other. The tension was so palpable, even over the internet, that I wouldn't have been surprised if it'd broken my phone screen. I believe Sebastian when he says he has no idea what happened to Jett—especially in light of all I know now, that he's alive and thriving here in Vermont—but I don't think it's a stretch to say that fight was Tyler's breaking point, the catalyst for all that came next.

I sigh, take a sip of honey nut latte, and click over into my email for a break.

There are a few new things, but only a couple of them look important. The first is a brief note from our editor, just checking in. I dash off a quick reply, telling her everything's going well and on schedule, how this change of scenery has been just what I needed to really focus on the book.

Back in my inbox, the subject line of the next email down catches my eye: *Open Invitation.*

I don't recognize the sender's name.

To: Alix Morgan (alix@alixmorganwrites.com)
From: Aspen Underwood (a.underwood@glossmag.com)
Subject: Open Invitation

Hi Alix,

I'm the coordinator for all things entertainment at GlossMag.com, and I came across the announcement in Publishers Marketplace for the Sebastian Green memoir you're working on (I know it's a bit hush-hush that you're ghostwriting for him, but publishing is a small world and I've got friends at your publishing house).

I'm sure you've signed an NDA and can't spill details related to Sebastian or his story, but I wanted to extend an open invitation—if you come across any juicy bits of news that don't fall under the NDA, please don't hesitate to reach out! I read that you covered True North pretty extensively back when you worked at *Starslinger Daily*, so thought you might have picked up some insider info at some point along the way.

Wanted to be proactive in reaching out—just say the word (and name your price) and we'd love to break any news you think the public might be interested in.

All my best,
Aspen Underwood

I blink, taking in the email on my screen.

Gloss is a *huge* deal.

Like . . . definitely not spam, definitely not a scam. Definitely a household name, thanks to their massive social media presence and their uncanny ability to spill celebrity secrets without spinning outright lies. I absolutely believe they have the resources for me to name my price (??!!), and given their long track record of breaking celebrity news, it's also not surprising that they'd go out of their way to hunt for potential leads like this. Searching the celebrity memoir section, digging for details about my own résumé as an entertainment journalist—it's a lot of work.

It's a lot of work, and they're willing to *pay*.

Before, the thought of selling Tyler's story was just some nebulous idea that could solve all my problems. This, though: *this* is an open invitation for me to share what I know with a reputable and respected site—and to get paid outrageously for it.

Honestly, I can't say it isn't tempting. But I've been feeling firmly on the side of keeping his secret ever since our talk. . . . Deep down, I think I'd regret it if I took Aspen up on her offer.

If my sister isn't able to get her coworker out of my apartment, though—and if I get evicted over it—

I slam the laptop shut before I do something I can't undo, then head up to the pastry case for a snack.

"How's the work going?" Makenna asks after handing off a drink to whoever ordered before me.

"Ugh," I say, scowling.

She laughs. "Sounds like something only a chocolate croissant can fix."

"It *does* sound like something only a chocolate croissant can fix," I agree. "How did you know?"

She pulls one from the case. "Warmed?"

"Isn't that the only way?"

"You'd be surprised how many people just don't want to wait," she says. "Tyler's one of them. He'll get it hot one day, then cold the next. And speaking of—"

I follow her gaze to the door and find myself staring straight at Tyler as he walks inside. His eyes light up, and my cheeks turn pink at his obvious attention—and the guilt I feel over the email in my inbox.

"After all these years," Makenna says in a low voice, "I finally know *one* thing he likes!" She gives me a pointed look before putting the croissant in the toaster oven.

Tyler joins me at the counter, gives me a shy smile.

I smile back, doing my very best to look innocent.

I *am* innocent, I remind myself. So why do I feel like such a traitor?

"What'll it be today, Tyler?" Makenna asks.

"Surprise me," he replies—to no one's surprise.

Makenna smirks. "I'll have it right out."

"You don't have to pay?" I ask as he follows me over to my table, where all my stuff is still spread out. Thank goodness I closed the laptop, so there's no chance of him catching a glimpse of Sebastian's name in Aspen's email.

"Perk of working on-property," he replies. "We get one free drink every day."

"Okay, so how do I get a job at the resort?"

"I'm sure Jules could hook you up with one if you really wanted it for more than just the free coffee," he says, grinning. His eyes study mine. "It's good to see you. Thank you—for Saturday. For everything."

He doesn't have to get specific: it's been almost two days, and his secret is still a secret.

"Speaking of Jules," he goes on, "she and Riv know that you know. You might have noticed, but they are embarrassingly excited about the fact that I've taken you on a few dates—and—you can say no to this—they invited us to dinner at Jules's place tomorrow night. It would be you and me, Jules and her husband, and Riv. Riv travels a lot, but he's back to help out with storm prep this week."

He looks so shy extending this invitation, definitely nervous. I guess it *is* the equivalent of meeting his family—and I'm the first person he's ever let in on his secret.

Maybe I'm the one who should be nervous.

Makenna comes over with my croissant and—I do a double take at the latte she sets before Tyler. There are *Froot Loops* on top.

Tyler raises his eyebrows. "This . . . is new . . ."

Makenna laughs. "Triple vanilla latte with a Froot Loop garnish, extra hot. Oh, and the milk is infused with Froot Loops, too—I let some soak in the fridge this morning since I figured you'd be in at some point."

"You," Tyler says, taking a sip and giving nothing away about how he likes it, "have a special talent."

"I'm taking that as a compliment!" she sings as she heads back toward her station.

"It actually is really good," Tyler admits when it's just us. "A bit on the sweet side. Want to try it?"

I take a sip, and wow, yeah, it's really sweet, even for me. But not bad?

"I'm surprised you like this, Mr. Naked Salad," I say, maybe the most awkward sentence that's ever come out of my mouth.

He laughs. "I wouldn't put it past her to make me a spinach cappuccino one day, honestly."

"Isn't that just called a smoothie?"

"Not when it's hot and has espresso in it," he says. "I think we've just invented the worst beverage idea in history."

"With soy milk," I add, laughing so hard I snort, which makes *him* laugh even harder.

"And nutmeg," he says.

"Stop it!"

"And—wait for it—*croutons*."

I'm in true danger of choking on my chocolate croissant; I close my eyes, focus on getting it down the right way. When I open them, there's Tyler, eyes bright, beaming.

"So let me see if I have this right," I say, now that I can speak again. "You actually *do* have preferences, but you let her make you whatever she wants just to mess with her."

"Correct," he says. "But wait, she actually *told* you I don't have preferences?"

"She said she's been trying for years to crack what you like and what you don't. You're such a closed book—you change the subject whenever it gets too close to something real."

He glances behind him, making sure we're still in the clear.

"I didn't think anyone paid enough attention to notice," he says quietly.

"Well, she did. And so did I."

He studies me for a moment, eye contact so intense it makes me want to sweep everything off this table so I can climb over it and into his lap.

"I'm glad you did," he finally says.

"Me too." I glance down, then meet his eyes again. "And I'd love to do dinner with your friends. If you're ready for that."

"The only thing I'm not ready for is how much shit they're going to give me over the fact that I've *finally* invited someone to one of our group dinners," he says. "But they'll give me shit no matter what, so it might as well be for a good reason this time."

"Can I ask—after all these years of not going out with anyone, why *did* you pick me?"

I've been dying to know. And it suddenly feels *important* that I know, given the temptation in my inbox.

"Honestly? It was your cat. And the fact that you were staying next door at all."

Of all the reasons he could've given, I admit that my cat is not one I ever expected.

"You asked me out . . . because of Puffin?"

He laughs, like he's only just now hearing how ridiculous it sounds.

"Riv owns the penthouse you're staying in," he explains. "No one ever stays there, so when I saw you that day waiting for the elevator, I knew you had to be someone special. Someone Riv had personally allowed into his space. And then when you told me they'd said yes to your *cat*—it just surprised me, is all. They only let me have a goldfish, and I've known them my entire life."

I try my best to cover my surprise: all this time, Sebastian has acted like it was *his* penthouse to share with me.

The fact that it belongs to River instead brings up so many questions.

River has to know I'm writing Sebastian's memoir, right? To allow a stranger to stay in one of his personal penthouses for a solid month—wouldn't he have to know? Surely Sebastian would have told him when asking for the favor.

Why would River say yes to an entertainment journalist moving in next door to his best friend—his best friend who's gone to great lengths to make himself disappear—all while continuing to keep his secret?

It doesn't make any sense.

"I still can't believe they only let you have a goldfish," I finally say. It's all I can manage.

"In Pete's defense, he is a very companionable goldfish," Tyler replies, not missing a beat, and I laugh.

Something he said earlier nags at me.

"You said I seemed like someone special because River had personally allowed me into his space," I say, "but at some point you must have figured out that I don't actually *know* River."

The corner of his mouth quirks up. "Riv and Jules get requests all the time for people to stay at the resort," he says. "Travel writers, athletes, food critics—all strangers, but almost always notable in some way or another. They usually stay over at the main lodge or in one of the lower suites." He shrugs. "I figured Riv knew someone at your publisher and that's why you got extra-special treatment—all he told me was that you were a writer with a good reputation."

It's all I can do to keep from blurting out that *Sebastian Green* is the someone who reached out to River for said "extra-special treatment"—but revealing that little detail would most definitely be in violation of the NDA I signed. Not to mention how it has the potential to set off an avalanche of drama between River and Tyler, and I'd rather not get caught up in it.

"Speaking of River," Tyler says, "I happened to mention your laptop disaster, and—"

From his backpack, he pulls a shiny rose-gold MacBook Air.

It looks brand-new.

"He wants you to have it."

I look at the laptop, then back to Tyler, then at the laptop again.

"River . . . bought me a new computer?"

"Apparently, people send him free stuff all the time—perk of being a social media influencer, I guess." He grins. "He said he had a couple of extras on hand and it's yours if you want it."

"Um, yes, I want it." I'm in a little bit of shock right now. "He doesn't want anything in return?"

River planted me right next door to Tyler, knowing full well that I'm an entertainment journalist working on Sebastian's book—and now he's dropping a brand-new laptop into my life so I can continue working on said book?

Interesting.

"Riv's got a whole closet full of stuff he's not sure what to do with," Tyler says. "You're actually doing *him* a favor by taking it."

"Well, tell him I'm happy to help," I say, laughing, even though I can't help but wonder if there's more to it than that.

More to it than Tyler knows.

"You can tell him yourself when you meet him tomorrow night," Tyler says, and that's when it hits me: I'm going to meet River Wu—*tomorrow*.

I could take or leave his celebrity status, and the fact that all the True North guys are pop culture legends. But the thing that's giving me a sudden surge of nerves is that I'm going to be meeting Tyler's lifelong best friend.

The guy he wouldn't join the band without—

The guy who helped him disappear—

The guy who invited Tyler's mortal enemy's ghostwriter to live in the penthouse next door.

So much for not getting in over my head.

SPOTTED:
Sebastian Green in Tuscany!

By Petra James // Starslinger Daily, *Staff Writer, Arts & Entertainment*

Pop star Sebastian Green was spotted over the weekend boarding his private jet at Teterboro Airport just outside of New York City—and spotted once again after arriving at Villa di Pratello, a secluded resort in Tuscany, via helicopter.

Known for traveling solo on a whim, Green did not appear to have any guests with him for the trip. Perhaps he's getting away for a writing retreat to work on his new book, or maybe he simply wished to put as much distance as possible between himself and the bad weather predicted for much of the Northeastern region of the United States later this week.

Whatever the reason for the getaway, please enjoy these gorgeous photos—and not just of Sebastian! Tuscany itself looks pretty stunning, too. We can't help but notice: even at a secluded resort in Italy, Sebastian Green can't shake the paparazzi . . . and judging by the way he's all but posing for the cameras, it looks like he not only doesn't mind their presence but like he's basking in the attention.

No complaints here—enjoy our gallery below!

22

At exactly seven o'clock on Tuesday night, Tyler and I knock on Julie's door.

Julie and her husband share the top floor over at the main lodge—I can tell it's going to be enormous by the fact that there's only a single door leading to what appears to be the entire east wing of the building.

"Tyler—and Alix! Come in!"

Julie has one of those smiles that lights up her entire face. She looks different here than she does when she's working—more relaxed. Her shiny dark hair is loose, framing her face instead of being knotted in a bun at the nape of her neck, and she's dressed casually in a faded concert T-shirt and stylishly ripped jeans.

"So sorry, but Justin isn't able to join us tonight," Julie says. "He's helping the kitchens prep for the Yeti."

Justin is Julie's husband, I learned on the walk over. They met at Brown and had already been dating for over a year when Julie got the call that changed her life, informing her that she and River had inherited Black Maple Lodge decades earlier than anyone anticipated. River was tied up with band obligations at the time, so Julie took on the entire weight of the resort alone.

"Thanks for having us," I say, following her into the palatial living room.

The view from the massive panoramic window is similar to the one from our building—it overlooks Black Maple Mountain, but from a higher vantage point and an even more postcard-perfect angle. It's twilight: all the lanterns and string lights in the village reflect in the shimmering ice of the skating rink.

"Riv should be here any minute," Julie tells us. "Can I make you a drink?"

She pours me a large glass of red wine, a cabernet sauvignon from somewhere near Sonoma; Tyler takes a whiskey on the rocks.

"How's the storm prep going?" he asks.

"We're fully stocked up for at least the next week and a half," she replies. "Now I'm just hoping the power doesn't go out for too long."

"They've got backup generators," Tyler tells me, probably because he sees the look of panic on my face—I knew power outages were a real possibility with the Yeti, but I hadn't considered how bad it would be if all the kitchens' refrigerators suffered a power failure.

"The kitchens will be fine," Julie explains. "But the concierge desk? Total nightmare. Last time we had a storm, we had an essential-use-only policy for the generators so they wouldn't get overloaded—the lines at my desk were endless, people wondering about our laundry service and when the water heaters would be up so they could take hot showers again."

"She hardly got a break for twelve hours that time," someone says behind me, and I whip around to see that River Wu has slipped in to join us, an unopened bottle of white wine in hand.

"Alix, River—River, Alix," Tyler says, heading straight over to River for a bro hug.

When they're done, River turns his full attention to me.

"So great to finally meet you," he says, eyes sparkling like only a former pop star's can.

River is polite and charming, with a quiet confidence that effortlessly communicates his celebrity status—unlike Sebastian, whose affect feels a bit forced, or Tyler, who's gone to great lengths to conceal his fame. His dark hair is short on the sides and swoops up in the front, and while his outfit is simple—slim-cut navy chinos and a white button-down, sleeves rolled up to expose his forearms, with a pair of suede loafers—it probably cost more than an entire month's rent on my apartment.

"Likewise," I reply. "And thanks for the new laptop, by the way—I'm sure Tyler's glad to have his back."

Tyler pulls me in for a side hug and kisses my temple. "Yeah, man," he tells River, "thanks again."

"Glad you can put it to use," River says, grinning.

River asks Julie what smells so good—roast chicken and veggies, apparently—and then they move on to talking about the Yeti, and the lodge, and all the logistics that go into prepping for a storm like this.

I smile and nod at all the right times, but inside, I'm sizing up the dynamics here—sizing up River for any indication that he might not have Tyler's best interests at heart. Clearly, he and Julie have kept Tyler's secret this well for this long; he could have told Sebastian the truth years ago if he'd wanted to.

Maybe, like me, River doesn't feel it's his secret to tell.

But eight years is a long time to keep a secret like that. I can't help but wonder if, deep down, River wants someone to find out.

If that's the case, you'd never know by the way he's smiling and laughing—they could all be siblings, family. Of course, I know as well as anyone that siblings can harbor all sorts of hidden feelings long before you ever find out about them. That's how it was with my brother: I'd been writing entertainment articles for more than three years when I overheard him telling our parents how disappointed he was in me, how he thought I should be *so much further* in my career, wondering out loud when I would ever get a "real job."

Things never quite recovered between us after that.

At dinner, the conversation is lively and fun—River's filling me in on the trip he took to Europe that inadvertently blew up his social media and turned him into an influencer.

"I was invited to speak at this conference in Switzerland," he says between bites of roasted chicken, "and I was told the audience would be full of 'rising stars'"—he exaggerates his air quotes—"of the luxury travel industry."

"I'm sensing a *but*," Tyler says.

"*But*," River goes on, and we all laugh, "as soon as I got to the resort, in the elevator, a lady whipped out an old True North poster and a Sharpie and asked me to sign it for her. And as soon as I got off the elevator, there were four more people who asked for autographs and selfies. Women, men, the cleaning staff—pretty much everyone I ran into the entire week asked me to do *something* for them."

"And did you?" I ask, most of the way through my first glass of wine.

"Well, I'm not a *monster*," River says with perfect comedic inflection.

"What he means," Julie cuts in, "is that he knew he'd be stuck at the conference for a week with these people, and he could either fight it or give in."

"I gave in," he says, sighing. "I learned a long time ago that it can take more energy to resist."

"So, what—the travel conference was, like, a front for some sort of fandom event?" I ask.

"Worse," he says. "Some True North subgroups had posted about the event, and apparently a few *hundred* side-hustle types suddenly decided they wanted to work in the hospitality industry."

"That's commitment right there," says Julie, topping off my wine.

"That's *concerning*," Tyler adds without missing a beat. "Wasn't that event sold out months in advance?"

"It was, until the fandom took to the internet and offered triple—or more—what people had originally paid for their tickets." River shakes his head. "The things people will do to meet someone famous—I'll never understand it."

"*Same*," I say, a little too emphatically, before remembering that half the people present in this room are celebrities. "No offense."

Tyler takes my hand in his, right there on the table for everyone to see. "I'd feel the same way if I were you," he says, eyes gentle but intense.

"This is the weirdest coincidence," Tyler goes on, leaning in toward Julie and River, "but Alix is an entertainment writer, and she interviewed me one time—*before*. I was an utter jackass to her. It's a miracle she hasn't held it against me."

River looks completely unfazed by this information—no surprise there. I'm pretty sure it's news to Julie, though.

"If it makes you feel any better, Alix," she says, swatting Tyler with her cloth napkin, "he was a jackass to everyone back then."

"Not everyone—"

"*Everyone*," Julie and River say simultaneously, cutting Tyler off.

"I was in a bad place," Tyler says. "At least these two knew me before."

"Yeah," River says. "The band turned him into someone else."

216

Tyler takes a sip of his whiskey. "It wasn't the band. It was *Jason*. Jason and Seb."

I glance at River, trying to gauge his reaction, but he deftly averts his eyes.

"Is that why you helped Tyler disappear?" I ask, then take a sip of wine.

All at once, their collective attention snaps to me. They obviously know I'm in on the secret—so why does it feel like I've crossed a line?

And then I realize: This is the very first time anyone has ever asked about what they did, let alone *why* they did it. It's new territory for all of them.

"Neither of us wanted to see it get any worse," Julie says solemnly. She takes a long sip from her tumbler of iced water as if to wash the memory down.

A thick silence falls over them. The longer it goes on, the more I want to break it—want *anyone* to break it.

Eventually, Tyler clears his throat. "They saved me," he finally says. "I'm in a much better place now."

Julie and River exchange a glance.

I catch it, but Tyler doesn't. He's looking at me.

"Well!" Julie suddenly says, a little too brightly, clapping her hands together. "Who wants dessert?"

She serves us each a generous slice of flourless chocolate cake, spooning warm raspberry compote on top. We migrate to the sitting room, where we eat and talk and laugh for the next two hours, never again circling back to Tyler's past. It's breezy and fun and all too easy to pretend the four of us are just on vacation at a gorgeous resort, no deadlines or secrets or unresolved tension between us.

At the end of the night, Julie wraps me in a tight embrace. Despite her birdlike frame, she's a strong hugger.

"You're good for Tyler," she says quietly when he's out of ear-shot. "I'm so glad you've found each other."

"He's great," I say when we pull back. "I'm so glad we've found each other, too."

And I am—

Even if it's feeling less like Tyler and I "found" each other and more like River put me next door on purpose, where we would almost certainly cross paths.

Tyler joins us in the foyer and pulls me in close, a look of contentment on his face.

"They loved you," he says when it's just us again, out on the moonlit path back to our building. It's a cold, clear night, no trace of the storm that's about to hit.

We take our time, enjoy the calm while it lasts.

APRIL 1, 2017

RIVER
12:54AM
Hey, Jules
Juuuuuules
I need your help

JULIE
12:55AM
Is this some sort of April Fool's joke,
Riv? It's the middle of the night . . .

RIVER
12:55AM
I'm coming to the lodge

JULIE
12:56AM
Like . . . after your tour is over?

RIVER
12:56AM
No, tonight

JULIE
12:57AM
I thought you had another show tomorrow
in Boston, that's not exactly a quick drive

Everything okay?

RIVER
12:58AM
Don't worry

I'm not staying, have to get back to Boston ASAP

Also, if anyone asks you any questions,
please tell them you don't know anything

JULIE
12:58AM
Questions??? RIV. What's going on??

RIVER
1:00AM
I'll explain everything

Don't worry

I'll call you as soon as we're in
the car and on the road

JULIE
1:00AM
Who's *we*??

Riv?

River??

23

By midafternoon on Wednesday, the entire resort is buzzing about the change in the forecast. Unfortunately, the change is not for the better.

Now they're predicting even *more* snow—and even sooner.

The Yeti has gathered more energy than expected, and instead of late Thursday or early Friday, some are saying it could start as soon as tomorrow morning.

The train is already running on a limited schedule, and they're booked solid today with people trying to get out in time. I'm guessing the opposite is true for the incoming trains they haven't already canceled—who would intentionally try to travel up this way with the massive blizzard on the horizon?

Chloe. Chloe would.

I pick up my phone, initiate a FaceTime.

She answers almost immediately.

"Aliiiiiix! This forecast is ruining my *life*."

"There's, like, one meteorologist still insisting it won't be terrible?" I say. "But I honestly think he's just trying to go viral."

"Trains run in the snow all the time, right? They have all sorts of protocols in place to keep them going twenty-four seven."

"Do they?" I say. "I'm honestly not sure. Even if the trains technically could run, they're anticipating power outages and significant delays, so they've preemptively canceled, like, ninety percent of their scheduled departures this weekend. You're still thinking you might try to come?"

I feel a sliver of hope that she'll still be able to visit as planned, but it's dulled by how unlikely it is to work out. I really don't want her making a treacherous journey on my account—what if she gets stranded somewhere between here and New York?

"Well, I did already pick up some rosé. And some cab. Oh, and also some sort of Italian white the cashier talked me into while I was checking out. And some stuff for a cheese board—"

"Chloe," I interrupt, before she starts in about Gorgonzola and goat cheese. "You know how much I want you here, right? But please . . . don't risk it if it looks like it's going to be too bad—I don't want you dying on the way over from the train station to the lodge."

She goes quiet, then sighs. "Text me the name of that optimistic meteorologist? If even he gets all doomsday, I promise I won't come."

Once we're off the call, I send her a link to the meteorologist's website, then dash off a quick text to Sebastian even though he never replied to my last one.

Heads up, the weather's looking really bad this weekend here at the lodge . . .

I know from his socials that he's in Italy right now, so I'm fairly certain our impending Vermont blizzard is the furthest thing from his mind. Still, I feel better just knowing there's about to be a gigantic buffer of snow between us (not to mention the entire Atlantic Ocean).

Puffin hops up onto my lap, stepping on my wrist in the process—it's been feeling almost normal over the last day or two, and this time I barely even wince under the pressure of his paws. I smooth my hand over the soft fur of his forehead, and he pushes back, purring, before leaping up to the table I've been using as a desk—and walking all over my keyboard.

Honestly, if Puffin could write this book for me, I would let him at this point.

I settle in to work on a fresh Sebastian chapter as best I can. This voice memo is testing my patience more than the others—it's a true challenge to sound neutral, unbiased, as I put his story onto the page.

A notable example from this particular voice memo: *"It was all just so hard—too many girls. Too much money. Too little time to go to every party I was invited to, too tight a schedule to jet off to Phuket at the drop of a hat, so much free swag I didn't even have time to open all the packages. But at the end of the day, I had the band, and the fans, and it was like the best dream of my life that I never wanted to end. It hasn't really ended, either: yeah, it's still hard to go out without getting recognized, without paparazzi on my tail at every single hour of every single day—I think that's something that will never go away—but it's a privilege, you know? I might want privacy sometimes, but there's no way around it. True North will always be a part of me."*

Eye roll, eye roll, eye roll.

I suppress the urge to add a ghostwriter's footnote: *Of course, Sebastian makes every effort to stand out—just look at his attire! He wears his pop star status like a neon sign. It's actually a shock he hasn't yet acquired an *actual* neon sign that says SEBASTIAN GREEN with a Vegas-style arrow pointing to his too-white teeth.*

If only.

If I weren't being paid to write this book, I would totally be submitting Sebastian-centered articles to places like Gloss instead—but alas.

It's possible I'm extra irritated by the fact that he's ghosted me ever since our last call—and despite my best efforts to stay neutral, I can't help but feel a bit disenchanted with Sebastian now that I know it was *Tyler* on the other side of their infamous rivalry.

I shut my laptop and pick up my phone.

Any chance you might want to take a certain stir-crazy writer out on the slopes this afternoon? I message Tyler. My wrist is basically perfect now

Almost immediately, Tyler replies, "basically perfect" lol

So my phone isn't broken after all.

I've got time at four, he writes back in a separate bubble. That work?

I check my watch. I *guess* I can wait a whole hour to see you again 😜

:)))))), he replies—Tyler and his emoticons.

See you then/there, I reply.

Can't wait <3

His little emoticon heart makes me feel all fluttery inside—the effort of it, the image of his strong hands typing out those two tiny symbols, just strikes me as beyond sweet.

I am in so far over my head.

Tyler is waiting for me outside the ski school when I arrive, just casually leaning against one of the big front windows. As soon as he sees me, his entire face lights up.

"Hey, gorgeous," he says, and—yeah—I could get used to

greetings like this. He takes my hand as soon as it's within reach and, in one smooth move, pulls me in close for a kiss.

His lips are soft and warm and taste like powdered sugar.

"Did I say I wanted to *ski* this afternoon?" I say between kisses. "I think I meant to say you should come over to my place."

He laughs. "Ahhh, yeah, I should have known you meant *let's stay in* when you asked me to take you out on the slopes."

"The weather's pretty terrible for skiing," I say, pointing to the lone cloud in the otherwise very blue sky. It's hard to believe we could be buried in snow by this time tomorrow.

"*So* terrible," he agrees. "How about this: we'll ski first, and then I'll make you dinner at your place and we can watch the storm roll in."

"That sounds amazing," I say.

A date night at my place with Tyler sounds like exactly what I need. I can picture it perfectly: lights as dim as they can get— fireplace blazing—the smell of herbs and butter and garlic heating up on the stove—a big mug of hot cocoa—his body pressed up against mine, as close as we can get under a fluffy down blanket while the sky outside the panoramic window turns progressively more ominous—Lauren calling—

Lauren. Is calling. Right now.

I texted her yesterday to check in since I hadn't heard anything after our last call. She insisted things were going okay—but quickly changed the subject when I asked how the conversation had gone with her presumptuous friend.

"So sorry, but I have to take this real quick," I tell Tyler. "It's my sister."

I pick up. "Hello?"

"Okay, please don't hate me," Lauren says.

My stomach flips. "What happened?"

"So, I have been looking for a good chance to tell Veronica she can't stay with me anymore, I swear, but she shuts me down literally every time I try to bring anything up—so I decided to try leaving the museum early again today, alone, and it worked. But it, um, kind of backfired."

"Backfired how, exactly?"

"She came back to the apartment anyway. I didn't answer the first time she knocked, or the second. But then she started banging on the door and calling my name, yelling for me to let her in, making this whole scene—and I didn't want her to get us in trouble by being loud again—so I finally answered the door. Which, it turns out, was a mistake. She asked why I left work without her and why I didn't come to the door sooner. I tried to be brave, Alix, I really did. I told her she couldn't stay with me anymore, especially because she has a tendency to be loud and I'm afraid it might get you evicted, and—um—she didn't take it very well."

I close my eyes, bracing myself. "What did she do?"

"She got even louder. And, um—she kind of keyed your door. It now says 'bitch' on it in gigantic ugly letters."

"*What?*"

"I'm so, so sorry—"

"Lauren. This is *not* okay."

"I know! I know. I tried to stop her, but I honestly think she would have scratched *me* with the key if I'd gotten any closer, and I just—I kind of froze. And then I left."

"Where are you now?"

"Hiding in the corner at a Starbucks."

"Did she leave, too?"

"I don't know," Lauren says. "I left first—I'm kind of afraid to go back."

I let out a long exhale. This is a mess. At least Lauren's in a safe place right now. Everything else, though . . . I don't even know where to start.

"She seemed so *nice* when I first met her," Lauren says ruefully.

"Some people are like that," I say, thinking of Blake: how charming he seemed on the surface, and how quickly that charm disappeared whenever anyone dared to question or challenge him.

"I don't know if I can go back to the apartment, Alix. What am I supposed to do if she shows up again?"

"Maybe you can stay with Chloe for the night?" I suggest, knowing that's far from ideal—and I would have to ask on Lauren's behalf, since Chloe blocked her days ago.

"I wish I could come stay with *you*. I think I made things weird with Chloe when I asked if Veronica could move in with her."

My heart sinks. Staying with me is absolutely, unquestionably not an option—I have too much work to do, not to mention the impending storm.

At least the snowstorm makes for a good excuse.

"I'm so sorry, but everything's a little chaotic around here right now—there's a huge blizzard headed this way. Chloe was actually planning to come up this weekend, but it's looking like she's going to have to stay in New York."

Lauren is quiet on the other end.

"You can handle this," I tell her. "It's going to be okay. Do you have any other friends from the museum who can make sure you get home safely? You could ask one of them to walk you up if you're afraid to go on your own."

"That's a good idea," she says.

"Call me if you need anything, okay? And worst case, I know Chloe will be there for you in an emergency, even if you feel awkward."

I make a mental note to fill Chloe in ASAP—and to tell her to unblock Lauren's number.

When we end the call, I look up to see Tyler rubbing out some smudges on his ski goggles, trying to pretend he hasn't overheard every single word.

"So, uh," he says. "That seemed . . . rough. Are you okay?"

I blink back tears. Now that I'm reasonably sure Lauren will be okay for the night, it's sinking in that I truly might lose my apartment over this—noise complaints, property damage, people staying there who aren't on the lease. I could have handled things more responsibly, *should* have been more on top of things somehow, shouldn't have let it even get to this point.

"Could be better," I admit. "Hanging out with you will help."

"Well, I'm glad I'm here, then."

Tyler pulls me into a tight hug, and I bury my face against the firm muscle of his chest.

"I'm really glad you're here, too."

Black Maple Lodge

Stowe, Vermont

Dear Valued Guest—

As you've no doubt heard, we're expected to get an unprecedented amount of snowfall over the next day or two. In the interest of keeping every guest informed, we want to make sure you are aware that the latest timeline for this week's weather event has been pushed up: Black Maple Lodge could begin to see snowfall as early as tomorrow morning, possibly even some flurries tonight.

Please know that we are doing everything within our power to ensure a safe and memorable stay for every one of our guests. We have generators on hand in the event that we lose power, and we've also stocked up on food and beverage staples above and beyond what we anticipate we will need. In short, you are in good hands with us, and we will do our very best to ensure that your stay is impacted as little as possible by events that are out of our control.

Should you have any questions or concerns, feel free to inquire at the concierge desk.

We look forward to serving you,

Julie Wu
Owner/Operator, Black Maple Lodge

24

Tyler seriously missed his calling as a chef.

My entire place is filled with the savory aroma of chili—garlic, onion, ground beef, a bottle of Blue Moon, roasted tomatoes—and I can already tell it's going to be the most perfect cozy meal for the impending snowstorm. Even though the worst of it won't hit until tomorrow, the wind has already started to pick up.

"You like things spicy, right?" Tyler asks as I watch from the kitchen island.

"In what context?" I say, just to mess with him. "Food or romance books or—"

He laughs. "Yes. All."

"I like it."

"And now, a controversial question for you," Tyler says as he rummages around in his bag of supplies. He pulls out a can of red beans and sets it on the island. "Beans in chili: genius or sacrilege?"

"Is it controversial that I have no strong opinions about it?"

"It would be in Texas," he replies, taking my lack of opinion as permission to go forward with opening the can of beans. "My mother grew up there, and this is her mother's recipe—except for one tweak. Red beans. The fight they had over it nearly tore the family apart."

"That sounds *serious*!" I say, mentally marking this down as the first time he's felt comfortable enough to mention his family around me.

"Oh, it was," he says. "I was ten years old, and we'd gone down for a huge family reunion on the Fourth of July. I thought my grandmother was going to have a heart attack right there in the kitchen when she realized my mother had just, like, nonchalantly added beans to her prizewinning recipe. Everyone turned on my mom except for my granddad, who made the mistake of saying he never felt quite full enough after eating my grandmother's chili, and—well."

"I don't understand how beans could be so divisive."

"Have you ever been to Texas?"

"I have not."

"Well, there you go," he says as he drains and rinses the beans, then adds them to the pot.

"So what ended up happening?"

"People were so hungry that they ate it anyway—and then they had to apologize when they ended up loving it."

I laugh. "Even your grandmother?"

"No," he admits. "My grandmother was lovely in so many ways, but she was also extremely petty. She was so offended she wouldn't even taste it, and she held a grudge about it until the day she died."

"Wow," I say. "Your poor mom."

"My mom was amazing."

His words hang in the air between us. The sizzle and pop of the bubbling chili now feels extra loud; he gives it a stir and it calms down.

"Was?" I say.

It felt like an invitation—or at the very least, an open door.

"She raised me on her own all the way up here in Vermont. Even before that reunion, we were always closer with friends— River and Julie's family—than with our actual relatives."

He adjusts the burner heat, sets the wooden spoon down.

"No one told me she was sick," he says quietly. "We were on tour, and *no one told me*." His eyebrows knit together like he's staring into the past. "When she died, Jason told me, 'Oh, shit, man. I didn't think it was that serious.'"

"Wait," I say as the weight of his words sinks in. "Your manager *knew* your mom was sick—someone trusted him with that information—and he just, like, decided not to tell you?"

"He'd known about it for a week, the whole time we were in Miami and Philly, but didn't want me distracted on tour. And then she was gone."

My head is spinning. How could anyone be so selfish, so cold? How could anyone have the audacity to withhold that sort of information?

And how did they keep it entirely out of the press? I was writing about the band that whole time and never heard a single tip about it.

I must have been processing out loud, because the next thing I know, Tyler's saying, "My publicist covered it up somehow—she said I was going through enough with my grief and everything with Jason. That I didn't need speculation and scrutiny from strangers on top of that. They wouldn't even let me do a funeral."

"I'm so sorry," I say. "That must have been terrible."

Terrible feels absolutely insufficient.

"It felt like someone had ripped the sky in half," he says. For a second, I think he might say more—but he leaves it at that.

Miami and Philly were the band's last stops before Boston—it makes more sense now, his disappearance. Why he left when he did.

When the chili is done cooking, we settle onto the living room floor with our bowls on the low, wide coffee table. There are at least three other spots in this place specifically designed for meals, but this one is the coziest, with the fire blazing and the view of the increasingly gloomy sky, the thick blanket of clouds growing darker by the minute. I can already see flurries on the patio.

I take my first bite of chili, making sure to get a little of the Greek yogurt and cilantro Tyler put on top—his bowl is also garnished with slices of fresh jalapeños.

"This is *so* good," I say. "Honestly, I see why your mom was willing to cut ties with her entire family over it."

"Fortunately, most of them came around in the end," he says, grinning. He takes a huge bite with more jalapeños than seems wise, but doesn't so much as flinch at the spice.

"So, your sister," he says. "Is it always like that with her?"

"Yeah." I sigh. "She leans on me pretty hard."

I've wanted to say so many things to Lauren for so long, especially that I think our well-meaning mother did her a disservice by treating her like she might break for her entire life—really, though, it was only the first few weeks after she was born early that Lauren was particularly fragile.

"You'd think by now she'd be better at handling the hard things on her own—she's like a magnet for drama. Honestly, though, I blame our parents for enabling her for so long."

It isn't Lauren's fault our parents have always fought her battles for her. I try not to resent her for it. Meanwhile, I've worked so hard for everything I have, yet *I* am the sibling who's treated like a disappointment with a questionable career. It's frustrating, to say the least.

"Have you ever felt invisible?" I ask Tyler.

As soon as the words are out of my mouth, I have to laugh at the absurdity of my own question. *No, Alix—a world-famous pop star will absolutely not relate to feeling invisible.* Millions of people tracked his every move until he decided to make himself disappear on purpose.

"What?" he asks. "What's funny?"

I gesture at his entire existence.

"You're . . . *you*. I almost forgot what your life was like before."

"You think famous people never feel invisible?"

My cheeks grow hot. "It's hard to imagine, that's all. The whole world knows who you are."

"The whole world *thinks* they know," he corrects. "But they never do. They know what they're shown, and then they draw their own conclusions. They don't know what's going on under the surface, not really. So I think maybe it's possible to feel even *more* invisible when you're famous—everyone thinks they know who you are, but they really, really don't. It's disorienting. If I had to pick, I'd rather not be seen at all." His eyelashes flutter as he glances down at his hands. "I guess, actually, I did pick that."

I take in his words. What he's saying makes complete sense.

"I know it's not exactly the same, but I kind of feel like that in my own family," I say. "It's like no one sees me for me even though I'm right there—it's like they see *potential*, but I'm never quite enough just as I actually am. My family has always disapproved of my career. It's not lucrative enough. Not stable enough. Not serious enough. I've worked so hard, but it's just never *enough*."

I stare into the fire, collecting my thoughts.

"And now I'm writing this book, right? This major book. But I feel like they'd still disapprove if they knew about it, because the only books my parents and brother approve of are ones on the 'classics' shelves"—I exaggerate my air quotes—"or ones that were written by dead guys more than a hundred years ago."

Tyler's eyes are wide.

Maybe I've said too much.

"You haven't even told your family who you're writing about?"

"I haven't told them about the book deal at all," I admit, feeling a wave of sadness. It's the biggest thing to ever happen in my career—I think it might actually kill me to tell them my big news only to be met with their not-so-subtle disapproval.

"I'm so sorry," he says, those thick eyebrows knitting together in concern. "About all of it. I still don't know who you're writing about, and I know you can't tell me. But I can already tell it's going to be *huge*. And that you're amazing—the perfect person for the job."

My eyes well with tears, I can't help it.

"Thank you," I say. "That . . . means a lot."

His holds my gaze. His eyes are gorgeous—but I miss his real eye color, the one the whole world knows but has most recently been seen by me alone.

"How are you feeling about the project?"

It's emotional whiplash, going from thinking about Tyler and his lovely eyes to . . . Sebastian.

I scrunch up my nose in a way that must be particularly telling, because Tyler laughs.

"No good?" he says, amused.

"Oh, my work is fine," I reply. "I'm just struggling to find a nice way to say, 'If I could throw this guy's voice memos in that fireplace, never to be recovered again, I might be doing the world a favor.'"

His mouth falls open, and I snort out a laugh.

"Okay, maybe I'm just being dramatic because the latest ones were super obnoxious. It hasn't been this bad the whole time—

though I am pretty irritated with him right now. We were supposed to plan a meeting, but he's been ghosting me for days. I feel like I'm the only one invested in making his life story sound good and that I'm basically all on my own."

"That must be challenging," he says. "Writing a book about someone you don't like."

It's the first time I've thought about it so plainly, but it really is that simple. The whole world might be in love with Sebastian Green, but I, Alix Morgan, am not sure I'm a fan.

"Challenging is one word for it."

Suddenly, the lights flicker. The night sky is fully dark now, but in the ambient glow of our building, the flurries are falling fast and furious, blown sideways by the wind.

"I know this isn't the same," Tyler says. "But when I was in the band, there were so many days when I just wasn't sure I could do it anymore." He smirks. "Spoiler alert, I know."

The lights flicker again, wind swirling so hard the decorative pillows fly across the patio. I probably should've brought those inside.

"But yeah," Tyler goes on. "For a long time, there was just this disparity between what I'd signed on for and what it actually became. I never wanted to be the guy who broke his contract or, like, ghosted people in the media. If I had known what I was in for when I agreed to it—"

He breaks off, lets out a sharp exhale.

"I thought the band would mean doing what I loved, having the time of my life, and getting paid enough that I'd never have to work again unless I just wanted to. I thought it would mean fans loved me too." His face goes dark. "I didn't sign up for all the drama, or for Jason's bullshit. I didn't sign up to be the bad guy to Seb's hero."

If only he knew Sebastian Green was at the center of *both* our professional problems.

"I'm so sorry," I say, but that's all I manage—I'm interrupted by an intense gust of wind, loud and howling just outside the windows.

The lights flicker three times and then go out completely.

The Yeti isn't even here yet: if this is only the beginning, I shudder to think of how bad it might get tomorrow.

We're drenched in darkness, everything pitch-black except for the warm glow of the flickering fire. When my eyes adjust, I can't help but marvel at the way the shadows fall on Tyler's face, making the cut of his cheekbones look exaggeratedly chiseled. His eyes sparkle even in near darkness.

"Well, *this* is an adventure," I say, my insides doing a little flip.

"It might be like this for a while," Tyler says. "Even with backup generators, it can take hours for maintenance to get the whole resort up and running again."

"If only there were things we could do in the dark to pass the time."

"If only," he says with a grin, and that's it—that's all the invitation I need to close the distance between us. His long legs are stretched out on the rug; I climb onto his lap, facing him, one knee on either side.

"Maybe something like this?" I say, as he settles his hands on my hips and gives a little tug so we're pressed even closer together.

I feel *everything*.

"Or even this?" he says, his lips so close I can practically taste them already.

He kisses me, soft and slow, his tongue flicking lightly over my bottom lip and my teeth—every teasing second makes me want to kiss him harder, deeper—but he takes his time. I savor the slowness for as long as I can, but at a certain point even he seems impatient for more, and once we give in, the kiss takes on a hungry new life of its own.

Tyler shifts, sitting up straighter, somehow pulling me even closer as I curl my legs around him. He's hot beneath me, every solid inch of him extremely present despite the layers of clothing between us. His hands find the bare skin of my back under the hem of my shirt; his touch is electric, and the feeling that courses through me only makes me want more.

And he gives me more—I think, honestly, he'd give as much as I wanted tonight. We stay in the heady space of this push-and-pull makeout session for now, though, the tease and tension of it all, his hands there and then not, his purposely restrained kisses giving way to a feast, all of it so bright and hot I'm surprised it hasn't restored power to the entire resort.

He's just started kissing his way down my neck when there's an unmistakable knock at my door.

In the middle of a blackout, in the middle of the night.

When we pull away, his face looks exactly how mine feels: perfectly disheveled with a touch of bewilderment. I imagine we're thinking the same thing, too, that it must be Julie or River—someone with exclusive access to our penthouse floor—maybe with an update about the power situation.

Together, we fumble our way through the darkness toward my front door.

When I open it, I see one of Julie's concierge desk assistants—the emergency lighting is surprisingly bright in the elevator landing—but she's not alone.

Lauren stands on the other side of my door, a huge smile on her face.

"What are you doing here?" I manage, thrown by her presence. "*How* are you here?"

"They had one last train going out tonight before the storm," she says brightly. "I caught it just in time and thought I'd surprise you. So—surprise!"

BEFORE

Sunday Brunch:
Jett Beckett's Erratic Behavior

By Aria Statler // Pop Culture Blogger, LifeLoveLattes.com

Happy weekend, everyone! Hope you've got a fresh cup of your favorite coffee/tea—I certainly do!

Is it just me, or has Jett Beckett's recent behavior seemed . . . *off* to anyone else? He's long had a reputation for being True North's most contrarian member, but reports from the band's latest tour note that Beckett has exhibited, for lack of a better term, a new and extreme level of diva behavior—and two tips we received over the weekend seem to confirm that.

The first mentioned a sighting of Jett and the band's manager, Jason Saenz-Barlowe, sharing a drink in the hotel lounge at the Ritz-Carlton Hotel in Philadelphia, Pennsylvania (the band played two sold-out shows there this weekend, and has another scheduled for tonight). The anonymous source reported that Jett began to raise his voice just as she took a discreet photo, so she proceeded to capture the entire debacle on video. Jett's outburst was fierce but brief, leaving his manager stunned, speechless, and alone at the table; Jett was reportedly *not* inebriated during the exchange, according to the bartender who was working at the time.

The second, unrelated tip was submitted by a tech who was called in to this weekend's concert venue to fix an issue with one of the band's soundboards. When he arrived, he heard a commotion in the men's restroom. Upon investigation, he found Jett Beckett smashing a Martin guitar against one of the urinals. When asked why, Jett merely replied, "Because nothing on the stage was hard enough to break it."

We sincerely hope Jett has a good support network behind the scenes.

If anyone out there happens to spot any newsworthy behavior from Jett Beckett or his bandmates, feel free to submit it at tips@lifelovelattes.com.

25

This is *not* what I had in mind for tonight. Not at all.

In fact, I think it's safe to say this is the furthest thing from what I had in mind. I should have explicitly told Lauren not to come instead of using the storm as an excuse—lesson learned.

"Did you not get my text?" I ask as Lauren steps inside.

"What text?"

"The one where I told you Chloe was all good with you crashing at her place tonight? I texted you, like, four hours ago."

"Wait, seriously?" She fishes her phone out of her tote bag, opens up our message thread to look. "Oh. No, I totally didn't get any texts from you today."

She holds up her phone so I can see it, its light too bright in this darkness. My text—which I distinctly remember sending, because I felt palpable relief at Chloe's willingness to help out—is very much not there.

"At least I made it here before the storm!" Lauren says, heading down the hall to give Puffin a chin scratch.

Tyler puts a hand on my lower back and leans in close.

"Rain check?" he murmurs.

"Yes, please. I'm so sorry."

"It's okay." He's so much more understanding than most guys would be if their hot date had just been interrupted. "I'll go find some candles for you—maybe we can do breakfast?"

I nod. "Breakfast would be amazing. Thanks for understanding."

He slips out, and I wave goodbye before shutting the door.

"I bet this place looks incredible with the lights on!" Lauren calls out from somewhere deep in the shadows of the penthouse, her voice echoing from the high ceilings. "Where should I sleep tonight?"

I find her in the living room, her face pressed up against one of the windows even though it's too dark out there to see much of anything.

"Lauren," I say, watching as she continues to just . . . make herself at home. "I kind of have a lot of work to do."

"In the middle of the night?" she says, genuinely clueless. "In a blackout?"

"No, I mean in general—this really isn't the best time for me to host anyone."

She glances over her shoulder, a teasing grin on her face. "Sure looked like you were enjoying your hosting duties with that random guy when I showed up."

"Tyler's not just some random guy—"

As if on cue, Tyler returns, two Target bags in hand. They're full of votives and tea lights and long white tapers still connected by the wick.

So. Many. Candles.

"Think this will be enough?" he says, handing the bags over.

Something about the ridiculous number of candles strikes me

as absurdly funny. "Looks like you robbed a candle factory—I think we'll be good."

Behind me, Lauren lightly clears her throat.

Because everyone who invites themselves over unannounced, interrupting one of the best kisses of the last decade, is apparently entitled to an introduction.

"Tyler, this is my sister, Lauren—Lauren, meet Tyler."

I'm thankful for the darkness. She was very into True North back in the day and took Jett Beckett's disappearance pretty hard. At least she won't recognize him tonight in such low lighting. Tomorrow, though, in daylight . . . that could be a problem.

"Good to meet you," Tyler says diplomatically, like he didn't overhear every word of our call this afternoon. "How was your trip?"

"Not bad at all," she replies. "I rushed to the station and got there just in time for their last train out—lucky, right?"

So lucky.

"Even luckier," she goes on, "the concierge knew exactly who Alix was. It was meant to be!"

She sounds so sincerely excited to be here.

There's no use fighting it: it's late, there's no power, and there's a ton of snow on the way. Like it or not, Lauren is staying here tonight.

"Guest bedroom is on the left," I say. "And you're on your own for breakfast—there's a café down in the village. I'll leave an extra key out."

She flings her arms around me. "Thank you, Alix! I'm glad I didn't get the text you tried to send—I missed you *so* much."

Her hug ends as abruptly as it began; she disappears down the hall, Puffin trotting happily behind.

Once I'm sure she's out of earshot, I let out a long sigh.

"If you need anything, you know where to find me," Tyler says quietly, and I feel his fingertips graze my lower back. "See you for breakfast?"

"Wouldn't miss it."

He kisses me, softly and way too quickly, and then he's gone.

I sleep like the dead, past the point of dreaming, and wake up to the Yeti. Everything outside is blanketed in thick white snow—and it's still coming down.

On my nightstand, the clock flashes. Probably too soon for the power to have been completely restored, I think, but I'm glad to have any at all.

I didn't bother plugging my phone in last night, given the lack of electricity, so it's still somewhere in the living room and very much in need of a charge—I have no idea if Tyler is awake yet. I brush my teeth, throw on a fresh pair of joggers and one of my softest racer-back tanks, and leave a serving of Puffin's favorite food in his dish.

I see no sign of Lauren. I'm guessing she stayed in, given the raging blizzard outside, and is still asleep—though I suppose it's possible she might have ventured out to get breakfast at the café.

I head over to Tyler's, eager to pick up where we left off last night. When I get to his door, though, everything feels too still. I don't smell coffee or waffles or bacon, don't hear the sound of anything sizzling on the stove.

I knock.

He doesn't answer.

The quiet is unsettling. I start second-guessing everything: Maybe it's earlier than I thought and he's not awake yet? Maybe Julie and River needed his help with something related to the storm? Maybe I should just head back to my place and get break-fast going on my own.

But then I hear the faint sound of footsteps on the other side of the door, and it opens. I smile on instinct, excited to see him—

It fades as soon as I *actually* see him.

Something's wrong.

He's got dark circles under his eyes, and his expression looks empty. Not angry . . . just vacant. Exhausted.

"What?" I say. "What is it?"

Tyler opens his door wider, gestures for me to come inside. On his kitchen island sits his laptop, a window open to his email inbox.

Or, rather, upon closer inspection: *my* email inbox.

No. No no no no no nooooooo.

I forgot to log out and close the browser before giving his laptop back, I realize, so of course it would have been on the screen when he opened the computer again. When I think back to the day I returned it to him—the day I traded it for the brand-new one from River—my stomach sinks.

Not only did I forget to log out, but I left the worst possible email open: the one from Gloss inviting me to spill whatever juicy gossip I might know—which also explicitly mentions the memoir. I clearly remember slamming the laptop shut so I wouldn't be tempted by it.

"The book you're writing is *Sebastian Green's*?" Tyler asks.

I was wrong before—his expression isn't vacant. It's *hurt*.

"Are there parts about me in the book?" he asks evenly.

As if he doesn't already know the answer.

"Tyler," I say, the first of us to break eye contact.

His name hangs in the air between us.

"I'm sure he has nothing but glowing things to say about me." His voice is tinged with sarcasm, a rare glimpse of the man he once was. "Hopefully you know me well enough by now to not buy into his bullshit."

Tears well up in my eyes; I blink them away.

"I don't have much control over *what* he says in the book," I say. "Just how it's written."

"So that's a yes."

I nod. "Yes to him painting you in a bad light. No to me believing it."

"But you're still writing it—*his* side of the story. Just his."

A statement of fact, not question.

"It's his memoir. It's my *job*," I counter. "You could tell your story if you wanted to."

Tyler's eyes meet mine, steely and hard. "I think it's a little late for that."

"It doesn't have to be."

He holds my gaze, like he's actually considering it: what it would be like to come out of hiding now, after all these years. How his side of the story would be *the* story of the year—how the attention and scrutiny would almost certainly be even more intense than before, at the apex of his fame.

"You don't have to be the one to write it for him, though, right?" he says, a flicker of hope in his eyes.

"And explain *why* I suddenly feel like I can't write it . . . how, exactly?"

"Tell them you're having a hard time writing the book since Seb keeps ghosting you, maybe? I don't know." His thick brows knit together. "I'm just saying, you could walk away if you wanted to."

"Easy for you to say—I don't have any childhood friends waiting to pay my rent for the next year if I break my contract."

As soon as it's out of my mouth, I know I've said the wrong thing.

"*Easy*?" Tyler says, incredulous. "Nothing about the past decade has been easy."

"I didn't mean it like that," I say.

Outside, the wind howls.

"It wasn't easy to be blindsided into joining the band," he says evenly. "It wasn't easy being made into a villain just so Jason could line his own pockets at my expense. And it sure as hell wasn't easy to realize my only shot at ever being happy was to leave it all behind and start over."

He shakes his head, looks away.

"I've tried so hard to leave all of that in the past, but this— putting it all in a book—it just *immortalizes* it. Who I was then, who Seb thought I was."

I reach out, take his hand.

He doesn't pull away, but he doesn't look at me, either.

"Tyler," I say gently, wait for him to meet my eyes.

Finally, he does. The frost of bitterness has melted away, but not the exhaustion.

"I know that isn't who you are. And I know it hasn't been easy—that none of this has been easy for you. I didn't mean it how it came out. I just meant that I literally won't have money for rent or food if I back out of my contract, especially since I'm on thin ice with my landlord as it is. Not to mention I don't want to burn bridges with the publisher." I sigh. "It's . . . just . . . complicated."

Tyler slumps onto a barstool at his kitchen counter, puts his head in his hands.

"I'm sorry," he says. "I know you're in a tough spot. And I know you're conflicted about it, I shouldn't have implied other- wise. But . . . I . . . I just—"

"Hate it?" I supply.

"Yeah."

I sit on the barstool next to his, wrap my arm around him. He doesn't fight me.

"I hate it, too," I say.

I feel the rise and fall of his thick, muscular shoulders as reality continues to sink in.

"If it helps," I go on, "I had a video call with Sebastian to get clarity on some stuff he said, and it turned out he'd just *worded* things badly. I don't think he's a good communicator, like, at all. But I think it's important you know I've been doing my best to make sure the book is fair to everyone mentioned in it. That conversation was before I even knew you . . . were you."

Tyler gives a half-hearted laugh. "I'm not sure if that helps or not, knowing some of what he's said was so bad you had to have a call about it," he says. "But I do appreciate you doing all you can to fix it."

"I'm amazed we had a call at all, honestly. He's so bad at getting back to me."

"Sounds like him." Tyler shakes his head. "His time is more valuable than everyone else's, always has been. Does whatever he wants, but only *if* he wants to. Made for fun band dynamics."

His words sound awfully familiar, just flipped. It's almost the exact same thing Sebastian said in one of his voice memos—but about *Jett*, not himself.

"I promise," I say, and wait for Tyler to meet my eyes. When he does, I start again. "I promise that I will do everything in my power to make this situation as good as it can be."

I won't be able to make it entirely painless for Tyler, I know that. But I can keep questioning the things Sebastian says that feel exaggerated or unfair, maybe talk him into a kinder edit.

Tyler puts a hand to my face, leans his forehead against mine, and closes his eyes. In a way, it's almost as intimate as a kiss—being this close, drawn together by mutual frustration and not just the heat of the moment.

Undeniably, though, the heat is still there, too. We both shift at the same time: he's going to kiss me, and I want it just as badly as I did last night. His lips find mine, soft and gentle and warm. He pulls me in close, tugs at my hips until I find myself sitting on his lap, both of us on a single barstool. He wraps his arms around me, strong and safe and so, so hot.

I kiss him more intensely, as if this magical snow globe world we've found ourselves in is about to break, as if this might be as close as we're ever able to get.

I want it to last, I realize. For all the ways I've been wounded in the past, for all the times I thought I only wanted something like this just for fun—to prove I was still even capable of fun—*this* is a man who treats me like I'm worthy of something enduring, something special. He didn't even question the part of the email where I had the chance to cash in on his secrets; he's been nothing but trusting of me, nothing but understanding. He didn't lash out at me when he was hurting like Blake always did—he pulled me in closer.

And he's kissing me like he never wants this to end, either.

His fingers tangle in my hair, and his five-o'clock shadow will almost certainly leave my lips red and swollen. I don't care. I want more.

His hands make their way down my body: neck, shoulders, sides, hips. I've just felt the graze of his fingertips, hot against the bare skin of my stomach, when a blood-curdling shriek from the elevator landing rips through the silence.

We jolt apart.

That was Lauren, no doubt about it.

Tyler runs to his front door, and I follow. I hold my breath, bracing myself for what we'll find on the other side of it. He whips it open and goes pale as a ghost.

Out on the landing stands none other than Sebastian Green, clad in the world's tackiest blizzard couture—and behind him, River Wu, looking sheepish but not altogether sorry.

In the open doorway of my penthouse, Lauren stares at them, jaw all the way on the floor like she is in complete disbelief that two-fifths of True North is *right in front of her in the flesh*. She shifts her gaze to me, eyes full of stars, and then to Tyler.

Oh. Oh no.

In slow motion, I realize this train wreck is happening whether or not I jump out in front to try and stop it. Context is everything: I didn't have it when I met Tyler.

Lauren does.

"Is that—*Jett Beckett*?" she says, confusion eclipsing her fangirl moment.

Sebastian turns his attention, for the first time, to Tyler; it's this that finally inspires him to take off his sunglasses. He doesn't even seem to notice as they slip from his fingers and fall to the floor.

"Holy shit," he says. "Look who's back from the dead."

Dewdrops · For You Page

#privatejet #whirlwindtrip #italy #tuscany #sebastiangreen
#celebrities #jetsetters

u/CelebJetTracker
11:15PM · March 8, 2025

SEBASTIAN GREEN—Flew from Tuscany, Italy, to
Burlington, Vermont, United States, via private
jet (Dassault Falcon900) / Approx flight time
7h45min / Touched down at 11:07 PM local
time / Weather: moderate wind, light snow /
Following disembarkation, Green entered the
back seat of a silver Audi SUV registered to
chauffeur service Drive Private / Headed east
on I–89 S toward Stowe, Vermont

26

Sebastian Green.

Sebastian is *here*.

A heads-up would've been nice. A text, an email, anything. In his defense, I guess it's possible someone tried to give me one—my phone is still dead back at my place.

Lauren's question hangs in the air.

Is that Jett Beckett?

I've never seen a person's head whip around as fast as Sebastian's did when he turned toward Tyler—never seen an expression shift so seamlessly from confusion to shock to recognition to fury.

"What are you doing here?" Tyler says, eyes darting from Sebastian to River and back again.

"I could ask you the same question," Sebastian replies, spitting the words like his mouth is full of acid. Gone is the shiny façade he puts on for the entire world—here, in the privacy of our penthouse floor, his bitterness is on full display.

"So, yes, then?" Lauren says from the doorway. "Jett Beckett?"

254

"He doesn't use that name anymore," I say quietly.

Lauren's eyes widen as she realizes this isn't news to me: that I knew—that I've *known*—and I've kept an enormous secret from her. More than one enormous secret, if you factor in Sebastian and his memoir.

But she's hardly the only one here who's been left in the dark.

"Riv?" Tyler says, a thousand questions in that single syllable.

Tyler's lifelong best friend—keeper of his most secret secrets, who went so far as to help him disappear—has just dropped his nemesis right on his doorstep.

River can't meet Tyler's eye.

Tyler turns to Sebastian. "How did you even get here in this snowstorm?"

"Flew in last night," Sebastian says, shrugging. "Roads weren't bad yet between here and Burlington."

Leave it to Sebastian to fly toward a blizzard, not away from it, just because he *can*. It dawns on me that my text warning him about the Yeti is probably the very thing that made him want to come—I should have known he'd be the thrill-seeking type who loves the drama of a storm like this.

"Showed up unannounced in the middle of the night," River finally says. "Said he needed to talk to Alix about the book—so I brought him to Alix. *Not* in the middle of the night, and you're welcome for that."

Tyler studies River for what feels like forever, presumably adding up all the pieces: that in order for River to hook me up with the penthouse like he did, he must have known who I was writing about this entire time.

I'm more convinced than ever that it's not serendipity that Tyler and I met the way we did—but that River put me in Tyler's path on purpose.

"You knew." It's Sebastian who turns on River now, furious. "All this time, you knew where he was? You could have *said* something." He cuts his eyes toward Tyler. "And you could have, too. I was drunk the night you disappeared, and there were times—"

He breaks off, and the silence he leaves in his wake feels like an apocalyptic wasteland.

Gone is the Sebastian who claimed Jett Beckett's disappearance was the best thing that ever happened to him. That may still be true, but he's clearly also got a lot of pent-up anger. Even if it did eventually change Sebastian's life for the better, Jett leaving the band affected all of them. It *ended* them.

"I always wondered," he goes on, voice breaking, "if I'd said something that pushed you over the edge somehow. I *worried* about you."

For a split second, I'm tempted to back into Tyler's place and let the guys work out their drama on their own—but then Sebastian turns on me too.

"And even *you* knew?" he says. "How many voice memos did I make talking about the hell I went through dealing with rumors and internet trolls?"

Approximately six hours' worth, my mind fills in automatically, but Sebastian keeps talking before I can give an actual answer.

"You didn't think, not once, that it might be relevant to mention that Jett Beckett is alive and well and, oh hey, living *right next door to you?*"

"She didn't know until recently," Tyler says, shifting ever so slightly to stand in front of me, as if his physical presence can protect me from Sebastian's barbed words.

"How would I have told you, anyway?" I speak up, bolder now thanks to Tyler's defense. "You couldn't even be bothered to text me back—"

"I'm here *now*," Sebastian says, arms spread wide like he's a gift to the universe. "I thought you'd like the surprise. Most girls would," he says with a smirk.

Lauren snorts. "Wow."

"It's Riv who has some explaining to do," Tyler goes on.

"Finally, something we can agree on," Sebastian says.

River, who's thus far been doing his best to blend in with the decor, pales under our collective attention.

"I, uh—listen," River stammers. "There are some things I maybe should have done differently—"

"Maybe?" Sebastian interjects.

River clears his throat. "I should have done things differently," he starts over. "But did either of you ever consider how hard it was to be in the group with the two of you? All I ever wanted was for everyone to get along. I never wanted to choose sides."

Tyler sucks in a sharp breath. I don't blame him—it would feel like a thorn in my side, too, if my lifelong best friend seemed torn between loyalty to me and my biggest rival.

"When you were at your breaking point," River says, glancing at Tyler, probably sensing the exact same tension I am, "I chose you, Ty. I helped you disappear. And I've kept your secret for all these years, and I've never complained—but did you ever consider how *hard* it was to help you start over? To stay quiet while the whole world demanded answers? I've lied for you for *eight years*, and at first I told myself it was helping you, but—"

River runs his hands through his hair, eyes shifting to Sebastian.

"But Seb's about to publish this, like, tell-all—and you guys hated each other, and everyone knew it, and I guess I was worried about what sort of stuff might make it into the book. When Seb reached out to see if Alix could write here for the month, it seemed like the perfect way—"

He breaks off, sorts out his words.

"I don't know," he starts again. "I guess it just seemed important for him to know the truth before everything went to print. For *both* of your sakes." River's gaze settles on Tyler. "It's been hard watching you spend so many years alone, Ty."

"I haven't been alone," he says, but his voice lacks conviction. "I've had you and Jules."

"And it's been a lot on us to be everything for you," River replies. "We love you, don't get me wrong. But we . . . want *more* for you."

"Well, I'm sorry I've been 'a lot,'" Tyler says with air quotes. It isn't lost on me that he doesn't argue with River's implication that his life is missing something.

The very fact that he and I have gotten so close proves River's point, honestly.

"You could have just told me," Sebastian says sharply, "instead of setting us up for . . . whatever's happening now."

"Sorry, bro, but I wasn't sure I could trust you to stay quiet," River says evenly. "I thought maybe if you could just see each other—here, where there aren't any paparazzi—you could have a chance to process everything and maybe talk it out a little."

"Um, I hate to interrupt your little boy band confessional," Lauren says, holding up her phone, "but, like . . . the paparazzi are kind of already here?"

Tyler shoots River a withering glare.

"What do you mean, they're here?" River says, moving over for a better look at whatever's on Lauren's screen. From what I can tell, it's a shot of Sebastian climbing out of a silver SUV at a resort that looks suspiciously like ours. "Seb?"

Sebastian raises both hands, a universal *Don't blame me.*

"Not my fault they follow me everywhere," he says like he

couldn't care less. "It's hard to lose them these days. They even found me in Tahiti. They must have tailed me last night."

Every muscle in Tyler's upper body looks tight, tense—like a headache in the making.

"I need a minute," Tyler mutters, and before I know what's happening, he's slipped past me and back through his own front door.

He doesn't let it close all the way, which I take as a sign that I could follow him if I wanted to. *Should* I follow him?

I guess we'll find out.

"I'm just gonna—"

I let my sentence hang in the air as I slip into his penthouse, carefully shutting the door.

I don't see him. He's not at the kitchen island, where his laptop sits, a reminder of this morning's first unexpected turn. I still haven't eaten anything—not that I have an appetite right now.

"Tyler?" I call out.

He doesn't answer, but it doesn't take long to find him in his living room, tuning his guitar. I guess we all have our stress outlets.

"Hey," I say, sinking into the closest armchair, its leather soft against my skin. "Do you want to talk about it?"

His brows pinch together as he continues tuning his guitar. I'm no musician, but he seems to be making things worse instead of better.

"I can go if you want," I offer when he doesn't reply.

"You can stay," he says.

But he doesn't say any more, so I stay quiet, too.

Finally, he gets his guitar in tune—relatively—and starts playing an intricate, delicate melody. The chords feel hopeful, then melancholy, before building into something that feels more like a question, unresolved and begging for answers.

It's utterly captivating, this front-row view of his talent. He doesn't sing, but I wish he would—if his guitar skills are any indication, his time in True North only showcased a fraction of what he's capable of, musically.

When he eventually stops, the silence feels too loud.

He perches lightly on the back of the armchair, twisting his guitar so it hangs by its crossbody strap like a backpack. I'm still sitting in the chair, but he feels much too far away. When I've made my way around to him and we're standing face-to-face, he tugs me in closer, one hand on each of my hips.

I drape my arms loosely across his shoulders and press my forehead to his; with him sitting like he is and me standing, we're pretty much the same height.

"Today has been a lot, yeah?" I say.

Tyler sighs, shifts his arms so they're wrapped around my lower back, and pulls me into a tight embrace. I bury my face in his neck, press a kiss to the soft skin where it meets his collarbone.

"I . . . don't know what to do." His voice is muffled in my hair. "I . . . *Shit*. Alix. Don't move, okay?"

Every muscle in my body tenses at his tone, but I do as he says.

"What?" I ask. "What is it?"

"Drone outside my window," he says, then mutters another curse.

"Do you think it can see us?"

"Any drone equipped to fly in weather like this has got to be some high-end gear. So . . . yeah. The camera's probably as good as it gets."

Would they even know who they were looking at? For Tyler's sake, I really hope not.

"They're probably just checking out all the windows to see if they can spot Sebastian," he adds, an afterthought.

Little do they know that Sebastian isn't the *only* paparazzi-worthy face around here. For the first time since arriving at Black Maple Lodge, it occurs to me that the world will be far more interested in what's *behind* these top-floor, panoramic windows than the majestic views outside them.

A moment later, I feel the tension melt out of Tyler's body.

"It's gone," he says.

We stay rooted in place for a long time—me holding on to him, him holding on to what very well might be the last day of his peace and privacy if we can't get Sebastian and his paparazzi friends off this mountain *fast*. But with how much snow has fallen—and how hard it's still coming down—I suspect we're all stuck here together for a while.

I want to tell him it'll all be okay.

I really, really want to.

But I'm not a fortune teller, and I'm not a liar.

I press another soft kiss into his neck instead. He melts into me, holding me in the silence like his world will fall apart if he dares to let go.

INTERN BESTIES

GROUP CHAT

LAUREN MORGAN • 10:21 AM
HI HELLO YOU WILL NOT BELIEVE THIS

RAE O'CONNOR • 10:22 AM
?????

SAMARA SHAH • 10:22 AM
Successfully intrigued . . .
What's going on??

LAUREN MORGAN • 10:23 AM
[image.jpeg]

LOOK
LOOOOOOOOK
(I took this photo)

SAMARA SHAH • 10:23 AM
IS THAT SEBASTIAN GREEN
LAUREN
WHAT
(?!?!)

Also, uh, did you forget we have a meeting
this morning? Where are you??

RAE O'CONNOR • 10:23 AM
STOP IT
Sebastian Green???
Like
Sebastian Green is like six feet away from you

SAMARA SHAH • 10:24 AM
WAIT THO
River is there, too????

LAUREN MORGAN • 10:24 AM
Staying at this amazing resort in Vermont with
my sister for a few days and he just, like, showed
up. River, too. Forgot about the meeting . . .
cover for me? 😫 I had some major drama with
Veronica last night and had to get out of the city.

RAE O'CONNOR • 10:25 AM
Ooooh, that explains it—V has been in a horrible
mood all morning. Be glad you're not here

LAUREN MORGAN • 10:26 AM
OH ALSO, I prob should have said this first,
but please don't share this photo . . . I kinda
snapped it in secret and my sister will kill
me if she finds out I sent it to anyone

SAMARA SHAH • 10:26 AM
LAUREN
Lauren
The other guy—not River, not Sebastian—who is
that? He looks kinda familiar but I can't place him

RAE O'CONNOR • 10:27 AM
WAIT
LOOK
[image.jpeg]
Okay, compare this with the guy in the photo . . .

SAMARA SHAH • 10:27 AM
IS THAT JETT BECKETT
?????????
LAUREN???

RAE O'CONNOR • 10:28 AM
I thought he was dead????????

SAMARA SHAH • 10:28 AM
Pretty sure the whole world kinda assumed that
Lauren? Confirmation??

LAUREN MORGAN • 10:30 AM
IDK, I could see it, but my sister
introduced him as Tyler

Just making sure you saw my message
about not sharing this with anyone?

Sami? Rae?

 Samara Shah has notifications silenced
Rae O'Connor has notifications silenced

RAE O'CONNOR • 10:29 AM

Looooook what this girl from my museum
internship just put in our group chat

ANICA BELL • 10:32 AM

STOP IS THAT 2/5 OF TRUE NORTH

RAE O'CONNOR • 10:32 AM

Yes, but LOOK CLOSER

ANICA BELL • 10:33 AM

Sebastian's pants are truly hideous

RAE O'CONNOR • 10:33 AM

Look past the pants
I know it's hard

ANICA BELL • 10:34 AM

WAIT
RAE.
JETT BECKETT???

RAE O'CONNOR • 10:35 AM

That's exactly where my mind went, too!!
He definitely looks different

THE LODGE

Older
But, like, still somehow the same?
I knew you would know better than me

ANICA BELL • 10:37 AM
No, I am 1000000% sure
He was my lock screen for like five years after he
disappeared, I would know that face anywhere
(even if it is older and his hair is different
and his eyes are the wrong color and his
nose is crooked and HIS EYEBROWS)

RAE O'CONNOR • 10:39 AM
THE EYEBROWS, RIGHT??
They have no right to be that hot

ANICA BELL • 10:40 AM
Who shared this with you again?

RAE O'CONNOR • 10:41AM
This girl from work
I don't know her that well but I know her
well enough to know this is legit . . .
She said not to share it, but I mean,
like . . . how could I not??

ANICA BELL • 10:42 AM
Agreed

Dewdrops · For You Page

#unsolvedmysteries #jettbeckett #truenorth #hottea
#celebritygossip

u/AnicaWithTheHotTea

Take a look at this photo and tell me what you see
[image.jpeg]

COMMENTS

⬆ **u/TruestNortherner**
IS THAT JETT BECKETT'S GHOST

↳ **u/AnicaWithTheHotTea**
Seems almost more believable than the
alternative, right—that he's out there after all this
time??

THE LODGE

↳ **u/TruestNortherner**
Also unbelievable: that Jett Beckett, River Wu, and Sebastian Green would all *willingly* be in a room together

↳ **u/jettbeckettconspiracytheorist**
Is this, like, AI generated????

↳ **u/AnicaWithTheHotTea**
HA, no. Friend of a friend took the shot at some resort up in Vermont. Said this guy's going by Tyler, so I did a deep dive—none of the websites were very thorough, but I found a review that mentions a ski instructor named Tyler Fox at Black Maple Lodge up in Stowe! And what a coincidence, River's family owns that resort . . . so . . . yeah.

27

It's blessedly silent outside Tyler's front door when I finally head back to my place. No sign of Sebastian or River or Lauren.

I'm still reeling from the last twelve hours or so; I wish Chloe were here. She might not know how to fix anything, but she would most definitely make everything feel better.

Back in my own penthouse, still no sign of Lauren, I find my dead phone and plug it in. As soon as there's even the tiniest hint of a charge, I initiate a FaceTime.

Chloe doesn't pick up, but a text lights my screen almost immediately.

Finishing up a meeting right now, can I call you back in five?

Oh, right. It's a regular weekday down in New York; of course she's at work. They're only getting rain today and not record-breaking amounts of snow.

Outside my own bedroom windows, it's a gorgeous wonderland, a blanket of white as far as I can see. The Yeti continues to dump thick, puffy snowflakes over everything, and I have the strangest sensation that time has actually stopped—especially since Chloe's five minutes turn into ten, and each feels eternal.

I pace my bedroom, anxious energy shadowing me with every step. An email alert on my phone makes me jump: it's not Chloe calling me back, but it's something to do while I wait.

When I check it out, I freeze.

It's Aspen Underwood again, reaching out on behalf of Gloss—but it's not just an innocuous follow-up.

It's my worst nightmare.

To: Alix Morgan (alix@alixmorganwrites.com)
From: Aspen Underwood (a.underwood@glossmag.com)
Subject: RE: Open Invitation

Hi again, Alix—

I hope this email finds you well! Just wanted to circle back in light of the posts that are popping up today on social.

There's a fair bit of speculation going on about this photo posted by u/AnicaWithTheHotTea over on Dewdrops—seeing as you're writing about Sebastian Green, I was wondering if you had any insight into the identity of the man on the far right? Everyone thinks he resembles Jett Beckett—and tbh, I agree—but we have a strict policy about verifying rumors before posting (unlike some of the tabloid outlets like Moondazzle), and I thought you might be my best hope of confirming them.

If you know anything and are willing to go on record about it and give us an exclusive interview, please reach out ASAP.

Feel free to text or call—my number is below. We can pay you
more than generously.

Best,
Aspen

Wait. What?

What photo is she talking about?

I tap on the link in her email, and my stomach turns to lead.
I've just started reading the comments when Chloe finally calls me
back. She's at her office desk, using her work laptop.

"Whoa, Alix, are you okay?" she asks.

I blink, dazed.

"I . . . am not. No. Hold on just a second—"

I grab my own laptop so I can send her the post Aspen sent
without leaving the call.

Her eyes shift away from the camera as she pulls up the link. I
watch as she scans the post, her face morphing from perplexed to
concerned in a heartbeat.

A minute later, she gasps—

Presumably, she's just gotten to the comment I was reading
when her call interrupted: *Friend of a friend took the shot at some
resort up in Vermont. Said this guy's going by Tyler, so I did a deep
dive . . . I found a review that mentions a ski instructor named Tyler
Fox at Black Maple Lodge up in Stowe!*

That isn't even the thing that's making me feel like I might
throw up.

There's only one person who could have taken this picture.
Only one person who could have *shared* this picture.

"Hang on just a second, let me close my door." Chloe disappears from the screen, then flops back into her desk chair a moment

later. "So, uh—Alix—is there something you've been meaning to tell me?"

My cheeks turn to fire immediately.

"I had no idea Sebastian would be here—"

"You know I'm not talking about Sebastian. Tyler—Tyler Fox—your *ski instructor*?"

"Okay, please don't be mad." I close my eyes, make a gut decision. Chloe is not my sister; Chloe is worthy of my trust. If I believe anything right now, it has to be that. "I only just figured it out, and I *wanted* to tell you, but it really didn't feel like my secret to tell. But then Lauren showed up last night unannounced—and then Sebastian showed up at my door this morning, also unannounced—and I have no idea when Lauren snapped that photo or why she would share it, but now the whole world is putting it together and I've even already gotten an email asking me to confirm the rumors."

Chloe shakes her head in awe. "I . . . don't even know where to begin with all that. She seriously shared it without even talking to you first?"

"Right?! What was she thinking?"

"Sounds like she *wasn't* thinking," Chloe says. "And I'm not mad at you, by the way—I get why you didn't tell me. Honestly, I'm impressed you were even able to keep a secret like that."

This right here: *this* is why I wish Chloe were here right now instead of Lauren.

From the far end of the penthouse, I hear the faint click of the front door.

I glance behind me instinctively, even though it isn't physically possible for Lauren to have made it all the way into my bedroom in the last half second.

"I think she just got back," I whisper, exaggerating my words in case Chloe can't make them out well enough.

"Good luck," she whispers back with a grimace. "Text me later?"

"You know I will."

When we end the call, the post fills my screen like a punch in the gut. Lauren's photo is so perfect it's almost staged—an unmistakably clear shot of Sebastian, River, and Tyler as if they're all characters in some kind of sitcom. Tyler's face is a mess of disbelief and confusion, much more reminiscent of his trademark Jett Beckett scowl than his laid-back ski instructor vibe.

And the comments.

The comments are wild.

Some people in the mix should work for the CIA, that's how good they are at tracking down personal information—though the whole screaming-it-for-the-entire-world thing would probably be a nonstarter for their careers as secret agents.

"Knock, knock!" Lauren says brightly, not actually knocking on my bedroom doorjamb. She's carrying two takeout coffees, one in each hand. "Brought you a maple latte, but you can have my vanilla one if that sounds better. I wasn't sure what you liked."

I stare at her like she's sprouted an extra head.

"Um . . . is everything okay?" Her face twists in confusion.

I think she legitimately has no idea. No clue what she started by coming to the resort—by taking that photo and sending it to whoever she sent it to.

"Maple latte sounds good," I say evenly, reaching out. "Thanks."

It's hot and sweet and comforting, exactly what I need right now.

Lauren sinks onto the bed beside me, one leg curled up underneath her.

"What's going on?" she asks, eyeing me over the top of her latte. "Why are you looking at me like that?"

I scroll up to make sure the Dewdrops post is fully visible, then hand my phone over. Her eyes widen when she realizes what it is. What's happened.

She looks up at me, panicked.

"I only told two people, I swear! And I told them not to share it! I have no idea who this person is who posted it."

"What did you *think* would happen? Of course they shared it. Of course it's going viral—no one has seen or heard from Jett Beckett for almost a decade, Lauren!"

"I didn't tell them it was him! And sorry, but, like, don't you spread celebrity news for a living? How is this any different?"

"It's *entirely* different," I fire back, even though there's probably more overlap than I'm ready to admit. "I am acting in a professional capacity. I don't upend people's private lives without their permission, for one thing."

"I didn't, though—I told them you'd introduced him as Tyler, not Jett."

I close my eyes, take a deep breath. How can she not see the way that detail only made things worse?

"All that did was give people a name to search in this part of Vermont. Do you not see how this photo could ruin his life? Did you even once stop to think that maybe he had good reasons for disappearing and no intention of ever resurfacing?"

"I'm sorry, okay?" she says, flailing a little bit; some of her latte sloshes out onto my white duvet. "I was just a little shocked to see so many famous people right outside your door—I had a fangirl moment and my brain blanked out. I had to tell *someone* about it. Thanks for trusting me, by the way. Did they say you're writing a book with Sebastian Green? Is that why you were always working so much back in New York?"

"This is exactly why I didn't tell you," I say, trying not to focus on the latte stain seeping into the luxe fabric. "And yes, it's why I was always *trying* to work so much. It's why I should still be working now. I'm on a huge deadline."

Her eyes grow steely.

"You could have told me, you know. I would have been really, really happy for you—and it would have made a lot more sense why you were always hiding out in your room instead of hanging out with me, just like you did when we were kids."

If she meant that to sting, well, mission accomplished.

"I know what happened today isn't the best example, but I'm actually pretty good at keeping secrets," she goes on. "Like, did you know Ian lost his job last fall and has been getting help from Mom and Dad?"

I—wow. No, I very much did not know that.

"Didn't think so," she says. "And did you know Mom actually got a job to help cover Ian's expenses? It's a huge reason I applied for the internship in New York, so I could finally start earning my own money instead of relying on them all the time. I wasn't sure Mom would even be able to get a job—she applied at, like, five different places the summer after my sixth-grade year, and literally no one gave her the time of day because she didn't have much on her résumé. Things were tight back then, but we just ended up cutting back on a lot until Dad got his new job."

All of this is news to me.

I was almost done with college that summer, already working in entertainment journalism. It was around that time that my parents started making comments: that I should consider something more stable, something more lucrative.

Those comments always felt like judgment and disapproval, but this new information—what they went through, how tight things were even with my dad's steady paycheck—makes me think maybe they were sincerely trying to be supportive, protective. Maybe it just came out wrong and I had no context to hear it in any other way. It's a lot to process.

"I've always thought you were so amazing, Alix," she says sharply, a dagger to my heart. "Living in New York, writing articles about celebrities—you've always made it look so easy. You've always known exactly who you are, exactly what you want. And I wanted to be like that, too. I still want to be that way. But, like, finding out you don't trust me? It *hurts*."

The dagger twists.

"Can you blame me?" I counter. "What happened today is exactly why I didn't tell you. Why I didn't tell *anyone*."

"You didn't even tell me you were working on a book. You didn't tell me anything! I'm your sister. Sisters are supposed to be close."

I sigh. "I'm not saying we can't be close. I'm just saying, the fact that this happened at all is why I was afraid to tell anyone. You took one picture and shared it with the wrong people—and now it's out there forever."

"I'm sorry, okay? I'm sorry I ruined everything." Abruptly, Lauren stands. "I need some space."

This conversation isn't over, but if she wants space, she can have it. She's stuck here for the foreseeable future thanks to all the snow—we'll talk again later.

I could use some space myself.

"I'm going to Tyler's," I announce too loudly, startling Puffin.

Lauren says nothing as I rip my charging cable out of my phone and tug on my boots. She picks at her chipped nail polish, not even bothering to look up when I leave.

Has Tyler heard there are rumors yet? Surely he hasn't seen them firsthand since he doesn't have social media.

I knock on his door, but he doesn't answer, so I try again. When he still doesn't answer, I send a text.

It's just me, I type out in a hurry. Come let me in?

But a minute passes, then two, and he doesn't text me back. Maybe his phone is dead like mine was?

Something feels wrong. It's quiet—too quiet. No signs of life, no sounds of his guitar. Nothing. Is it possible he managed to slip out of the building without anyone spotting him?

He's kept himself hidden for eight years, I remind myself. I guess anything is possible.

I give up after ten minutes, my gut full of dread. Where is he? Why isn't he answering? I could try Julie or River, I guess, see if they know anything. If he knows that photo is circulating, they would have been the ones to tell him.

I turn around, intending to head to the elevator, but my own door catches my eye instead: there's an envelope taped to it. I definitely missed it on my way out.

My hands shake as I open it, as I pull out the handwritten note.

Alix,

I'm so sorry. You were the best thing to happen to me in years, and nothing in me wants this to be over. I need to go clear my head. If we don't see each other again, I know you'll understand why—I just hope you'll forgive me.

Love,
T

What?

Excuse me, *what?*

I read it three times before it fully sinks in. Tyler isn't simply out for a few minutes—it sounds like he doesn't intend to come back.

On my fourth read, the word *if* hits me in a new, more hopeful way: *if* we don't see each other again.

If means there's a chance, however small, that this isn't the end for us. Every instinct in him might be telling him to run, to hide, to start over again—but maybe he's trying to fight it this time. Maybe there's a part of him, deep down, that wants to resurface.

Wishful thinking, I know. I'm not biased at *all*.

I have to find him—he can't have gotten far in this snowstorm.

But if he's not here, where is he? And how did he get out without being spotted by the paparazzi drone from earlier? If it's not circling like a vulture already, on high alert for any sign of him, it will be soon.

I have to get to him first.

WJKS News Update:
The Yeti, Jett Beckett, and More!

Trevor Jones, News Anchor, on location at Black Maple Lodge

TJ: Good afternoon, everyone—we hope you're holding up well under the Yeti, which has already dumped as much as twenty-eight inches of snow over the last ten hours in some of the hardest-hit parts of Vermont! I'm Trevor Jones, and I'm coming to you live from Black Maple Lodge, not only to bring you a glimpse of the snow but also to catch you up on some breaking news that's unfolding here at this very ski resort.

When we brought the team out here yesterday ahead of the storm, we never anticipated we'd be talking about anything other than the weather—but we're hearing rumors that a certain missing pop star might have resurfaced right here at Black Maple Lodge! While we have yet to spot him with our own eyes, we thought it might be fun to chat with some locals here at the mountain to see what they have to say.

Behind me is the Village Café, where guests and staff alike go for coffee and other sweet treats here at the resort. Their lead barista, Makenna Monroe, has agreed to give us a peek inside. Let's go take a look!

Hi, Makenna. Thanks for having us!

MM: Hi, Trevor. Happy to show you the café.

TJ: Black Maple Lodge has gotten some *serious* snow today. Have you been slammed, or has the weather kept the guests away?

MM: It was pretty quiet this morning, honestly. Now that the blizzard is finally letting up a bit, though, we're getting busier. I wanted to mention, for anyone watching who might be snowed in here at Black Maple Lodge, we have all the usual coffee shop beverages along with some Yeti specials, and—

TJ: Actually, I was wondering if you might be able to talk a little more about your experience with the guests!

MM: The . . . guests?

TJ: Sure! Like you said, you have all the usual coffee shop beverages, so I thought we could talk about what sets Black Maple Lodge apart.

MM: I mean, if you want to know about that, I'd probably talk about the maple candies we put out every day, or the view of the mountain. Or the Yeti specials I just mentioned. The guests are pretty great, too, though.

TJ: Have you ever encountered anyone . . . unusual?

MM: Unusual how?

TJ: You know—like—

MM: Famous?

TJ: Yes, exactly! Have you heard what people are saying? That Jett Beckett has been spotted here on the property?

MM: Jett Beckett—like—from the boy band?

TJ: Yes! Here, I'll show you the photo that's circulating. I was wondering if you've seen this guy around, and if you can confirm whether it's him?

MM: I'm sorry, where are you from? I thought we were doing a segment on the café?

TJ: Oh, uh, yes, I'm from local news station WJKS—

MM: If Jett Beckett is here, he probably came for a reason, and I'm guessing he wouldn't want people trying to pry his secret out. If he's not, he's not. I couldn't say, really. Would you like a latte on your way out?

28

My one and only idea right now is to go find Julie—if there's anyone who knows where Tyler might've gone, it's her.

I call Chloe while I walk over to the main lodge.

"Hi again," I say, keeping my voice as low as possible. There's a small group of resort guests lingering just outside my building, no doubt hoping to get a glimpse of the True North guys—especially Jett Beckett.

When I'm sure I'm out of earshot, I fill Chloe in on Tyler and his note.

"So, what, shit gets real and he leaves?" she says, protective instincts kicking in hard.

Heat fills my cheeks. "I'd like to think he wouldn't. Or, that he couldn't—we've gotten so much snow, it has to be impossible to get in or out of the resort right now."

The storm has lightened up considerably, but still, 30 percent of the Yeti is still comparable to a regular snow day in New York.

"You have to go find him," Chloe declares.

"Yeah, that's what I'm trying to do now. But I just don't understand how he could've left our building without being spotted—can you look and see if there are any new photos?"

"I was made for this," she says, and it's true: if anyone knows how to find up-to-the-moment celebrity gossip, it's Chloe.

I hear her tapping on her laptop keyboard.

"Hmm," she says a moment later. "I'm seeing approximately two zillion reposts of Lauren's photo. There's also one of River and Sebastian leaving the building—that one's starting to blow up, too." She pauses, and I hear more tapping. "No new ones of Tyler yet, from what I can tell."

It's both unnerving and a relief that no one saw him leave the building. But where *is* he?

"Okay, I'm almost to the main lodge," I say. "Text me immediately if you see anything else pop up, okay?"

"On it," Chloe says. "Anything else I can do to help from here?"

"Unfortunately, I think that might be a full-time job as it is."

"You've got this, Alix. Keep me posted, and I'll do the same."

The main lodge is cozy as ever, a beacon of warmth amid the thick snowbanks, aglow with lamplight and crackling flames in oversized fireplaces. I keep my head down, trying not to call attention to myself, and make a beeline for the concierge desk.

Someone I don't recognize stands behind it, a thin man with a smile bigger than his whole face.

"Can I help you?" he greets me.

"I'm looking for Julie Wu. Any idea where I can find her?"

A look of relief floods his face. "Can I just tell you how refreshing it is to talk to someone who's not asking about when the hot water will return? One guy demanded I turn the snowstorm off."

He makes a face. "Sorry, though, I haven't seen Julie since first thing this morning. I think she's hiding from the guests."

"Ah, thanks anyway. And just to be clear, you *can't* turn off the snowstorm?"

He laughs. "I'll keep trying and let you know."

I head back to the grand lobby. I *think* I remember how to find Julie's place—I retrace my steps to the centermost elevator bank and take one all the way up to the top. As soon as I step out, I know I'm in the right spot—immediately confirmed by how I collide with Julie herself, her eyes glued to her phone.

"Aghh, I'm so sorry!" I say, and she looks up.

Her eyes brighten when she realizes it's me. "Oh, hey, sorry about that—Riv told me about the tense moment you all had with Sebastian, and I was just texting him back. I tried calling Tyler, but he hasn't picked up."

That's not a promising sign.

"He's not answering his door, either. And, uh, he left me this note."

I hand it over, watch as she reads, the concern on her face quickly shifting into a deep scowl.

"Yeah," I say when she looks up, speechless. "I was coming to see if you know where he might have gone—he somehow got out of our building without anyone spotting him. I have no clue where to even start."

Deep down, I think I was hoping he might be hiding out *at* Julie's. Clearly, though, she's just as much in the dark as I am.

She bites her lip, thinking. "It isn't common knowledge," she says, "but we've got an underground tunnel system connecting a few points of the resort for electricians and other maintenance workers to use—all the main buildings are on it, and so are the lifts. We used to get in trouble for playing down there as kids."

"And there's an access point from our building?"

Julie nods. "If you take the stairs all the way to the basement, there's a way to get in from there."

"I didn't even know there *was* a basement," I reply.

"None of it is marked," she says, grinning. "As for where he *went*, though . . ."

"Think there's any chance he's just hiding out in the tunnel system?"

"Probably not? It's not impossible—it's just not the most comfortable place to hide out for a long time. I can check our security feeds, though, and I can also send some guards to do a sweep."

Something pulls at my memory. "You said the ski lifts are also connected to the tunnel?"

This is where I go when I need to clear my head, I can hear Tyler saying the night he took me up to look at the stars. It's too similar to what he wrote in his note to be a coincidence.

Julie's eyes light up like she knows exactly what I'm getting at: that Tyler might have gone up to the mountaintop lookout.

"Can the gondolas even run in this weather?" I ask.

"They're pretty tolerant of snow—it's the wind that makes them dangerous." She taps on her phone and pulls up her weather app. "We're well under the wind threshold now that the worst of the storm has passed. They'd be fine."

"Do they have power?"

"They're connected to a dedicated generator that kicks in automatically," Julie says. "If you want to go up and check, I can get someone to operate the lift for you."

We exchange numbers so she can reach out—or so *I* can—if I'm wrong. As we wait for the elevator, she dashes off a text to whoever will be helping me.

The elevator chimes, and we step inside. It's a long, slow ride to the bottom, both of us anxious and trying not to show it. When the elevator doors open again, we're met with a riot of noise: every stir-crazy guest at this lodge has apparently made their way down to the lobby, and they're all swarming the front door. There are so many smartphones obscuring my view that I can't make out what—or *who*—they're filming.

My stomach drops.

Is this it?

Is this the moment Tyler resurfaces, like it or not?

The sea of people parts and—sigh of relief—I see a flash of Sebastian Green and his tacky, tacky pants. *Only* Sebastian Green.

For all the years they were forced to share the spotlight, at least one of them still wants to bask in its warmth.

This will buy me some time, at least. It's the perfect diversion: if this many resort guests are here in the lobby, hopefully that means there won't be as many . . . wherever Tyler is.

Julie tells me to stay put, that the gondola lift guy should be here shortly. A few minutes later, I see a man in a Black Maple Lodge uniform approaching, a maintenance badge dangling from a tool belt at his hip.

He glances down at his phone. "Alix?"

"That'd be me," I say.

He nods, then motions for me to follow him.

We make our way through the main lobby and push through the crowd of Sebastian fans (Sebastian himself is taking a selfie with one).

We've just left the building, trading the cozy warmth of the gigantic fireplaces for the frigid, snowcapped wonderland, when a text from Julie dips down from the top of my screen.

Checked the security vids—saw footage of T using the tunnel system, and he def took the branch that leads to the lifts. The lift operator found you?

Oh, excellent, thanks for the update! I write back. And yes, with him right now.

Though am I really "with" him if he's three feet ahead of me and almost entirely silent?

It's a miserably cold walk to the gondola station.

"All right," he announces once we're finally there and I'm clear to use the lift. He scribbles something on a hot-pink sticky note and hands it to me. "Here's my number for when you're ready to come back down again."

I thank him and slip inside. The gondola doors close behind me, muting out the lingering sense of noise and chaos down at the resort.

He gives me a thumbs-up, and then I'm off.

To: Alix Morgan (alix@alixmorganwrites.com)
From: Aspen Underwood (a.underwood@glossmag.com)
Subject: RE: Open Invitation

Hi, Alix—

Just circling back to let you know I've been in touch with
another firsthand source that sounds promising—it's not a
done deal yet, though, so if you have any relevant information
to share, now's your chance. (If not, please disregard, and
don't hesitate to reach out in the future if there's anything you
feel might be of interest to Gloss!)

Best,
Aspen

29

This trip up the mountain is nothing like the first time.

For one, it's a lot quieter—and lonelier—without Tyler here to keep me company. Instead of a sky full of stars and a clear view of the glowing village below, it's like I'm in a freshly shaken snow globe: the higher the gondola ascends, the less I can see down in the valley. And even though Julie said we're below the wind threshold, it's still unnerving every time even the slightest gust picks up.

I've almost figured out what I want to say to Tyler by the time I reach the top. The doors open, and a swirl of snow rushes in as I step out.

It's otherworldly up here, entirely white and eerily silent. No one's been up to clear the sidewalks—and if Tyler left any footprints earlier, they've already been filled in with more snow.

Fortunately, I remember how to get to the lookout from here, not to mention that everything is clearly marked with Black Maple Lodge's official signage.

The walk isn't far. I stay steady on my feet, determined not to land in the medical center this time, silently going over the words I've planned in my head. Even once I get there—when I see him sitting on the bench, alone, his back to me, the oversized hood of his coat flecked with snowflakes—I'm still running through it all, reluctant to actually say anything.

But it doesn't matter, because Tyler speaks first.

"You got my note."

He hasn't turned around; he must have heard me, or the lift on its way up.

I make my way over to him, boots crunching through the snow. He continues staring off into the distance—or what *would* be the distance if we weren't currently inside a cloud—even when I join him on the bench. I sit close, turn my body to face his.

He stares at his gloved hands.

"Yeah," I say, careful to keep my voice even. "I got your note."

He still doesn't look at me.

I have a strong urge to pull his hood back so I can see more of his face, but I resist. For now.

"Tyler," I say, and finally—*finally*—he turns.

The look on his face breaks my heart.

I don't know what I expected, exactly, but this isn't it: an expression so numb, so void of emotion, it's in danger of getting frostbite.

The more I take him in, though, the more I see that it isn't so much the absence of feeling as it is too many conflicting ones at the same time.

Anger, simmering just beneath the surface.

Panic—fear.

Sorrow.

Exhaustion.

"I'm sorry, Alix," he says, voice low and crackling. "I . . . I can't."

"You can't *what*?" I push.

He blinks, looks away, like it's physically impossible to meet my eyes when he says, simply: "Stay."

I grit my teeth, summoning the speech I went over on my way up the mountain.

"But you're still here. You wrote, 'Nothing in me wants this to be over,'" I continue, quoting his own letter back to him. "So *stay*." I take a deep breath, look him right in the eye. "You don't have to be someone who runs from problems when they get too hard—who makes himself disappear rather than face them. I don't think you actually want to leave so much as you're just . . . afraid . . . to face the world."

His jaw twitches, and I know I've struck a nerve.

"Of course I don't want to leave," he says, skirting around my more pointed comment. "I've made a life here, one I actually enjoy. I love where I live. I love what I do. I love—who I do it with."

"This isn't the same as when you disappeared the first time, Tyler," I say, a new edge in my voice. "You left for good reasons. You were trapped in your contract, surrounded by toxic people you couldn't trust, and you found a way to get yourself out of that life. You shouldn't be afraid to share that story with the world. Some people will never understand—but I think you underestimate the number of people who *will*."

I take another deep breath, plow forward before he can say anything. "If you run this time, it's officially a pattern. You become *someone who runs*. You'd be turning your back on your closest friends, the ones who saved your life by helping you go off the grid—and you'd be running from me too. I'm fully aware that I haven't been in your life very long at all, but I know enough to recognize that this kind of connection we have? It doesn't come along all that often. There was something about me that made you trust me enough to let me in. Maybe I'm wrong, but I think that should count for something."

The snow is picking up again, thicker flakes instead of the delicate ones. It's absolutely freezing out here, and I'm shivering, but there's no way I'm heading back down the mountain until we're done with this conversation.

"It *does* count for something," Tyler says with fresh intensity. "You are the best thing that's happened to me since I left the band, Alix. I didn't realize how much—"

He breaks off, looks away.

River's voice flits through my memory: *It's been hard watching you spend so many years alone. We want* more *for you.*

". . . how much I'd been missing," he finally finishes. "I didn't realize how many parts of me I'd left for dead until you came along and made me feel alive."

"So *stay*."

"It's not that simple—"

"It doesn't have to be that hard, either."

His expression darkens. "You don't know what it's like to have your every move scrutinized," he says bitterly. "You don't know how it feels to have the entire world salivating, just waiting for you to make a mistake so they can feast on it. You don't know how it feels like *fire* for people to pass judgment on your life when they don't know the first real thing about it—and how it burns your soul to ash when no one sees you for who you actually are. You don't know what it's like, Alix. So forgive me if I don't want to show my face after *eight years* only to be torn apart all over again—I let the entire world think I was gone for good and dragged my best friends into lying for me. Some people will say that's unforgivable."

His words hang between us, like he's just painted a black streak through the bright white sky, until the wind whips them away.

Silence takes over, thick and heavy.

"I never said I thought it would be easy," I say carefully. "I just think you're strong enough to handle it—stronger than you give yourself credit for." I inhale, the cold air sharp and stinging.

Tyler considers my words.

"Also," I go on, while I still have the boldness, "I truly believe that for every person angry with you for the choices you made, there will be more who understand. People who'd be *thrilled* to see you back—and not just because they write clickbaity articles, but because they loved and missed *you*, Tyler. Not everyone is a Sebastian fan, you know. You could tell your own story."

When he finally looks at me again, those gorgeous eyes are filled with more sadness than I've ever seen on him—but otherwise, he's unreadable.

"You said it yourself," Tyler says evenly. "You haven't been in my life long at all. I appreciate the confidence—but I'm not sure I'm as strong as you think I am. I'm sorry, Alix. You should go somewhere warm before you get hypothermia."

I should. I really should.

But I'm frozen, and not just in the literal sense.

"Where will *you* go?" I ask.

I want so badly for him to see that he *is* strong enough.

"Wherever I end up," he says, "I'll find some way to let you know I'm safe. I trust you, Alix—"

His voice breaks. I hate this for him. I hate it for *me*.

But it was always going to come down to this, wasn't it? There's no way we could ever have been together for more than just a fling unless he left his life of reclusion behind—I can't imagine loving someone so intensely in secret for the rest of my life.

Still, there was part of me that hoped we'd sparked something special enough, rare enough, to make him consider abandoning his life of perpetual anonymity and loneliness.

I leave him alone on the lookout bench. It takes everything in me not to turn around for one last glance.

Dewdrops · /TrueNorth

#theories #JettBeckett #SebastianGreen #JettIsAlive

u/jettbeckettconspiracytheorist
12:08PM · March 9, 2025

Okay hi, hello, what is happening—

That photo of the True North guys making
the rounds today: LET'S DISCUSS. (Jett
Beckett?????!!?)

COMMENTS

🔺 **u/TruestNortherner**
TOP
I HAVE NO WORDS

↳ **u/TruestNortherner**
Except that OBVS you were 10000% correct
this whole time and you were the first person I
thought of when I saw it

296

↳ **u/jettbeckettconspiracytheorist**

So you think it's really him, too?

↳ **u/BoiiiBandBoiii**

IDK, that guy looks SO DIFFERENT

I don't think it's him

Jett Beckett doesn't have brown eyes

And something seems off about his nose

↳ **u/TruestNortherner**

That's what my brother's looked like when he
broke it

↳ **u/jettbeckettconspiracytheorist**

DO WE THINK HE BROKE IT JUST TO CHANGE
HIS APPEARANCE OR

↳ **u/TruestNortherner**

that is some true dedication

↳ **u/BoiiiBandBoiii**

Still not convinced it's him tho

↳ **u/TruestNortherner**

Okay but imagine if this old photo of him had
thick eyebrows (and brown eyes)

↳ **u/jettbeckettconspiracytheorist**

And long dark wavy hair instead of it being
bleached within an inch of its life

↳ **u/BoiiiBandBoiii**
But, like, in what universe would Seb, Riv, and
Jett ever be hanging out *on purpose*

↳ **u/TruestNortherner**
I mean, to be fair, Jett doesn't look HAPPY about
it . . . so that kinda still tracks?

↳ **u/BoiiiBandBoiii**
Ugh I don't know
I concede it is *possible*
How, though? How does a guy like Jett Beckett
make himself disappear (at all/for so long)??

↳ **u/jettbeckettconspiracytheorist**
It's what I've thought all along
Here's a post I made a while back re: how
someone could *hypothetically* do it. He
would've needed help for sure, but IMHO it's
possible.

↳ **u/TruestNortherner**
Yeah, sorry, bro. I never bought your theory
until now
But I think you're right

↳ **u/BoiiiBandBoiii**
Thx for the link, I'll check it out

↳ **u/jettbeckettconspiracytheorist**
No prob.

↳ **u/jettbeckettconspiracytheorist**
Did you see this yet? New photo just leaked:
moondazzle.com/jett-beckett-back-from-the-dead

RUMOR MILL:
Jett Beckett Back from the Dead???

By Rylee Jay // Senior Editor, Moondazzle.com

Sebastian Green, fresh off a whirlwind trip to Tuscany, has been spotted numerous times today by guests snowed in at Black Maple Lodge in upstate Vermont. Which begs the question: Why would one of the biggest pop stars of our time make such a sudden departure from Italy—where it's currently sunny and mild—just to fly into a record-breaking blizzard?

The answer, it seems, is Jett Beckett.

A very-much-*alive* Jett Beckett.

Earlier this morning, <u>this Dewdrops post</u> sparked a viral rumor: that Jett Beckett is back from the dead and just may be working as a ski instructor in Stowe, Vermont. This is pure speculation at this point, and we await confirmation from either Jett Beckett himself or a firsthand source.

However! We've just gotten our hands on some brand-new drone footage from the resort; the photographer reports he was trying to get more shots of Sebastian, but after seeing the aforementioned viral Dewdrops photograph, he realized he'd caught a fresh image of the man in question instead.

So what do we think? Could this long-haired, thick-browed, slightly scruffy man be our long-lost Jett Beckett? He lacks the ultra-polished pop star vibe he was known for, but otherwise, we think the resemblance is there. (Admittedly, we never would've expected him to resurface at a ski lodge—but it's as good a place to hide out as any, we suppose.)

Our inquiring minds also wonder:

- Is that a guitar strapped to his back? Since when does he play the guitar?

- Who is the mystery girl? We've got very little to go on since all we can see is her back.

- Does she know she's up close and personal with Jett Beckett (if it does turn out to actually be him)?

We want to know *everything*.

Theorize away and blow this post up, y'all! And if you have any tips/sightings from around Black Maple Lodge, our inbox is always open!

30

I'm halfway back down the mountain, staring off into the haze of snow, when my phone buzzes in my hand.

Chloe.

"We've got a problem," she says as soon as I answer. "More stuff has popped up—are you alone right now?"

I sit a little straighter.

"Yeah. Why?"

"One of these stupid tabloid posts has a picture of you. Well, *I* know it's you—but it's just the back of your head. And, uh, you're with Tyler. They're calling you his 'mystery girl.'"

Oh *no*.

That drone we saw must have gotten something after all.

"Has anyone gone on record to confirm the Jett Beckett rumors yet?" I ask. "Check Gloss specifically. They seem really invested in breaking the story." I saw the follow-up from Aspen as soon as the gondola doors closed.

"I'm not seeing anything there or anywhere else yet, no," Chloe says. "But Alix, I'm worried about *you*—do you have any sort of hat, or, like . . . sunglasses?"

I snort.

"As in the classic celebrity disguise? Because that *always* works."

"Hey, it might help," she says, laughing. "Here, I'll send you the link. I just don't want people to, like, mob you. *You* know the truth. They *want* the truth. They're snowed in with nothing better to do—I feel like they'll do anything to get to you since they can't get to Tyler."

She's right.

I hate that she's right.

I've never been on this side of celebrity news before: *in* the story, not just writing it.

It feels way more invasive than I ever imagined, and I haven't even left the quiet cocoon of this gondola yet—I know it doesn't hold a candle to what Tyler's been through, but even just the idea of people trying to track me down makes my skin crawl.

"Promise you'll be careful?" she says.

"I will. Thanks, Chlo."

"Always. Just wish I could do more from here."

When we're off the call, I check out the link she sent over. I can tell it's me, but other than my back and hair, there are no identifying details. I do wish I'd grabbed a hat before leaving in such a rush earlier—a hair tie, anything.

I sigh, leaning back. I'm almost at the bottom of the mountain, and then I'll have to make it all the way through the village and back to my penthouse without being recognized. My one consolation right now is that my face didn't make it into any photos. Also, Gloss hasn't posted anything Jett Beckett–related yet, so I suspect they're still awaiting confirmation from their "promising source."

For now.

Which means—maybe—there's still time for me to convince said source to *stay* quiet.

Even though Lauren leaked the original photo that started this whole mess, I don't believe she'd share more about it, especially not after our conversation earlier. And besides, how would Gloss have known to reach out to her? She's no celebrity, and not obviously connected to the situation unless you dig pretty deep. Could Aspen have approached more obvious sources—namely, River or Sebastian—like she did with me? I could see either of them selling Tyler out: River, since he set this entire thing in motion in the first place—or Sebastian, because he was blindsided by it all.

I take a shot in the dark, follow my gut.

Can we talk? I type out to Sebastian. Meet at the penthouse ASAP?

I keep my head down and walk as quickly as I can through the village. I pass the café, busier than before, more people out doing things now that the worst of the storm has passed. A few resort guests mill around the ice-skating rink and along the sidewalks— fortunately, they're mostly looking at their phones, probably scrolling social media in pursuit of their next Jett Beckett leads. I manage to make it past all of them without sparking anyone's attention.

Just outside my own building, though, a larger group has assembled by the front door—which they clearly assume is the *only* door. I nod hello, figuring it would look blatantly suspicious if I just ignored them, and keep going until I'm well past them. The path curves past the far side of the building; I dart around the corner and head for the private penthouse entrance, which—mercifully— is both unmarked and unattended.

I slip inside as fast as I can.

Back in the penthouse, I find Lauren right where I left her: sitting on my bed, staring at her phone, scowling. Puffin is stretched out beside her, his soft fur pressed up against her leg.

She must have moved at some point, though. The stain from her latte earlier has all but disappeared, only a faint hint of brown remaining.

"Hey," I say, settling onto the bed. "Thanks for cleaning the duvet."

Finally she looks up.

Her eyes are red and puffy, as if she spent a decent portion of the time I was gone in tears.

"I'm so sorry," she says, her voice barely more than a whisper. She holds her phone up, shakes her head. "I really didn't know it would turn into all this. I'm so sorry, Alix. I wish I had never taken that photo. I wish I could fix it."

For as much trouble as she's caused, my heart still breaks to see her upset: she's my little sister, after all.

"Do I even want to know what people are saying?" I ask.

"About him or about you?"

"I don't want to know *anything* they're saying about me." I make a mental note to throw my phone over the edge of my balcony at some point in the near future. "But what about Tyler?"

"Lots of speculation—tons of people who believe he truly is Jett Beckett, others who argue he can't be because he looks too different. Some people are also being kind of mean, saying he's a selfish coward if it really is him. And then there are some who think we should leave celebrities alone and let them make their own choices."

I snort. "If only."

Even as I say it, though, I recognize that I'm part of the problem. Writing about celebrities has been my literal job for years: had

I been on the other end of it before now—*in* the headlines, not just writing them—I might have thought twice about some of the articles I submitted for publication.

Lauren wasn't altogether off base when she asked how what she'd done was any different from the work I do every day.

"But yeah," she goes on, idly stroking Puffin's fur. "I can see why Tyler just wants to hide in a hole forever."

I hate the idea of Tyler thinking his only options are to live a miserably public life . . . or to run and hide and somehow try to reinvent himself again. And I hate that I finally, after all these years, opened myself up to someone—someone *incredible*—only for it to fall apart like this.

It isn't about me, I remind myself. If anything, everything that went down between us today is proof that he cares quite a lot, even if the reality of him leaving feels like the opposite.

Tyler didn't have to leave a note. Didn't have to word it in such a way that hinted at where to find him. Surely he could have found some way to leave the resort, even in this weather—cross-country skis exist for a reason, and I know they have some at the ski school. He could have headed off the beaten path and made himself disappear without a trace.

Without a goodbye.

But he stayed. He stayed long enough, at least, for us to talk one last time . . . and maybe I'm wrong, but I think that has to count for something.

At the end of the day, though, it *was* a goodbye.

It's the fact that I'll never see him again—that he'll never again make me laugh, or make me dinner, or kiss me late into the night in front of a blazing fire—he'll never take me up to look at the stars, or buy me a pretzel bigger than my face, or confide his deepest hopes and fears—

It's *that* I can't get over.

I understand his choice. And I know he doesn't want to hurt me. It doesn't stop it from hurting.

"I'm moving back home," Lauren says suddenly. "To Iowa."

The abrupt subject change throws me for a loop. "Like—after your internship?"

"Like, after this weekend," she says, eyes low. "Everything I've touched since I moved to New York has . . . just . . . fallen apart. I'm terrible at my internship. I'm terrible at knowing who to trust—and you might get *evicted* because of that. The people I thought were my friends are obviously not. But I really did think I could trust the ones I texted, Alix, I never would have sent that photo otherwise. I thought they'd just fangirl with me, you know?"

She takes a deep, shaky breath.

"And I've totally screwed things up with you when all I ever wanted was to get to know you better. For you to finally see me as an adult—someone you might want to spend time with, be friends with, if I ended up living in New York for good like you one day." Her eyebrows knit together. "But I just don't know if I'm cut out for it. For *any* of it."

Her gaze flicks up to meet mine.

"For . . . a really long time now," she goes on, "I have been *intensely* afraid that I have no idea how to take care of myself." She makes a face, looks away. "I thought doing the internship would help me get over my fear, help me prove that I'm capable of making it in a city like New York. Mom's always bragging about you to people around town, saying how impressed she is by the life you've made there, so I thought maybe I could do it, too."

"Wait—sorry—but Mom brags about me? She's *impressed*?"

This is news to me, but Lauren gawks at me.

"Um, yes. Definitely. She brings it up to anyone who'll listen."

"I honestly had no idea."

Maybe she's spent so much time saying nice things to other people, she doesn't realize she's never actually said them to me.

"But . . . yeah," Lauren goes on, looking down at her chipped nail polish. "Maybe I'm just not cut out for the city like you are, or for city people. I have no idea what I'm doing."

My heart breaks all over again.

"Hey," I say, nudging her. *"Hey."*

Finally she meets my eyes.

"No one knows what they're doing, not really. It's not like people are born knowing how to handle every single thing—it takes work to figure out your own life. I know it has for me, anyway. You're *going* to make mistakes. Everyone does. But you have a choice: you can face the hard things, or you can run from them. You have to risk making mistakes in the first place if you're ever going to get better at dealing with them."

She's quiet, probably thinking—like I am—about how our mother has spent Lauren's entire life solving every one of her problems for her before she even gets a chance to try.

And I think about Tyler, who ran when things got too hard before—who could very well be running away again right this very minute.

Puffin climbs lazily over Lauren's lap and onto mine, then raises his chin until I give in and start scratching it. He leans into my fingers, purring loudly, and then flops his entire body upside down like he's lost all his bones. His huge green eyes stare up at me like I'm the sun at the center of his universe.

Lauren's eyes on me feel almost the same. I don't know how I never saw it before this spring—how much she looks up to me.

"You're the last person I ever wanted to hurt, Alix," she says now. She shakes her head and sighs. "Maybe I should start by getting you an apology latte since you barely touched the drink I brought earlier?"

The corner of my mouth quirks up. "And maybe some apology maple candies, too?"

There's a knock at my front door. I'm not exactly motivated to answer, given that there's only one person I want it to be and it's almost certainly not him—but maybe it's Sebastian, even though he still hasn't answered my text.

Lauren follows me to the door, pulling on a puffy coat as she walks. "Maple latte again?" she asks.

"Tell the barista to surprise me."

I open the door, hoping against hope that Tyler's there, leaning artfully against the doorframe in one of his trademark V-neck shirts—

But no such luck.

It's Sebastian.

Lauren slips out the door with a little wave.

"You said you wanted to talk?" he says. "Let's talk."

He came all the way to Vermont to discuss his memoir, but this is about to be an entirely different conversation. Which, ironically, we would not be having had he not shown up at the resort in the first place. It's not like he had any idea he'd be setting off a chain reaction that led to the implosion of our numerous secrets, though, I remind myself. I may not be his biggest fan, but at least I can acknowledge that he didn't put Tyler's privacy at risk on purpose.

"Come in," I tell him.

"Nice place," he remarks as we pass through the living room and turn off into an area where I haven't spent much time, the game room.

"I could live here, honestly," I say. "I really appreciate you arranging for me to stay here this month."

Sebastian gives a cursory glance to the myriad seating options in this room—barstools, armchairs, a couch upholstered in emerald-green velvet—and chooses, instead, to lean casually against the pool table.

It's the most blatant attempt at a power position I've ever seen, and I'm not even sure he's aware he's doing it. I think that's just how he *is*.

Every seat I could take would result in him looking down on me, and the barstools are a bit too far away for conversation, but the pool table looks more than sturdy enough to hold my weight and then some. I climb up and make myself comfortable, crossing my legs and letting them dangle over the edge.

"Busy day for you," I comment.

He rubs a hand over his jaw. "I'm used to it."

"Have you seen everything that's happening online?"

"My manager called, yeah. To talk about Jett."

His expression is hard to read. It's hard, period—steely, impenetrable.

"And?" I say.

"And I told him to piss off."

If I had a drink, I'd be choking on it.

"He can tell I know something," Sebastian says, shaking his head. "He wants me to talk—to confirm the rumors about Jett. He's gotten a lot of calls today, a lot of interview offers." He makes a gesture with his fingers that can only be interpreted as *cold, hard cash*.

Ah.

"And . . . are you going to?"

It's not like he needs the money—but then again, his constant jet-setting has got to be burning a hole in his pocket. The fact that he seems to be on the fence gives me hope.

In all likelihood, Tyler's peaceful days of hiding out at the lodge have ended. Until one of us confirms he's really Jett Beckett, though, there's a chance—however small—that the truth might remain a mystery. Maybe the fandom will decide he doesn't look similar enough or that it's too unlikely that he's flown under the radar for this long. Maybe it will all blow over.

"Maybe?" he says. "Probably. I don't know."

He shifts, and it sounds like plastic crinkling.

I think it's his pants.

"I can't decide if it makes more sense to take the cash today," he goes on, "or make them wait to read the whole story in the book."

"I'd rather not write *anything* about Jett's secret life in the book, honestly."

"It isn't *your* book," he counters. "It's my story to tell."

"Not this part—this part is Tyler's."

"Who's Tyler?"

I guess he hasn't read *everything* being said online, only the broad strokes.

"That's the name Jett is going by now," I say.

His eyes light up with recognition. "Huh. Well. I think the publishing house would agree it's relevant to my story."

It would sell books, I'll give him that.

A pit forms in my stomach.

When it comes down to it, is this not what I signed on for? To write Sebastian's story in the most accurate way possible—which, I reluctantly admit, might include this week's compelling turn of events?

I don't think there's any way out of this: my only options are to break my contract or to write the book however Sebastian and our editor see fit.

It's an impossible choice.

Nothing in me wants to ruin the career I've worked so hard for—but at the same time, if the rumors *do* manage to blow over somehow, could I live with myself for being the one to officially betray Tyler's secrets to the world?

Maybe it won't ever have to come to that.

There's always a chance Sebastian will change his mind. Maybe, in time, I can convince him.

If someone else writes this book, I'll have no control. No control over what's said, how it's said. Didn't I *just* tell my sister not to run when things get hard? Didn't I just tell Tyler the same thing?

Nothing in me wants to do hard things, but I can do them.

I can if I have to.

"Okay," I finally say. "You're right—it's your book. Your story."

My best option right now is to convince Sebastian to wait to confirm the Jett rumors rather than selling out to Gloss or whoever else is vying for an interview. If Tyler's determined to make himself disappear again, the least I can do is buy him some time—as soon as this snowstorm ends and the roads clear up, the paparazzi will multiply like cockroaches.

"If I were you," I go on, "I wouldn't cash in today. You'd make more money in the long run with book royalties, I think—*and* you'd get the credit for telling the world exactly what happened to Jett Beckett. People will be dying to read about that."

I hold my breath, wait while he considers it. His pop star–perfect face creases between the eyebrows (and nowhere else).

If I know Sebastian—and I'm pretty sure I do at this point—appealing to his ego should work.

"Good call," he says, nodding. "I can see that. You think you can work it in?"

Unfortunately, I can already tell the Jett Beckett reveal is the missing piece that will make the entire book come together. Sebastian's story started with his rivalry with Jett—and then his life drastically changed course when Jett disappeared and the band fell apart—and now that Jett's resurfaced as Tyler, Sebastian can finally get closure, finally has the context he needs to process his own life story.

As much as I hate to admit it, their stories really are inextricable.

"Yeah," I say. "I can." After a beat, I add, "Don't tell Maribel yet, though? Let's wait until the draft is done—less risk of anything leaking that way."

He stands, straightening his worryingly tight pants.

"Sounds like a plan," he says. "Should we get to work?"

WJKS News Update:
A Moment with Sebastian Green

Trevor Jones, News Anchor, on location at Black Maple Lodge

TJ: Welcome back, everyone! We're still on location at Black Maple Lodge, where it's been quite the eventful day. We've just run into someone who's featured prominently in today's main conversation online and here at the resort—Sebastian Green! Sebastian, thank you for your time. Have you seen the photo that's going around?

SG: I've posed for lots of photos today, Trev—you're gonna have to be more specific! [wink to the camera]

TJ: [laughs] Here, let me show you. *This* one.

SG: Oh, hey, great photo. Shout-out to whoever sent me these pants.

TJ: Care to comment on who exactly you're with in this photo?

SG: That's River Wu. We were bandmates back in the day—his family owns this resort.

TJ: And the other guy?

SG: [pauses, leans in to study the photo, shrugs] Couldn't tell you. Pretty sure he works here.

TJ: People are saying that's Jett Beckett, another of your former bandmates. You really don't know him?

SG: I've only been here since last night. I don't know every person at this resort.

TJ: But when you met this guy, did you think he looked familiar? Like Jett?

SG: Look, Jett's a sensitive topic for all of us, man. I try not to think about him too much.

TJ: [nervous laughter] Right, sorry about that. You've got a book coming out later this year, is that true?

SG: Yes, sir! That's why I'm here in Vermont, to work on it for a bit. I just finished nailing down some of the material with my team, and if I do say so myself, you won't want to miss it.

TJ: Best of luck with it—and thank you for your time!

31

I'm curled up in bed, Puffin stretched out beside me, trying my very best to resist the temptation to scroll social media for updates on Tyler.

I sent him a text as soon as Sebastian left, though I have no idea if he even has his phone on him at this point. After several awkward first drafts, I finally settled on this novel of a text message:

Sebastian wants me to write about what happened this morning—how he was shocked to discover you here at the lodge—in his book. There's not much I'll be able to do about it, so I wanted to give you a heads-up. I think I at least convinced him not to confirm that it's you *today* . . . so that should buy you some time.

I'm so sorry for what all of this has come to—

I'm not sorry I met you, though. I'm only sorry that it has to end if you choose to start over somewhere else. It was worth it, though, for me: there's no one else like you, and I'm lucky to have gotten the chance to know you, even if it wasn't for long enough.

x, Alix

My cheeks are still hot with tears. I didn't come here for romance—if anything, I was reluctant to dip my toes back into the water until Chloe encouraged me to just go have fun, try something new—but then there was Tyler, and his smile and his laugh and the way he put me at ease right from the start, and I—

I ended up ruining his life. Indirectly, of course, but it wouldn't have happened if I had never come here.

SO MANY NOSY RESORT GUESTS, Lauren texts me, along with a photo. And these are just the ones INSIDE the coffee shop. Still no sign of him, but people keep asking if I know anything. Got stopped outside your building, too.

Oh, crap.

It didn't even occur to me that people might think Lauren is Jett Beckett's mystery girl—but our hair is very similar. In good news, a wavy blond bob is not the most remarkable of hairstyles. In not-so-good news, guests with nothing better to do have been staking out our building all day, no doubt on the lookout for Jett or anyone who could possibly be the girl from that invasive drone photo.

Ohmygosh Lauren, get out of there! I don't need coffee that badly

I do, she replies. They're mostly leaving me alone at the moment . . . but I can accidentally bump into someone and spill coffee all over their phone if I need to . . .

Is this going to be my life now if the world finds out I'm the mystery girl? Unable to go get coffee for fear of being swarmed? No wonder Tyler would rather keep a low profile. I can't imagine how intense things must have been at the height of his fame—and the relief he must have felt after he went off the grid, finally able to live his life in peace.

And now it's all come crashing down. My heart hurts, and not just because I want him in my life—but because I know, deep down, that even if he tries to start over, he's never going to be able to get away with it like he did before. For one, he had River and Julie helping him the first time. For another, now people know to look out for him, even in the unlikeliest of places.

I trust you, Alix.

It was the last thing he said to me up on the mountain. It might be the last thing he *ever* says to me.

Puffin stretches up to rub his face against mine, as if he can sense how much I need a little comfort. His purring intensifies when I scratch between his ears, like there's nowhere else in the world he'd rather be.

If only human relationships were so simple. Aside from Chloe, Puffin's been in my life longer than any of my friends—and there's a reason for that. I don't let people in easily.

But I let Tyler in. For the first time in years, I let my guard down and allowed myself to get close to someone else. I let myself consider the possibility of a relationship after so many years of trying to keep myself from getting hurt.

We're *both* learning how to do this again, both learning how to take risks when we're used to playing it safe.

I would very much like to continue being a person who's worthy of Tyler's trust.

I head into the kitchen, look for a snack. All I have on hand are olives and cheese and crackers, the last of what was stocked in my fridge when I first arrived. I head to the living room, careful to keep my distance from the windows in case any more drones are trying to get a look inside.

After my snack, I start to get antsy. Lauren's been gone for thirty, forty minutes now—I know she said the café was busy, but that seems like a bit too long even given the circumstances. It's not that far of a walk, and her last message was more than fifteen minutes ago.

I open my messaging app, planning to send a check-in text, and am surprised to see the three-dot bubble in the window that indicates she's already typing.

ALIX YOU HAVE TO GET DOWN HERE RIGHT NOW, she writes.

My skin prickles. Are you okay?? I reply.

I'm fine. Just get down here

And then she sends a link, no context, to a Dewdrops post. I click through.

To the untrained eye, the photo might look like it came straight from one of those public domain websites: the snowcapped mountain would make the perfect desktop wallpaper or a great addition to one of those moody aesthetics people post about their favorite books and films.

But I know better. It's not just *any* mountain—and it's not just some generic postcard view from the valley below.

This photo was taken from the lookout. *Tyler's* lookout.

I glance at the username—u/Jettsetter—and everything falls into place. The most recent post before this one is from eight years ago, the night of Tyler's disappearance.

Beneath the snowy mountainscape, there's a simple caption: *Took some time to clear my head. See you again soon, world. Xoxo*

My heart leaps to my throat. What time did he post this? Six and a half minutes ago, according to the time stamp. He does have his phone. Did he see my message? I tap over, see a little *read* notification under my text where before it only said *delivered*.

This can't mean what I think it does. Right?

The briefest search—*Jett Beckett mountain picture Vermont*—yields a handful of fresh image results: from what I can tell, all the guests who were hoping to spot Jett at the café are now migrating toward the base of the mountain where the gondola lets out.

Everyone wants to be the first to snap a shot of him.

Everyone wants to confirm the rumors.

Surely Tyler wouldn't resurface like *this*, would he? Knowing full well there will be people awaiting him at the bottom of the lift? Then again, the fact that he's posted online at all from his long-dormant account proves anything is possible.

If I'm right—if Tyler is heading down the mountain as we speak, working up the nerve to show his beautiful face on his own terms for the first time since his disappearance—then I have to get down there as soon as I possibly can.

It's mercifully quiet outside my building, but the ski village is even busier than I expected. There's a group making its way down the path that leads to the lifts; I follow, keeping my head down, doing my best to not call attention to myself. The closer we get to the base of the mountain, the thicker the crowd gets, countless smartphone cameras poised and ready.

Lauren stands out in her hot-pink puffer coat. She spots me immediately, waves me over.

"The ski lift started up a few minutes ago," she says, "so everyone's convinced he's on his way down."

Sure enough, the gondolas are in motion. The lift tech powered everything down before we left earlier, and since the slopes are all closed for the day, I can see why this has caught everyone's attention, especially given Tyler's social media post.

The WJKS news crew members have their cameras trained on the gondola cars, looking out for any sign of him. If he's still in the jacket with the oversized hood—and he'd have to be, right?—they might not be able to see much.

Soon, though, a flurry of excitement ripples through the crowd.

More and more people pull out their phones, as if we're about to witness a moment that will go down in pop culture history. And maybe we are—but Lauren and I are in the minority, neither of us even attempting to capture the moment.

I just want to see it with my own eyes.

I want to see *him* with my own eyes.

I don't truly believe it's happening until the gondola doors open and he steps out.

Time slows as he lowers his thick, black hood. He pulls off his knit hat, too, shaking out the wavy hair that no one but me currently associates with him—everyone else is used to the bleached-blond highlights of eight years ago, no doubt, short and spiky and gelled within an inch of its life.

Whispers build to murmurs, everyone frozen and unsure what to make of Jett Beckett 2.0. They watch as he scans the crowd. He's nervous—I can tell by his tight smile that doesn't quite reach his eyes.

As soon as he spots me, though, he relaxes, his eyes lighting up. A handful of people glance over their shoulders, trying to figure out what—*who*—he's seen.

Before they turn their full attention my way, though, Tyler clears his throat. The whispers fall silent.

"Um . . . hi, everyone," he starts, with a small wave. "It's been a while. You might remember me from a band called True North."

The crowd erupts.

Everyone wants a picture, everyone has a question. They shout at him, voices blending together in cacophony, their collective volume growing louder by the second.

He nods politely at them but keeps his head down as he makes his way toward the crowd—

Toward *me*.

People move just enough to let him pass but close in around him again as soon as they can. They snap photos and reach out to touch his jacket, still asking so many questions; the television reporter shoves a microphone in his face.

Tyler barely seems to notice.

He's clearly on a mission, and that mission is me.

"Do you want me to record this moment for you?" Lauren asks, holding up her phone.

I shake my head. "I kind of just want to pretend no one else is here," I admit. "But on the bright side, I don't think there will ever be a shortage of footage if I want to relive it."

By the time Tyler gets to me, all eyes—and cameras—are on us. He takes my face in his gloved hands, which most definitely must have hand warmers inside, and presses his forehead to mine.

"What happened?" I say quietly, wrapping my arms around him. My voice is so low I'm not sure even Tyler can hear me, but it's the closest we're coming to privacy right now. "I thought you were going to disappear again?"

"I know," he says. "I'm sorry. Everything you said on the mountain this morning—and then your text—" His thick brows furrow. "It was the clarity I needed. I don't want to be the sort of person who runs when I'm afraid things will be too hard to face. I had good reasons the first time, and I'm not sorry I did it. But this time—today—"

I feel his rib cage expand as he takes a deep breath.

"This time," he goes on, "I wouldn't have been running for any good reasons. And I would be missing out on—on *this*. On you." His hands move gently, fingers finding their way up into my hair. "I know we only just came into each other's lives recently, but you've changed mine, Alix. I thought I was fine before I met you, but now—now I see what I've been missing. You make me laugh more than anyone. You weren't starstruck when you figured out what I'd been hiding, and you never used my secret for your own gain, even though we both know you could have, and—"

His voice breaks, but he's said enough.

My phone vibrates in my jacket pocket; we're pressed together so close that I know he feels it, too. I take a quick glance, see a message from Tyler that apparently took its sweet time to come through: I'm on my way down. Meet me at the bottom?

"I got your text," I say, and he laughs.

"Kiss her already!" someone yells from the crowd, setting off a wave of laughter.

We're already so close: it doesn't take much to close the distance. I tilt my head just enough, and he meets me halfway. His lips are chapped from the cold, but I don't care—I only hope it doesn't hurt him.

My worries melt away as he kisses me, sending dueling sensations of heat and chills coursing through my body. His hands tighten in my hair, and I wish, really wish, that we weren't surrounded by a crowd of onlookers right now.

Screw it, I think, as he continues to kiss me in front of the entire world. Let them watch.

When he finally pulls away, he only has eyes for me.

"It's weird when you're famous," he says, not realizing—or not caring—how many people are hanging on his every word. "Everyone thinks they know you, everyone has an opinion. Everyone wants to control you and use you and they start to forget you're an actual person. But I . . . just . . . I don't know. I was just thinking about how long I sat back and let everyone believe what they wanted to believe. After we talked, I thought a lot about how I could continue to let that happen—at the expense of actually *living* my life—or I could choose to finally take control of my own story. It doesn't have to be like it was before."

I tuck his hair behind his ears, search his eyes for any sign that he might regret this, but he's fearless. Determined. Brave.

We might both have uphill battles from here, dealing with the fallout, but life isn't perfect. Life is messy and hard and complicated. Even if you go to great lengths to outrun it, to completely reinvent yourself like Tyler did, it will almost always catch up eventually.

But neither of us will have to work through it alone this time: we can face it together, the good and the bad and the shady. And *that* will be worth it.

"I'm done, Alix," he says, pressing one more kiss to my lips. "I'm done hiding."

Hundreds of thousands of eyes could be on us right now, maybe millions.

In this moment, the only ones that matter are his.

"Welcome back," I say, and he grins.

The world is about to find out exactly what they've been missing.

MORGAN FAMILY

GROUP CHAT

ALIX

Um, hi, is this thing on?

I know it's been a while, but I have some news
and thought you might want to know about it

publishersweekly.com/sebastian-
green-to-publish-memoir

I've been working on a book this year—a memoir

LAUREN

:) Proud of you, Alix

MOM

This is an article about Sebastian
Green's book, is that the right link?
I don't see your name anywhere

ALIX

Yes, that's the right one

I'm ghostwriting it

DAD

That name sounds familiar. Lauren, is he from
that band you begged us for tickets for that
time? True . . . something. True Direction?

ALIX

True North. :) That's the one.

MOM

Wow, honey! Will you get to sign copies
even if your name isn't on it?? When can
we buy it?? Will you do a book launch?
Will Sebastian Green be there, too?

IAN

Of course he'll be there, it's his book . . .
Congrats, Alix

DAD

How exciting, Alix! Yes, please tell us
when we can order a copy and any
other details. I'll pass it on at work

THE LODGE

ALIX

:) :) :)

Thanks, everyone

I'll send all the links when I have a minute

Yes, there will be a release party.

And yes, Sebastian will be there.

MOM

We're so proud, honey. Congratulations.

Mike, do you think we should order a

new bookshelf for the living room?

Epilogue

EIGHT MONTHS LATER

It's almost time.

Everything is red: the thick curtains serving as a backdrop on the iconic New York City stage; more than six thousand sold-out seats waiting to be filled; RADIO CITY spelled out in neon on the famous marquee, our names in white just below.

And everything *gleams*—the brass railings throughout the building; the arched ceiling, brilliantly lit to resemble the golden rays of the sun as it sinks beneath the horizon.

Sebastian is dressed in a bespoke navy suit, looking stunning—a far cry from his usual preferences thanks to our publicist, who talked him into a more polished look for our book launch event. A gigantic poster of his book cover—*our* book cover—looms behind him, as if anyone needs reminding that it exists. It only just came out, but we've known for months that it would be an instant best-seller all over the world due to its record-breaking presales.

I watch from the wings as Sebastian steps forward to test the mic. He's a pro surrounded by pros, so it only takes a few minutes to get the levels right.

"I'm good," he says, turning to the man behind him onstage. "You want a check?"

Tyler's hunched over his guitar, making sure it's in tune—a posture I've seen more times than I can count at this point.

"Sure," he says, stepping up to the mic. "Thanks, man."

It's been eight months since our lives turned upside down that day in Vermont. There have been moments where it's been a roller coaster—close your eyes and ride it out until it's over—but never, not once, have I regretted the days leading up to this new life.

Leading up to *today*.

"One, two?" Tyler's voice reverberates through the room. His guitar gleams under the spotlight; his face is bright and beaming and radiant. "One, two, three—yeah, that's good, Jack, thanks. How's my guitar in the house?"

If he's nervous, he doesn't let it show.

Someone joins me in the wings, but I can't tear my eyes from Tyler, who looks like he's never been more comfortable on a stage. He looks *happy* up there in the spotlight, just him and his guitar and a mic.

"You ready?"

I glance over to see that it's Maribel Tovar who's joined me, looking every bit the editorial powerhouse in her black tailored dress and stilettos.

"I think I will be once we get started," I say quietly. "I've never done anything like this before."

Maribel gives me a comforting smile, her eyes twinkling even in the relative darkness of this backstage lighting. She's calmed me down more times than I can count over the past several months.

"You'll be perfect," she says. "Just remember, everyone who'll be here *wants* to celebrate the book with you and Sebastian."

It helps.

The stage is set with two wingback chairs where Sebastian and I will be in conversation about his book, along with a rug and a low coffee table to make it feel even cozier. Behind that whole setup is the aforementioned fifteen-foot poster of our book cover. After my talk with Sebastian, Maribel will introduce Tyler as our special surprise guest: he's been working on some music over the last six months or so, and tonight he's going to announce his upcoming solo album—and perform an acoustic rendition of its first single.

All of this, shockingly, was Sebastian's idea.

He and Tyler have been working through their differences in the months since everything went down at the lodge. Once the shock wore off, they had an intense heart-to-heart (in Fiji, because Sebastian is incapable of staying in the same hemisphere for longer than a few weeks at a time). Turns out they have even more in common than either of them realized and actually do enjoy each other's company now that no one's manipulating them into a rivalry at every turn.

This will be the first time since before True North broke up that they've shared a spotlight—and the first time ever that they've shared one *willingly*.

Maribel and our publicist thought the idea to include Tyler was genius, no doubt because there's a *second* enormous book cover waiting in the wings, ready to be revealed—tonight's audience is about to be absolutely swimming in surprises.

One night a few months ago, when I was at Tyler's place for dinner, he pulled out a stack of paper.

"What's this?" I said, eyeing the familiar logo at the top, thinking surely it couldn't be what it looked like.

But it was.

"I've been talking with Maribel," Tyler told me. "She asked if I might want to do a book like Sebastian's—and I told her yes this morning. I'm thinking I'll make a companion album to go with it."

Finally, *finally*, Tyler would get a chance to tell his story to the world.

Sure, the whole world knew the basics by that point—that he'd made himself disappear, only to resurface at the lodge eight years later. And Sebastian's book goes into slightly more detail, but mostly as it relates to Sebastian, not Tyler.

To have the opportunity to tell the why behind everything that happened, not just the what—it's something Tyler wants to do, he told me. Something he *needs* to do.

And he's writing every word himself.

"I love it," I told him that night he broke the news. "I can't wait until we can tell people about it."

The waiting ends today.

Maribel and I listen as Tyler rehearses the song he'll be playing this evening. It's good—*very* good. He had nearly a decade's worth of songs to choose from; he never stopped writing after leaving True North. This time around, he'll get to release music on his own terms.

My phone vibrates in my pocket: it's Chloe.

We're here!!!!!!! Ohmygosh, Alix, your name is on the friggin MARQUEE!!! Do not let me leave without us getting a photo with it

Once my name became inextricably linked with Jett Beckett's all over the internet, our publicity team thought it might actually be good to play up my part in creating the book. Hence: my name is on the marquee right under Sebastian's.

YESSS, I write back. I'll come around to make sure you get inside okay!

Security has been instructed to keep the doors closed—people have been lined up on the sidewalk since six a.m.—but Chloe, River, Julie, and Julie's husband, Justin, are all on the VIP list along with Lauren and Ian and my parents.

We find each other in the grand foyer, a space that stretches four stories tall and is every bit as opulent as the rest of the theater. Chloe gives me the most enthusiastic hug on the planet; we haven't seen each other in weeks.

Over Chloe's shoulder, I see River, along with Julie and Justin—and Grace, the tiny baby girl in Julie's arms.

"She'll probably wake up right in the middle of your talk," Julie says, a callback to a running joke we have about Grace always interrupting at the most inconvenient times, starting with Julie's water breaking two minutes after we arrived at a restaurant to celebrate Tyler's book deal.

I've gotten to know Justin and Julie well over the last year.

That fateful, chaotic day—the day our collective secrets exploded for the world to see—had blurred into an exhausted, emotionally electric night. In the aftermath of Tyler resurfacing and the subsequent viral social media posts, Tyler and I went back to his place for some much-needed alone time. Our room service delivery had just arrived when I got an email from my landlord: an eviction notice. The damage caused by Lauren's coworker was the final blow after all the noise complaints.

The next morning, I found Julie outside my door. She wasn't wearing her usual concierge uniform—just light-wash jeans, ripped at the thighs, and a Fair Isle sweater so big it swallowed her. I didn't know it at the time, but she was already twelve weeks pregnant.

"Tyler told me about your apartment," she said. "I've been thinking: long-distance relationships can be really hard—and it's been so good to see Tyler finally let someone in." Her smile was warm. "River and I talked things over. We won't be hosting any more guests in this penthouse now that Tyler's news is out in the open, so—if you'd like to stick around for a bit—we'd love for you to stay."

So I did.

Over the last eight months, Tyler and I have spent countless late nights and early mornings—and every other part of the day—at either his penthouse or mine. River suggested we tear out some walls and transform our homes into a single living space, so that's exactly what we'll be doing as soon as the book tour ends. He and Tyler have grown closer than ever now that they've worked through years' worth of things that had gone unsaid—a friendship tested by fire that's only come out stronger.

"You *can* help pay for the renovation," Tyler had told me one night, when he found me working out numbers on a spreadsheet, "but please know you don't have to."

I stood my ground until he showed me the numbers in his old bank accounts—the ones from his True North days, which would have gone dormant from inactivity years ago had he not continued to receive regular royalties from all the book and merch deals True North had accumulated at the height of their fame.

It was . . . an extraordinary amount of money. Like, astronomical.

It gave me a new appreciation for all he'd walked away from when he left the band—and for his discipline all these years, his commitment to keeping a low profile.

Chloe takes my hand and gives it a squeeze, pulling me out of my head.

"We're *so* proud of you, Alix," she says, and it means so much to hear her say it. It's been hard on us both to not live in the same city—or even the same *state*—this past year. She practically lives in my guest bedroom on the weekends, though, and has become a pretty decent ice skater, so I think she'd say it's working out just fine.

Behind me, someone clears his throat; when I turn around, tears well up in my eyes almost immediately. It's my dad, dressed in a nicer suit than I've ever seen him in, four copies of *The Grass Is Always Greener* tucked under his arm. My mom and Ian and Lauren are all right there, too, looking like they've robbed a bookstore—they're probably holding twenty hardcover copies between them.

"Congratulations, honey," my mom says, leaning in for a hug. She smells like the cinnamon candles she's put in our guest bathroom for as long as I've been alive.

Lauren hangs back, looking nervous but happy—she melts in my arms when I pull her into a hug. It's a contrast to Ian's greeting in every way; he and I are still warming up to each other after years of silence, but he gives me a deep nod of approval, like I'm one of his accounting clients who's done a particularly good job of itemizing her expenses.

I'll take it.

The stage manager, wearing a headset to match her all-black attire, pokes her head out of the auditorium.

"Alix Morgan?" she says. "You're needed onstage."

I've already done my sound check, and the doors open to the public in twenty minutes—I thought I was done until we entered with a full audience, but I guess not.

"You can come in if you want," I tell Chloe and the others. "I'm sure this will only take a minute."

They trail behind me as we head back inside from the foyer, and Chloe lets out a loud gasp. This place is truly breathtaking—never in a million years did I imagine doing an event here, let alone a sold-out one that I'm headlining along with two famous pop stars.

"This way," the stage manager says, gesturing for me to follow her since there isn't an easy way up to the stage from this part of the theater.

"Be right back," I tell Chloe, but she's preoccupied with taking a 360-degree video of this gorgeous place. My family and friends make their way down the aisle toward the row we've reserved for them, some of the best seats in the house.

I pass Sebastian and Maribel in the wings.

"Is this, like, another sound check?" I ask as I walk out onstage.

The view from here is overwhelming—I try not to think about how many faces will soon be staring back at me.

"Just take a seat in your chair," the stage manager directs me. "We're going to check the lighting."

I do as I'm told.

Chloe's filming *me* now, grinning from ear to ear. She tilts her head, and I follow her gaze to the far side of the stage—

And there's Tyler, no longer in his sound check clothes. He's now dressed in a trim suit that makes him look like a million bucks—we picked out the color together, a forest green so dark it could be mistaken for black, but this is the first time I've seen him wearing it. His wavy hair is parted in the middle, the tips of it grazing his shoulders, and he's got a dark five-o'clock shadow like always.

He was already the most handsome man on the planet, but I've never seen him look quite *this* good.

Whoever's working the lights has trained a spotlight on him, too, and it follows him as he makes his way across the stage, eyes locked on mine. I've been so preoccupied with getting ready for tonight's event that I don't suspect a thing until it happens: Tyler completely bypasses the other wingback chair and, instead, drops to one knee on the ornate rug, so close I can feel the heat radiating off him.

Oh.

Oh.

"Alix," he says, no microphones in sight, for my ears only, "I don't know what I thought life was before I met you, but if there's anything I've learned in the last year, it's that I had no idea what I was missing. Even before, in my days with the band, I never truly knew what it meant to let someone in—it's why I didn't hesitate to disappear. I only ever really confided in Riv and Jules, and as long as I didn't have to lose them, I was okay with losing everything else."

He takes a deep breath, pulls a box from his pocket.

"You helped me learn how to live again—and I don't want to live another day of my life without you in it."

Tyler opens the box, and inside is the most gorgeous engagement ring I've ever laid eyes on: a sparkling pear-shaped emerald surrounded by a dozen glittering diamonds, the design a stunning vintage art deco.

"Please, Alix—say you'll marry me?"

I nod, too overwhelmed to speak. He slides the ring onto my finger, and I just manage to say yes before his lips find mine. Together, we find our way to our feet, and he kisses me under the spotlight like we're the only ones in all of Radio City Music Hall. I'm vaguely aware that we're not; Sebastian and Maribel are beaming from the wings, my family and friends are celebrating out in the audience, and Grace is still miraculously asleep (or at least not crying).

In this moment, no matter how many people are looking on, everything feels exactly as it should: the two of us, center stage, ready to take on the world—together.

After a few long, lingering minutes, the spotlight dims.

"Doors will open in five," the stage manager informs us from the wings.

Tyler doesn't move.

"You look beautiful, Alix," he says as he tucks a piece of hair behind my ear. "Are you ready?"

Tonight might just be the biggest night of my life. With Tyler beside me, though, I feel more settled than ever. No trace of nerves, no second-guessing the road that led us here—only excitement for what's ahead.

"Yeah," I tell him. "I think I am."

Acknowledgments

It's that time again—the part of the book where I get to shine a spotlight on all the people who had a hand in helping this story go from idea seed to the finished copy you're reading! Writing might *seem* like a solitary endeavor, but that's a total illusion. It takes a village to make a book happen, and I'm incredibly grateful for everyone who's had a hand in this one.

Holly Root and Taylor Haggerty: Thank you, as always, for championing this book right from the start. And actually, in Taylor's case, thank you for championing it even before that—the entire reason *The Lodge* exists is because you told me you wanted me to write the coziest thing ever, so thank you for that! Thank you, too, to Mary Pender-Coplan and Heather Baror-Shapiro for the work you both do behind the scenes in the worlds of film and foreign rights.

Kaitlin Olson, you continue to be my dream editor! Your notes always resonate perfectly with my vision for any given project, and I know my work is immeasurably stronger because of the impact you've had on it. Thank you for everything.

What an absolute joy it is to work with the entire team at Atria Books! I'm always shouting about how excellent you all are to anyone who will listen, but here's my chance to do it with an even larger captive audience—I'm thankful for each one of you, and am constantly impressed by how good you all are at what you do. Thank you to the following S&S/Atria Books team members and supporting freelancers for their various impacts on *The Lodge*: Megan Rudloff (publicist), Dayna Johnson (marketing), Chris Lynch (president and publisher, Simon & Schuster audio), Morgan Pager (marketing and social media), Jolena Podolsky (marketing and social media), Ifeoma Anyoku (editorial assistant), Morgan Hart (production editor), Bee Johnson (cover illustrator), Kyoko Watanabe (designer), and Stacey Sakal and Alison Cherry (copy editors).

And to all the various Atria Books people I spent time with at Book Bonanza, including the inimitable Libby McGuire (senior vice president, publisher) and Gary Urda (senior vice president, sales), I had a blast with you down here in Texas.

Publishing is a marathon, not a sprint, and I'm very thankful to have had good friends to encourage me at every step of the way. Emily Bain Murphy, you have been such a blessing in my life for so many years now! I'm so glad to have you as my friend, and so thankful we get to experience author life with each other. Erin Bowman, thank you for your support and encouragement throughout the various drafting, revision, and copyedit stages of this book. Carlie Sorosiak, thank you for flying all the way to Texas to join me for my launch party for *The Reunion*—I love that you're writing romance these days, too, and hope we get to do many more events together. And Alison Cherry, thank you for your patience with all of my copyediting questions, and for squeezing *The Lodge* into your tight schedule when we decided to do an extra pass.

Chrystal Schleyer, Liz Griffin, Ande Pliego: thank you for all the kind words you've sent my way over the years—it's been so exciting to watch you all work so diligently toward your writing goals, and I can't wait to fill my shelves with your books.

Huge thanks to the #bookstagram community for so many gorgeous photos of my books . . . and a very special thank-you to the readers who participated in my cover reveal for *The Lodge*: @bookcasebeauty, @bitofeverythingbooks, @mapuamade, @brooks readsbooks_, @bookshelvish, @savvyrosereads, @whatmaddieread, @bookswithbresmith, @parkhopandpages, and @m_lockreads!

I'm also incredibly grateful for all the independent bookstores that've supported my work—a special shout-out is in order for my local store, Patchouli Joe's in Denton, Texas. Joe and Diane—and Charlie and Stephanie—thank you for all the love you've shown me (and my books)! Looking forward to teaming up for many more events in the future.

Michael Slezak, thank you for taking the time to answer my questions about what it's like to write for an online entertainment outlet!

To my tennis community—especially Emily McClendon, Constance Alexander, Brandon L'Heureux, and my cardio/drill friends—thank you for being a healthy distraction and a huge part of my life! I'm so glad to have a physical outlet to contrast the sedentary/cerebral aspects of writing a book, and I'm so glad I have such fun people to spend time with on the court.

I'm fairly certain our cats can't read (but then again, how do I know for *sure?*), but I want to give a special shout-out to our sweet tuxedo girl, Rouki: she showed up to work with me every day for months, waiting outside my office so she could follow me inside and sit there while I worked—her presence is always so calming and comforting, and was a big help while writing this book.

To all the Hahns, Holubecs, and Olsons: thank you, as always, for being excited with me about the worlds I create—I love that every single branch of my family is full of creative people who understand the desire to dream about things (and then *do* them).

Andrew and James, I love you so much! There aren't enough words for how much you both mean to me, and I can't say thank you enough for your love and support. We'd be here for a while if I were to list all the ways I'm thankful for you, but fortunately, I know where to find you so I can tell you in person.

As is my tradition, last but not least: thank you to Jesus Christ for being my peace throughout every season, the good days and the hard days and all the other days in between—I've revisited Psalm 23 a number of times while writing this book, and am thankful for the green pastures and still waters that fed my soul when I needed them most.

And finally, to all my wonderful readers—thank you for spending time with Alix and Tyler at Black Maple Lodge! I hope you enjoyed this little snow globe of a book, and that it helped to bring a touch of glittery, sparkly magic to your life. If we ever meet IRL, please be prepared to tell me who your favorite boy band is . . . Now please go do yourself a favor and get a soft pretzel and some hot cocoa ASAP. ♥

About the Author

Kayla Olson is the author of two books for young adults and *The Reunion*. Whether writing at her desk or curled up with a good book, she can most often be found with a fresh cup of coffee and at least one cat. Visit her at KaylaOlson.com or at @authorkaylaolson on Instagram/TikTok.